Awakening

Part 1 of the Living Myth Saga
Gabriella Creighton

Gabriella Creighton

ISBN Information

Kindle: 979-8-2990618-6-4
eBook: 979-8-9931454-2-6
Print: 979-8-9931454-3-3

You can find more books by this author at:

GabriellaCreighton.com

To my brother, Brian. You knew my madness better than most. You embraced it.
Siblings hold the line together, even in the most bleak moments.

About The Author

Gabriella Creighton is a life long lover of the Fantasy and Science Fiction Genres. She has been fascinated by Dragons and other mythical creatures from a young age and grew up dreaming of being a writer. Inspired by great authors like Jane Yolen, Anne McCaffrey, JRR Tolkien and Phillip Pullman, she loves to take an alternative view of myth and weave her own versions. After a long life of working, gaming and enjoying the works of others, she has finally decided to put her nigh on useless Masters Degree in English Literature to work to tell stories of her own.

Growing up in Rural New York and around many of the real life versions of the locations in this book, as well as having been thrown all over the United States, Gabriella has learned she has only three desires. To write until the nail her coffin shut, to never answer the phone and for a cool glass of Salted Caramel Crowne Royal mixed with Cream Soda and Dr Pepper, which she calls a magic elixir.

It helps get the writing done.

You can find more of her works at:
GabriellaCreighton.com

Contents

Fire and Brimstone

PROLOGUE

> Perhaps home is not a place but simply an irrevocable condition.
>
> James Baldwin

THE HOUSE WAS BURNING.

The night split open with fire, flames roaring skyward, casting orange and crimson shadows through the tall trees surrounding the old country home. The fog that had clung to the treeline turned to steam in the heat, curling like spirits fleeing the inferno. Ash danced like snow in the suffocating air. The world hissed and crackled beneath a sky gone black.

The shriek of splitting wood and the sharp pop of glass shattering mixed with the distant wail of sirens, mundane and magical. Emergency wards sparked to life in the treetops, crackling with soft blue light that did little to ease the chaos.

Inside the collapsing house, smoke thick as tar filled every room. The nursery was a ruin of smoldering wood and crumbling stone. A woman knelt on the scorched floor, her blonde hair matted with soot, eyes wild as she scanned the debris through stinging tears.

"Peter!" she screamed, her voice raw and panicked. "Peter, where is she!?"

A man staggered into the room, his form ghostlike in the haze. One arm covered his mouth, the other cradled a small bundle wrapped in a singed baby blanket.

"I've got her!" he coughed, stepping over debris.

Mariah Mason struggled to her feet, hands trembling. "Where's Mia?"

Peter looked down at the child, Sia, barely a year old, whimpering softly, and for a moment, he didn't answer. His face was cut, soot-streaked, eyes filled with guilt.

"Peter," Mariah said again, her voice cracking. "Where is our daughter?"

The ceiling groaned above them. A beam snapped and crashed down in the next room, spraying sparks and embers. The fire surged, flaring with a low, hungry roar.

"She's gonna be okay," Peter said, though his voice wavered. "We got Sia out. Mia's still inside, I'm going back for her."

Mariah grabbed his arm, desperation in her grip. "Peter, no! The whole house is coming down, "

"She's still alive!" he barked. "I won't leave her."

Another crash from overhead. Flames licked down the hallway, curling like fingers around the doorframe.

"I'll find another way in," Peter said, eyes burning. "Get Sia out of here."

He turned and vanished into the choking smoke.

Mariah staggered to the back door, cradling Sia against her chest. The baby coughed weakly, then began to cry again, high, thin, terrified. As Mariah burst through the doorway into the night, a wall behind her collapsed with a deafening crack, sparks shooting skyward like fireworks.

Outside, the air wasn't much clearer. Sirens howled. Magic shimmered through the smoke as wards activated, enclosing the house in protective glyphs meant to contain the blaze. Fire crews arrived on broomsticks and armored trucks alike, shouting spells and commands over the roar.

From the treeline, two dark silhouettes watched.

They were tall, unnaturally still, dressed in black suits without a speck of ash on them. The shorter of the two wore a permanent, frozen smile. The other's eyes glowed faintly, red-orange embers in the dark.

"She was supposed to die tonight," said the smiling one.

"She still might," said the other, his voice low and gravelly.

They both turned as Peter reemerged, coughing, his clothes scorched and hair singed. In his arms, wrapped tightly in his coat, was a second bundle, Mia. Alive.

"She's tougher than she looks," the ember-eyed one muttered.

"And the bond between them grows stronger for it," said the smiling one. "We'll try again."

Behind them, the woods were quiet. The stars above them blinked out, one by one, as if the sky itself mourned what had almost been lost.

A short distance away, Peter collapsed to his knees beside Mariah, both girls now in their arms. Sia still whimpered in her mother's grip, and Mia stirred faintly in her father's, her tiny chest rising and falling.

Mariah pressed her lips to Sia's soot-smeared head and whispered something wordless, trembling.

Peter's voice was hoarse. "That wasn't an accident. The wards were triggered from the inside. Something breached the defenses."

Mariah nodded. "Demons. I felt them. They didn't care about the fire... they came for the girls."

Peter looked down at Mia, then at Sia. "They know what they are. Even this young."

"We can't stay here." Mariah's voice broke with fury and fear. "They'll come again."

"I know." He exhaled, long and shaky. "We'll leave tonight. I'll contact the old network. Dobahold will take us. It has to."

Mariah tightened her grip on Sia. "They'll be safe there. They'll grow up far from this madness. They'll have time."

Peter met her eyes. "They'll need each other. Whatever's coming... we can't let them face it alone."

The fire behind them howled, its roar rolling through the trees like a voice from some ancient mouth. Ash drifted upward into the sky as if to blot out the stars, the last remnants of the house burning like a funeral pyre for a life already lost. The image of flame and smoke faded, dissolving into black.

A HEARTBEAT. A SINGLE beat of silence. Sia opened her eyes into the Dreaming. Or at least, something shaped like it.

The marble beneath her feet cracked and glowed with heat, veins of molten red pulsing outward like blood under skin. The air was thick and choking, metallic with the scent of iron and sulfur. Around her, the remnants of a ruined furnace room stretched wide, walls scorched black, vents hissing with intermittent bursts of steam, chains dangling from rusted hooks above long-dead firepits.

It felt like the belly of a beast that hadn't finished digesting. Each breath felt stolen. She turned slowly, the shadows flickering and alive across the jagged floor. Somewhere beyond the ruined furnace wall, something groaned, massive, slow, like stone grinding over stone. And then she saw it: scrawled across the blistered wall in scorched hand-print smears, glowing faintly through soot and smoke.

Sia, this is real.

The words pulsed once, then again. Her throat tightened. The world pulsed in time with her heartbeat.

"Mia?" she whispered.

No answer came.

But the heat pressed closer. Something unseen moved beyond the veil of firelight, pacing just out of sight. The Dreaming never waited for permission and tonight, it brought a warning. the sky above her a twisting sea of violet and indigo, stars hanging too close and too bright. Towering pillars of broken stone stretched around her like the skeletons of a forgotten temple. The air hummed with static and something older than sound.

She didn't remember falling asleep. She did not want to sleep and experience these nightmares, but night after night they came. She did everything to avoid them.

But the Dreaming never waited for permission.

CHAPTER 1
The Umbrella Prophecy

Storm crow descending, winter unending.
Storm Crow departing, summer is starting.

An Old Nursery Rhyme

A VOICE RANG OUT from downstairs, warm, familiar.

"Sia!"

Sia Mason opened her eyes to the pale ceiling above, her breath catching in her throat like it always did. Her room was still. Quiet. Morning light filtered in through the window, cutting long stripes across the far wall. Her hand instinctively drifted downward, checking the skin of her arm, her side, her stomach, no burns. No marks. Nothing that proved the dream had happened at all.

She let out a long, shuddering breath.

Fifteen now. A freshman in high school. Still small for her age. She hated that about herself, how her limbs never seemed to grow at the same rate as everyone else's. She was thin, short, built like a child someone had pressed fast-forward on but forgot to let finish. The teasing had died down over the summer, but it never really went away. Not for girls like her.

She sat up slowly, the sheets whispering against her skin, and looked across the room to where her violin rested atop a chair. The case sat beneath it, waiting. She rose, barefoot, and padded across the floor to close it gently, her first daily ritual. The room around her was spotless. Spartan. Everything had a place, and she needed it that way. The violin, the sheet music stacked neatly on the desk, the lone lamp, it was a space where chaos wasn't allowed in.

Not even dreams could follow her here.

She made her way into the bathroom, flicking on the light, its hum joining the soft patter of the faucet. Leaning close to the mirror, she peeled back the curtain of messy hair from her face and stared.

Lines of sleeplessness etched shadows beneath her eyes. Her skin was pale, almost waxy in the bathroom light. Her irises were a cold blue, closer to ice than sky, wide and sharp in a way that made people uncomfortable if they looked too long. And that hair... tangled waves of dusky brown, streaked with sunlit blond, like someone had smeared paintbrush bristles through it without asking.

She didn't dye it. People thought she did.

They thought a lot of things about her.

She touched her reflection gently, not for vanity, but to feel that she was still here.

Still normal.

Still... real.

The Mason family was, on the surface, as normal as they came.

They lived in a restored 18th-century colonial tucked along a quiet road in the wooded edges of Apple Grove, a small, New York countryside town with more trees than people and the sort of quiet that felt like it had to be borrowed from a postcard.

The Masons had dark hair, pale skin, and the faintest traces of heritage that no one quite knew how to place. As Sia once described herself during an uncomfortable classroom icebreaker: "a mutt." A mix of Italian and German descent. Her father, Peter Mason, came from a long line of Ellis Island Italians, now thoroughly Americanized. Her mother, Mariah Mason, was fourth-generation German-American. Neither held tightly to old customs. Their roots had been sewn into American soil long before Sia or her sister were ever born.

Peter worked for Intel, tucked behind a desk solving the kind of problems no one else wanted to. A software engineer, clever, quiet, and thoughtful. Mariah was the school nurse at nearby Taft Elementary, a woman who could smile through anything but whose hands were always a little too still when she worried.

They had one daughter now. And a golden Labrador named Truth.

One child short of the classic nuclear family, and yet most neighbors considered them "well-off," if perhaps a little reserved. Their house sat just a few streets away from the local highway, distant enough to remain peaceful, close enough for a fifteen-minute drive to the mini-mall or the nearest diner. Apple Grove's heartbeat was slow and steady, one main street, a handful of restaurants, a library older than the town charter, and a population that still used paper checks and gossip as their primary currencies.

It was a place where the worst crime in recent memory had been a hit-and-run by the town drunk three years ago. The kind of place where everyone knew each other's names, and stories. And secrets, too, though they never said them aloud.

It was, by all outside appearances, the perfect neighborhood to raise a child.

Sia had lived here her whole life, and she couldn't remember a single time she'd ever truly felt like she belonged in it.

Slinging her backpack over her shoulder and popping her earphones into her ears, she walked down the road toward the main highway; only a short fifteen-minute walk would take her to school. The earbuds played music from her phone, a device her parents insisted she carry so they could keep track of her, as if she were the kind of girl who would ever go out. Classical violin filled her ears, a strangeness for someone her age, but Sia preferred the order of string instruments over the chaos of pop.

She glared as a minivan made its way down the road along which she walked, some soccer mom hauling her kids to school. She absolutely hated motor vehicles of any sort, only bearing to ride in her parents' cars when absolutely necessary. Something from her dreams. Something from her nightmares. The growl of engines too often mirrored the guttural roar of beasts that stalked her in the dark, the same snarl that echoed in the corners of her dreams where fire kissed metal and voices whispered behind her eyes.

Each step she took on the pavement felt just a little too loud, the sun too pale against the edges of shadows that clung longer than they should. A crow watched her from a fence post and didn't blink. The breeze had a bite to it despite the clear sky, and every now and then, the hairs on the back of her neck rose as if she were being followed, though the street was empty.

She kept walking, one hand tightening around the handle of the umbrella, as though it might do something, anything, if whatever was watching decided to step closer.

This was not some environmentalist measure, either. The glare she gave to passing cars held a small degree of phobic detraction. It limited her social life, but Sia was not a very social person. She preferred the quiet. Or at least, the lack of noise that wasn't born of orchestra or cello string.

The clouds had begun to gather, subtly. There was no thunder yet, no obvious warning. But she knew. Before the first drop hit, she paused at the edge of the school lot, raised her umbrella, and clicked it open just in time for the rain to start falling in earnest. The rising torrent soaked the pavement in seconds.

Sia remained dry, untouched beneath the dome of dull black fabric.

To anyone else, it was just luck.

To Sia, it was instinct.

Or prophecy.

CHAPTER 2

When the Sky Fell Quiet

It moves at its own measured pace, for it has no reason
to hurry. Tomorrow will come in its own good time.
Sidney Sheldon

SIA'S SAFE PLACE HAD always been the library.

After dropping off her backpack in her locker and brushing past
the cliques of chattering students, she made her way there without
thinking. The quiet corridors of Apple Grove High faded into soft
shadows and hushed pages. The library's warm lighting fell in golden
squares across polished tile, dust floating lazily through the air like
magic trying not to be noticed.

She dropped her notebook on one of the side desks near the back,
sliding into the chair like she'd rehearsed it. Her pen hovered for a
moment before scrawling two words across the first line:

Nightmare Log.

She paused, tapping the pen against her lip, then started writing.
No one had told her to do it. No therapist had given her a journal. It
was just something she needed. A way to prove, to herself, to something watching, that she was still tracking the dream. Still in control.

Today's entry was short. Just bullet points.

Fire.
Chains.
Furnace room again.

> Something moved in the smoke.
> Mia's name written in blood.
> "Sia this is real."

She stared at the last line. Underlined it. Twice.

The screen of her school-issued tablet glowed beside her, open to a search page she hadn't quite hit enter on.

> Dreams of fire and prophecy?
> Dreams that predict the future?
> Nightmares about a sibling calling out to you?

She sighed and deleted the whole line. It felt silly. Not for the first time, she wondered if maybe she was losing her mind.

"You know," said a familiar voice, "you'd probably get better search results if you didn't delete them all."

Sia's head jerked up.

Ella Archer stood a few feet away, arms folded across her chest, one brow raised like a queen catching her handmaidens gossiping. She was tall and regal in posture, with honey-gold blonde hair braided down her back like spun sunlight. Her hoodie was a rich red that contrasted sharply with the green of her eyes, bright and striking, like spring leaves caught in sunlight. A messenger bag hung at her side, worn casually over one shoulder, as if ready to vanish at any moment.

Sia blinked. "You're early."

"I could say the same thing about you." Ella dropped her bag in the chair across from her and sat without asking. "You didn't answer your texts."

"I was writing," Sia muttered.

Ella leaned forward. "You've had another one, haven't you?"

Sia's silence was enough.

Ella's voice softened. "The furnace again?"

"Worse this time." Sia rubbed her wrist absently, though there was no pain. "There was a message."

Ella frowned. "What kind of message?"

Sia hesitated. Then: "From Mia."

That name hung in the air like smoke.

Ella didn't say anything for a long moment. She just reached across the table and, gently, closed the notebook.

"You're not crazy," she said. "Even if no one else believes you, I do."

Sia felt something tight in her chest begin to unwind.

Ella didn't move her hand from the notebook right away. She left it there, steady, an anchor in the storm of Sia's thoughts. Then she gently slid the notebook aside and rested her chin on her other hand, elbow propped on the table like this was just another one of their usual morning meetings, like this wasn't the moment Sia needed someone most.

"Hey," Ella said softly, her voice all warmth and velvet. "You don't have to carry this alone. I know you act like you can, but I know better."

Sia offered a small, tired smile, and Ella returned it with one of her own, bright and slow-spreading, like dawn cutting through fog.

The chair creaked faintly as Ella shifted closer, resting both arms on the table. "Scoot over."

Sia blinked. "What?"

"I said, scoot."

Sia complied without argument. Ella stood, moved around the table, and settled next to her, knees brushing under the wood. She slung her arm loosely across the back of Sia's chair without making a thing of it.

They sat there like that for a few long minutes, side by side, letting the silence fill in the spaces words couldn't.

Sia leaned into her, just slightly, enough to make the contact real. "I hate feeling like this," she murmured. "Like the world's fraying at the edges and I'm the only one seeing it."

Ella nudged her shoulder gently. "Then we'll hold the threads together. One stitch at a time."

Sia exhaled slowly. The storm inside her hadn't passed, not fully, but Ella's presence dulled the lightning.

"Thanks," she whispered.

Ella leaned her head against Sia's. "Always."

The bell hadn't rung yet, but the volume of the halls suggested otherwise.

Ella and Sia stepped out of the quiet safety of the library and into the storm of lockers slamming, voices overlapping, and the rhythmic squeak of sneakers on waxed floors. The morning crush of Apple Grove High was in full swing, and the two girls navigated it with practiced ease, close enough to look casual, silent enough not to invite questions.

They passed the usual cliques clustered like weather systems, jocks orbiting the vending machines, theater kids speaking in half-accented quotes from last night's rehearsal, a group of band kids squabbling over brass maintenance like it was national policy. None of them looked their way.

Not yet.

"Your fan club's at it early," Ella muttered under her breath.

Sia followed her gaze.

Two boys stood near the end of the hallway by the double doors, engaged in what looked like a very animated debate over a half-crushed coffee cup.

The first was tall and lean, all elbows and knees, with a mop of dark hair that looked like it had lost a battle with a hairdryer. He had startlingly bright blue eyes and a grin that practically glowed with mischief, a grin made to get him into trouble, and one he wielded like a weapon. Eric Sinclair. Resident class clown, part-time magician of detention slips, and full-time agent of chaos.

He spotted them immediately and lit up. "Ladies! Did you know the vending machine still owes me two dollars and a bag of shame?"

Beside him stood someone who made a very different kind of impression. Marcus Duvall was almost as tall as Eric, but broader in the shoulders and far more put together. Soft auburn hair framed a face that would've looked just as natural behind a football helmet as it would in a coding tournament. Hazel eyes caught the light as he glanced their way, a quiet confidence in his expression that was never smug, just assured, like he knew who he was and didn't need to explain it.

He gave them a nod that was both casual and warm. "Morning, Ella. Sia."

Ella offered a polite nod. "Marcus. Eric."

Sia mumbled a greeting under her breath, her fingers twitching slightly around the strap of her bag. She never quite knew what to do with Marcus's attention. He wasn't teasing. He wasn't mocking. And that, somehow, made him harder to deal with than the people who were.

Eric leaned back against the locker like he lived there, arms folded. "You look like you both saw a ghost. Or burned one at the stake. Wanna trade stories?"

Ella rolled her eyes. "Only if we can skip the part where you pretend you're helpful."

"You wound me," Eric said, dramatically pressing a hand to his chest. "And here I was going to offer my unmatched insight on social dynamics and poor cafeteria decisions."

Sia couldn't help it, she laughed. Just a little.

And that, she realized, was probably why Ella tolerated him.

The bell rang overhead in two sharp bursts, snapping them out of the moment like a needle through silk.

Eric's voice preceded his arrival. "Time to pretend we care about public education again."

He was waiting for them just outside the library doors, his usual smirk firmly in place and a backpack slung over one shoulder like it offended him. Marcus stood beside him with a relaxed air, hands tucked into his jacket pockets.

"We're late," Ella muttered, slinging her bag over her shoulder.

"Technically we're fashionably delayed," Eric countered, falling into step beside them as the four headed down the hall. "It's a power move."

Marcus chuckled. "Says the guy who once tripped over his own shoelaces trying to make a power move."

"Strategic stumble," Eric corrected. "Kept expectations low. It's all part of my plan."

They turned the corner toward their first class. The hallway buzzed with noise, students darting in and out of classrooms, teachers calling out reminders. Colorful posters lined the bulletin board by the office, the largest one practically glowing with forced enthusiasm: FALL FORMAL - Friday Night! Theme: Starlight Soirée!

Ella made a face. "That again?"

Marcus laughed under his breath. "Didn't they just do a Spring Fling?"

Eric leaned close, mock-whispering to Sia. "It's all a ploy. Lure the teenagers in with music and sparkles. Then boom, emotional break-downs and poorly executed slow dances."

Sia rolled her eyes. "Yeah, hard pass."

Ella nodded. "We're not the dancing type."

"Nope," Marcus said quickly, though he glanced at Sia a second too long before adding, "Definitely not."

Eric shrugged. "Not yet anyway."

Sia caught the subtle look exchanged between Ella and Marcus, and a flutter of something she didn't want to name stirred in her stomach. She couldn't explain it, not exactly, but something about this odd little quartet felt... right. Like threads quietly being woven into something bigger.

And none of them knew yet just how tightly they'd be tied together.

The rest of the day after that however, moved like molasses.

Sia sat near the back of her literature class, staring out the window more than she watched the board. The clouds outside had thickened into a low gray ceiling, rumbling softly with the promise of rain. Miss Halpern was droning on about foreshadowing in nineteenth-century Gothic fiction, which might have interested Sia on any other day. But not today. Not with Mia's name still echoing in her mind.

She kept one hand on her desk and the other curled loosely around her umbrella, which she'd propped against her seat like a faithful pet. Her fingers tapped the handle in rhythm with her heartbeat.

Something felt wrong.

When the bell finally rang, she didn't wait for Ella, Marcus, or Eric. She slipped out of class, weaving between the crowd, past the noise and lockers and laughter that felt too loud in her ears. She made it outside just as the sky opened.

The rain came all at once, sheets of cold water soaking the sidewalk in seconds. But Sia was ready. She opened her umbrella without missing a step and ducked her head beneath it. Her shoes splashed through puddles forming in the cracks of the pavement as she walked across the empty school yard, putting distance between herself and the crowd.

She wasn't sure where she was going. Only that she needed air. Space. Solitude.

She found it under the old maple tree behind the school. It stood like an old sentinel on the edge of the property, far from the main walkways and hidden behind a curve of fencing and overgrown hedges. Its branches stretched wide, limbs gnarled with age, leaves thick and green even under the gray sky. The roots jutted from the ground like the bones of the earth itself, bursting through cracks in the concrete where the lot had tried to contain it.

The space beneath it was more than just dry, it felt sacred. A hush hung there, broken only by the rhythm of rain against her umbrella and the occasional roll of distant thunder. It was the kind of place stories wanted to happen. The kind of place that waited for significance.

Sia stepped carefully between the roots and stood in the hollow they formed, her shoes brushing damp moss. Her breath came in quiet shivers. It wasn't just the chill. It was the dread curling behind her ribs. The sense that something was building again. Watching. The dream hadn't ended, it had followed her here, threading its way into the waking world.

"You always run when you're overwhelmed," came a voice behind her.

Sia didn't turn. "You always follow me."

Ella stepped up beside her, not even wearing a hood. She didn't seem to mind the rain. Her honey-blonde braid had soaked through, clinging to her jacket, and droplets beaded on her lashes as she looked at Sia.

"Because I know what it feels like," Ella said quietly. "To want to disappear for a while."

Sia tightened her grip on the umbrella. "It's not getting better, El. The dreams. The feeling. It's like I'm walking through something only I can see, and it's getting worse."

Ella stepped closer, brushing their arms. "Then we'll walk through it together. Even if it's storming."

Sia blinked, and for the first time that day, let herself lean into someone else's warmth.

The rain didn't let up, but it didn't feel quite so cold anymore.

CHAPTER 3

Where Secrets Stir

In doing what we ought we deserve no praise, because it is our duty.

Saint Augustine

PADDINGTON STATION WAS AS it ever was, filled with people, milling about in their daily lives. Men and women coming and going from work, families reuniting after children had gone off on long trips, travelers and tourists both coming and going. It rang softly with the sound of water hitting the windows of the upper shed windows. Light from the gloomy day leaked down, illuminating the scene, still other lights shone down, making it seem brighter than the day outside. It was truly small effort in such stormy weather.

A man stood smoking a cigarette by the 20A Terminal. He wore sunglasses to hide his eyes, his long blonde hair tied back in a ponytail, and it was cut neatly, respectable almost. His shirt and most of his slacks were hidden under a closed, tan duster, the collar of the duster pulled up in the old fashioned detective style out of noir mystery movies, shielding his neck from view. He took another drag of his cigarette, the only thing truly pulling him into focus in the scene of milling travellers were the fingerless leather gloves about his hands and his stoic position, a stone in the middle of a stream of travelling people. The gloves were barely visible under the long sleeves, but with the rest of his outfit they were a stark contrast, a 'punkish' decoration on what could otherwise be the clothing of a respectable businessman.

He watched people milling back and forth along the station. None paid him much attention, save those who looked at him rudely for smoking in such a busy causeway. He didn't seem to care however. Thin lips drawn in a serious expression, his eyes hidden as to where they focused, making it hard for a passer-by to see who or what he may be watching for. He continued to lean, his head following a man in his mid-thirties, short cropped brown hair, hazel eyes and wearing a business suit.

The man's eyes, under the glasses, peered at the back of the businessman's neck as he walked along. If one was watching such as the duster clad man was, they would have noticed the inked dragon delicately tattooed into the passer-byer's skin, a mark almost hidden by his hair and the collar of his shirt. Slowly he fell into step behind the man, he walked with a trained yet casual ease which did not immediately alert the man as to his intentions. They walked, the man still seemingly not taking notice to the stranger who had flicked his cigarette aside and casually walked in the same direction he was. However, as they parted the crowds into the busy London Streets, the man took a sharp left for the nearby alleyways. His pursuer adjusted his black sunglasses and followed after him at an increased pace.

The two headed into the darkness of the alleyway, the stone cobbles of the street giving way to concrete. The man slowly turned to eye his follower and glared. His eyes in the darkened alleyway seemed to come alive, a slight red glow behind them and his position becoming more apparent as he seemed to grow. "Who the bloody hell are you? Why are you following me?"

The duster clad man did not speak, instead he slowly opened his long coat, revealing his loose white shirt underneath, his slacks held up by a heavy belt. Hanging across his chest was a rosary, made of shining silver. The man took a step back, frowning. "If its money you want, I don't have much. Someone will hear me screaming!" He yelled out, his hands falling to his sides.

The silent man adjusted his belt, the silvered hilt of a sword falling into sight. Its handle wrapped in fine black leather, the pommel a simple rounded circle providing the counterweight to the blade itself. His gloved hands gripped the handle and drew it out smoothly, the metal shined in the light as though the weapon we made of pure silver or chrome, yet it did not look like a vanity weapon, it was worn with use and fitted the man's hands as assuredly as those fingerless gloves firmed the grip he had on the handle. The businessman's eyes grew wide as he saw it and put his hands out. The glow of his eyes increased as he embraced some hidden arcane power, the darkness behind him flared just a little as that dragon tattoo illuminated the brickwork behind him. What should have astonished the swordsman was fire gathering in the palms of the businessman.

It was no natural fire, darkness flitted inside the glowing red and white of the superheated flame, it moved unnaturally, guided by no wind, it smelled faintly of ever burning sulphur. He held out his palms towards the swordsman, sending a jet of burning flame out at him, the alleyway lit up with the intensity of the gout. The swordsman held out his sword before him, his blade straight in front of him as though holding it as a shield, he began to chant. It became quickly evident that he was praying.

"In nomine Patris, et Filii, et Spiritus Sancti."

The sword seemed to glow against the light of the fire, where most men would have leapt away and guarded their faces; the swordsman took a step forward into the fire. The fire began to part aside, like the Red Sea parting for Moses. On the flat of the blade, letters began to appear as though etched into the metal by gathering points of light, the light itself not from the flames at all. Letter after letter formed, creating the word VERITAS. The businessman's gaze fell on him and he narrowed his eyes in focus, the flames burning brighter, flames licked the brick sides of the alley and the ground around the swordsman. Never once did the hellfire touch him as he continued to pray, each word flowing from his lips with a step he took, slowly and deliberately he closed the gap between himself and the businessman, whose palms began to boil from the sheer heat of the magical flame's recoil, losing room to burst outward.

The swordsman's words began to reverberate about the alleyway, echoing and repeating, growing stronger like a wave of force, causing the flame wielder's knees to buckle, shaking he struggled just to stand up, the words cut him like knives. *"Sicut erat in principio, et nunc, et semper, et in saecula saeculorum. Amen."*

At "Amen", the golden haired swordsman stood within striking range of the fire wielding businessman. The fire faltered and went out; the man took a step back, the wild light in his eyes was no longer one of power, but the sheer fright of a man facing certain death. He choked out his protests in growing disbelief. "How... that was hellfire, who the bloody hell are you!?"

The swordsman said nothing, his first stroke smote the air in front of him, the heat from the flames and the glow of his sword creating a streak of light in the air, the man stumbled back, his chest a growing well of red blood that began to soak his shirt, the cut through the fabric so fine it seemed non-existent save for the effects of the blade parting skin and bone as though they were butter. The swordsman once again raised his sword, and he brought it down on the man's skull, splitting through bone, brains and flesh, destroying his head beyond any form of recognition, beyond any form of restoration and resurrection. Blood spattered, it flew into the man's face, stopped only by the glasses and his coat slicked with blood, bone and brain matter, the man's eyes never wavered under those dark lenses. He had no mercy for a sinner. No mercy for the sin.

And yet...

Tobias stood still, the blood cooling on his coat, his blade held loose at his side. The sinner was gone, struck down, body broken beyond resurrection, but the sting of it lingered.

He did not regret the act. The flame-bearer had chosen his path, signed away his soul long before this moment. But that didn't make the killing clean.

Tobias turned his gaze skyward, as though the rain might wash away more than the crimson staining his boots. The sword slowly lowered. There was satisfaction in his work, yes, but not joy. He never took joy in the kill. Only in stopping the spread.

Demons corrupted everything they touched. They whispered lies into wounded hearts, and he had seen the aftermath, whole villages undone, churches burned, families torn apart. This was justice. This was defense.

But he still remembered the weight of younger eyes watching him return from hunts, how innocence recoiled from the scent of ash and iron. He had grown used to being a shadow in the service of light, a sword for a cause that called for silence and precision, not applause. He knew the justness of his calling, but justice was not the same as peace.

He took a breath. Inhaled the ash, the smoke, the lingering scent of sulfur. It never quite left him.

But neither would the duty.

He sheathed his blade with a practiced movement, and as it locked in place beneath his coat, his expression hardened once again.

The rain whispered around him as if trying to wash the alley clean, but it could not touch the weight that lingered in the air. Tobias stepped over the body and back onto the street, his footfalls muffled on the wet stone. Somewhere nearby, a church bell began to chime the hour, its echo distant, solemn, like a benediction spoken too late.

As the final toll faded, so too did the weight in the air. The city exhaled. The time for reflection was over. There were more names in the file. And one girl, above all others, whom he would not allow to fall.

Far across the ocean, in a quiet library untouched by rain or blood, another force stirred awake...

Walking through a small library, a man with long dark hair walked into the back door to the office normally occupied by librarians. The two young women who worked there didn't as much as glance up at him. The man wore a simple oxford shirt and black slacks, black socks showed a little, which blended into the black leather shoes he silently tread over the ground. His dark hair was pulled back in a tail, his eyes were a deep hazel, he walked to the far back wall of the office and touched a framed picture of a Victorian era woman. As he touched it, the image seemed to bend and twist a little, and the wall opened like a hidden doorway.

He stepped into the darkness beyond and shut the door, this was well out of view of any common patrons looking for books in the front. He continued to walk through the darkness as though the hallway he trotted down was lit with fluorescent overheads. A few moment and he stepped into a large candlelit study, leather-bound books lining the walls on large shelves. In the centre of the room a woman with short red hair worked on a tome nearly the same size as herself, the pages were a dark brown, worn with age, the ink black and oddly fresh looking in comparison to the age of the book, with occasional brownish red markings. The markings were clearly not ink, but blood. She turned to peer at him and scowled.

"Crowley, you're late. I've been here over an hour already reading the Word. What kept you? Messing around with another woman are you?" She spoke in a thick British accent, northern in quality, her eyes were glaring points of green under her too red shade of hair. She wore a pale green dress, a two piece affair with a knee length skirt and matching blouse, it was cut to show off what was a most womanly body. She smirked a bit at the man, who adjusted a pair of square framed glasses he had pulled out as she spoke.

"Now, now, Lilian, you know there is no other woman in the world worthy of my attentions but you. Did you get all trussed up like that for me? Did you actually bring yourself to use a mirror for once?" He smirked, the final part of his riposte was sarcastic, meant to burn, and to an outsider might seem confusing. To her however, it caused her to recoil.

"Did you slither here on your belly then, Crawley?" She hissed a bit, turning and putting her hands on her wide hips to peer over the tome again, as though dismissing him. Crowley merely chuckled and studied her instead of the tome, he walked up by her.

"Again, with all due respect to a lady, My Dear Lilian, let's not go throwing about names. I rather like Crowley, you know." He turned his attention to the tome just as her head snapped, catching the emphasis of her own chosen name. Her eyes seemed to glow in the dim light a moment with green to match her dress and irises.

"Forget that. Read the Word and tell me you're seeing what I'm seeing." She spat out her words and turned back to trace the tome with him, what she apparently called The Word. Crowley traced the lettering with his eyes, the letters were not composed in any language known to ordinary man, intricately written scratches in the shape of runes, maddeningly, the bottom of the right page appeared to be being written even as they glanced, red blood covering the page to form letter after letter in the strange text. Crowley mumbled the long forgotten tongue under his breath.

He smiled, then peered at her. "I see it. The Word tells us, the seals are breaking. The Last Prophet is awakening and the time is coming soon when we will be able to change the outcome of God's plan. Do the others know?" He peered at her through the glasses, trying to catch her eyes. "Have the other Lords been informed, Lilith?"

Lilian scowled as he broke his own word in naming her, the red haired woman sighed. "I've told them all to check into their Word, they'll know soon enough. "Astaroth is already in the area that she's in. And we have Sonneillon trailing after the Templar who the Church thinks will be able to protect her. Neither will last long. The Morn-ingstar will be pleased."

"Be sure he is, Lil, because if we fail, no degree of whoring will save you from his wrath this time," Crowley purred, circling her like a cat eyeing a coiled serpent. "And don't think he's forgotten that little 'incident' in Apple Grove, either. That house fire nearly cost us our chance at the twins."

Lilith's expression soured, her hands curling slightly as she leaned in, smile sharpened like a blade. "Funny you bring that up, Crawley. As I recall, it was your little tantrum with a fireball that scared the mother into running. If you'd aimed your spell with more than just your ego, we might not be cleaning up your mess now."

Crowley's eyes narrowed behind the glass. "And yet here you are, still sniffing at my heels like a hellhound hoping for scraps." He hissed a little, putting his hands in his pockets, his attention gone from the Word and focused entirely on the woman before him. Lilian, or Lilith, sighed as she crossed her arms under her breasts and gave him a confident sneer.

"What Crawley, worried he won't remember his little snake who started all this?"

The Word went still.

In the silence that followed, the room felt heavier. Not with fear, but with the gravity of what had been spoken, names, fates, blood. A breathless moment passed as if the world itself exhaled, briefly pausing its spin.

And far away, across the sea and beneath a storm-laced sky, the weight of purpose settled once more on a man already carrying too much.

The swordsman stepped out of the alleyway, his weapon once again hidden, his coat strangely and remarkably clean. But even as he walked, the weight of the act lingered. He could feel the blood drying beneath the lining, the scent of char still clinging to his clothes. His boots struck the cobblestones with the rhythm of a man walking in time with old burdens.

Three men ducked into the alleyway after he left, dressed like city maintenance workers, blue jumpsuits and yellow gloves. They moved like professionals. One carried a plastic jug marked with acid warnings. Tobias did not look back. These men were not street cleaners. They were his order's janitors, cleaning up the stains that couldn't be left for the world to see.

He lit another cigarette, letting the warmth in his lungs blunt the ache in his shoulders. The cold mist of the rain gathered in his hair, his coat, but he barely noticed. He walked in silence, down back alleys and through empty crosswalks, until he reached the front steps of a quiet Roman Catholic church nestled in the heart of London. Far fewer of them remained than once did, hidden between Anglican parishes and modern indifference, but this one, this one still opened its doors at every hour.

Tobias paused on the steps, gazing up at the simple wooden cross over the entrance. He drew one last breath through the cigarette, the embers briefly flaring as he exhaled smoke like incense from some grim ritual.

A door creaked behind him.

"You know," came a voice from the shadows within, dry and unimpressed, "you're not technically supposed to smoke on holy ground."

Tobias didn't turn. "Add it to the list."

The priest gave a tired sigh. "You Paladins are all the same. Kill a demon, light a cigarette, track blood through the vestibule. Saints, the lot of you."

Only then did Tobias drop the cigarette, grinding it out with his heel. He stepped inside.

The chapel was dim, lit only by votive candles and the dim glow of the altar. The sound of the old wooden door swinging shut behind Tobias echoed through the space like the final beat of a drum. The air was thick with incense, aged wood, and the faint metallic tang of polished brass. Somewhere overhead, the faint creak of the building settling groaned in harmony with the low, mournful whistle of wind outside.

Tobias moved forward with quiet steps that didn't quite silence the soft scuff of leather on tile. The worn pews stood like forgotten sentinels, shadows dancing over their backs from the flickering votive flames. At the front, an iron-wrought crucifix hung in reverent stillness, its silhouette wavering in candlelight like a memory barely clinging to form.

He knelt in the second pew, the action slow, bones complaining softly. His hands folded around the hilt of his sword like a monk's at prayer.

"Ave Maria, gratia plena, Dominus tecum..." he murmured, low and precise. The Latin rose from him like breath through parchment, measured, memorized, fatigued. His voice was hoarse from smoke and chanting. Each syllable curled upward like ghostly ash.

Silence followed the final word.

The faint rustle of fabric signaled another presence. Another priest knelt beside him, the scent of cold wool and old manuscripts wafting off his robe.

A folder slid onto the bench.

"You've done proud service, Paladin," came the whisper, reverent but brisk. "The Holy Father has another request."

The voice bore the cadence of cathedral stone, northern and unwavering, shaped by scripture and secrecy.

"Go with God's grace, and know your works pave your place beside Him."

Tobias did not speak. He simply nodded, the movement small but absolute.

The priest left without ceremony. Tobias finished his prayer, slowly rising. His knees ached. His joints cracked. The fire fight had taken more from him than expected.

He cursed inwardly, not the magic, not the hellfire, but his own waning endurance. Ward Ways or no, he was beginning to feel the cracks in his armor.

Still, he stood. Still, he moved. The sword at his side was not light, but it never had been.

He took the folder and left without looking at it, not until he was past the chapel's doors and under the night sky again.

Only then did he open it, and when he did, his step faltered.

A girl. Sixteen at most. Hazel eyes. Unkempt brown hair. A mundane name: Sia Mason.

He frowned. Of all the things he expected, this was not it.

The sword was moving again. had he had better proficiency in the Warders Ways, the art his order practiced in defense against magic, he would not have had to work so hard. He turned and began moving to step out, tucking the folder under his arm, not daring to open it under the eyes of the man hanging on a cross at the head of the chapel. He stepped into the street and towards his hotel, as he opened the file. His eyes widened a little; the target was little more than a girl. Definitely no older than fifteen or sixteen years, mussed up brown hair and cold hazel eyes. He looked at the picture of Sia Mason, as he began to read the file.

His plane touched down at 3:02 AM, the tarmac of Stewart International shrouded in low fog. The terminal lights buzzed softly, sterile and too bright for the hour. Tobias disembarked with a quiet grace, his boots tapping softly on the waxed floors.

He slipped the dossier back into his duffel, the file now worn from handling. He knew it by heart. Sia Mason. Prophet or pawn, it didn't matter, only that someone wanted her protected, and someone else wanted her dead.

By the baggage claim, a portly priest in a wrinkled black suit waited like a misplaced relic. Tobias nodded. No words. The man took his duffel with practiced efficiency and disappeared into one of the service doors behind a security checkpoint. Paladin travel was no longer protected by old oaths or divine seals. These days, they moved in shadows and subtext.

Tobias bought a coffee from the kiosk, cradling it in his gloved hands. The heat bit pleasantly at his knuckles. His phone buzzed.

> You better not ghost me again. You promised.

He smirked faintly and thumbed out a reply.

> I'll be by in the morning. Try not to set anything on fire until then.

He passed through customs using his real name for the first time in years. The name Hendricks had served well, but this mission called for honesty. For something closer to home.

Outside, spring air clung to the streets like a memory, damp and cold, rich with pine and the distant hush of dew-wet tires rolling down early roads. His cab pulled up, old and boxy, and rumbled through the sleeping towns of the Hudson Valley. Porch lights blinked through thick trees. Diner signs glowed like forgotten stars.

By the time they reached Apple Grove, the sky was starting to blush at the edges. Main Street was quiet, the kind of quiet that only existed in places where everyone knew each other's middle names. The library's clock tower stood like a sentinel, watching.

Tobias stepped out, duffel slung over one shoulder. He didn't make it to the porch before the front door flung open.

"Tobias!"

She crashed into him like sunlight.

He caught her easily, the duffel sliding from his shoulder to the porch as he held her. Her hair still smelled like sleep and lavender. Her arms wrapped tight around his neck, no questions, no hesitation.

She was safe. Still smiling. Still his sister.

He closed his eyes for just a moment and held her.

"Hello, Ella," he said.

CHAPTER 4
Dreams That Remember

Deep into that darkness peering, long I stood there, wondering, fearing, doubting, dreaming dreams no mortal ever dared to dream before.

Edgar Allan Poe

SHE WAS IN A dark, strange place. A humid, living dark. The air reeked of damp straw and wet stone, overlaid with a metallic tang like raw meat left too long in shadow. The scent didn't just fill her nostrils, it overwhelmed her, burned into her skull. She could smell color. Feel emotion through scent alone. Her senses had shifted, become something more, something other.

Ella tried to sit up, but her limbs felt foreign, thicker in some places, thinner in others, her muscles unsure how to move. She collapsed to her side with a dull, muffled thump that should've hurt, but didn't. The ground beneath her was soft, warm, damp. She blinked and shapes came into focus, a dark cavern, glistening walls veined with bioluminescent threads. The distant drip of water echoed, slow and rhythmic, like a heartbeat.

It should've been terrifying. But it wasn't.

Somehow, this place felt safe.

A presence pressed against her awareness. Not with sound, but thought.

<Awaken, young one.>

The voice shimmered like silk through her thoughts, not spoken but known. It pulsed through her chest, resonant and warm. A memory that wasn't hers. A mother's voice that had never belonged to the woman who raised her.

Ella turned her head slowly, breath rising in cold clouds despite no chill in the air. The cavern flickered with a strange, dusky glow now, as though the walls breathed light. The ceiling arched far above her, carved from black stone veined in silver and gold, patterns moving like molten script just beneath the surface.

A figure stood at the far edge of the chamber.

It was tall, taller than any man she'd ever seen, and cloaked in darkness. Not the absence of light, but the suggestion of it. The shape was indistinct, as if shadow bent to its will and not the other way around. No features, no face, only the glint of two pale eyes like dying stars.

Ella felt no fear. Only stillness. A weight, ancient and watching.

"Wh... Who are you?" Her voice cracked like a branch underfoot. Her throat felt raw, her words strange, as though she were speaking through someone else's lips. Her tongue seemed heavier, her breath echoed within her chest.

The figure did not move, but the voice returned, calm and inescapable.

<You must wake up, young keeper. The Hold calls you. Awaken.>

"I don't... understand..." she whispered, even as her vision began to fold inward, the dream curling at its edges like burnt parchment.

The figure remained still, watching.

And then the world fell away.

"I don't understand..."

"...don't understand..." Ella murmured, her voice trailing out of sleep.

A louder voice snapped her from the haze, her mother's.

"Ella! Up! You're going to miss the bus again!"

It wasn't soft or mysterious. Not warm silk in her chest. Just her mom's usual blend of exasperation and urgency. The stark contrast made her blink hard and rub at her eyes, trying to shake off the dream, the cavern, the voice, the shadowed figure that watched her. It clung like fog behind her eyes, already slipping away as dreams always did.

She sighed and sat up, glancing blearily at the blue glow of her alarm clock.

"Twenty minutes... fantastic."

Not tired in the sleepy way, Ella always slept well, but in the "I could definitely stay wrapped up in these sheets forever" way. But her dream had left her heavier than usual. Something about the dark figure... No. No time to think about that now.

Tobias had gotten in late. She'd tried to wait up. She barely remembered hearing the front door click shut before she'd dozed off on the couch. He was probably still asleep in the guest room, which used to be his room, before he left for Europe all those years ago.

She scrambled into the shower, worked the knots from her hair, and changed in record time. A slice of toast in hand, she bolted downstairs, grabbing her bag and jacket with her mouth full. She paused just long enough to kiss her dad on the cheek, earning a chuckle from behind his newspaper, and waved at her mother who watched with amused eyes.

"You always do this to yourself," her mom said.

"Worth it," Ella mumbled through toast. "Dreamed of dragons."

That wasn't true, but it was easier than explaining what really stirred her. Behind her, her mother's smile dimmed for the briefest moment. The word 'dragons' hung in the air like a thread pulled too tight. A flicker of something passed through her eyes, concern, recognition, but she turned back to the counter before Ella could see it. She said nothing, though her fingers clenched just slightly around the rim of her coffee mug.

She hit the sidewalk running, toast in hand, hair slightly damp, the morning chill sharpening her senses. A few houses down, she spotted a familiar figure: Sia, walking the same path she always did, early, quiet, already in motion. It was strange. Usually Ella had to catch up with her at school. But today, as if sensing her, Sia slowed and drifted to the edge of the sidewalk, making space.

Ella fell into step beside her, brushing her still-wet hair back with one hand, breath still catching up with her body.

"You look tired," Sia said quietly, without looking.

Ella smirked. "Takes one to know one."

It was classic Sia, direct, observant, and just a little detached. Most people didn't notice Sia's way of greeting wasn't through words, but attention. A glance. A shift in pace. Her presence was quiet, but sharp.

Still catching her breath, Ella smiled and dropped her news like a pebble in a pond. "Tobias came home last night."

Sia's breath hitched, not that most would have caught it. Ella did. Her best friend didn't like Tobias much, though she'd never said why.

"How is he?" Sia asked. There was something under the words. Hesitation. Unease.

"Well enough," Ella replied. "Brought back some souvenirs."

Sia's eyes stayed forward, but Ella could feel her calculating something, always working things out in silence.

"What does he actually do?" Sia asked, tone light but clearly fishing for a distraction.

Ella laughed softly. "Some kind of corporate errands guy. No idea, really. He sends photos from all over Europe. Cathedrals. Old castles. Always says he's on a job."

Sia gave her a sidelong glance. "Maybe he's a secret agent. You know, takes out terrorists, seduces spies, the usual."

Ella giggled, humming the tune to "Secret Agent Man." "Please. My brother's more likely to talk someone to sleep than shoot them."

"Or pray them into a coma," Sia added.

Ella smiled fondly. "He's not that bad. He's just... Tobias."

She said it like it explained everything.

By the time the first few periods passed in a blur of routine, Ella had finally settled into her usual rhythm. She and Sia had made it to class just in time, navigating the morning chatter and lockers with practiced ease. The second bell echoed through the halls like a distant chime, ushering them into English.

English had always been one of Ella's favorite classes. She loved words, their weight, their shape, the way they lingered when spoken with meaning. Mr. Forrester's lectures, with their sharp insight and theatrical delivery, made every lesson feel like a play being staged just for her. Today, they were reading from Sir Arthur Conan Doyle's The Final Problem, and she found herself swept up in it again., and she found herself swept up in it again.

Mr. Forrester strode across the front of the classroom like a conductor before an orchestra, his voice rich and deliberate. "Moriarty didn't need to frame Holmes; it was misdirection. He blurred the truth with believable lies. The most dangerous lies," he said, pausing to look over the tops of lowered heads, "are the ones people want to believe."

Ella leaned forward slightly, letting his words sink in. It wasn't just about Holmes. It was about belief. About loyalty.

Mr. Forrester's gaze swept the room and landed on her. "People, in general, are stupid," he added, voice dry and not without humor. "They follow what's easiest to believe. Not what's right. Not what's true."

Ella flushed under the attention. She wasn't one to crush on teachers, not really, but Mr. Forrester had a gravity to him that made her want to be smarter. To have better answers.

He continued. "Holmes once said, 'When you have eliminated the impossible, whatever remains, however improbable, must be the truth.' That kind of thinking? That kind of clarity? It's rare. Even Watson faltered in his belief."

Ella raised her hand, hesitating before speaking. "But what about Watson? Didn't he trust Holmes? I mean, they'd been through everything together. Wouldn't belief matter more than probability?"

Mr. Forrester smiled genuinely. "A good question, Ella. Watson did believe, but belief wavers when fear creeps in. That's the true test of friendship. When the truth seems impossible... will you still choose to believe your friend?"

Ella glanced sideways at Sia, who was busy doodling in her notebook, half-lost to the world. A soft smile tugged at Ella's lips. She turned back and said quietly, but with conviction, "I'd believe anything my friend told me."

It's always been hard for me to accept that my brother wouldn't be around much.

When I turned ten, Tobias left home. He never really said where he was going, just that it was far away, somewhere overseas. Every time I asked, he'd dodge with a joke or a cryptic answer. I used to think he was just being mysterious. Now I think he was protecting something.

He changed after high school. He used to be like Sia, quiet, withdrawn, thoughtful. But when he came back last night, he was so different. Bright-eyed. Confident. Still my big brother, but somehow... more.

We stayed up for hours. He told me stories about the places he'd visited. Cathedrals in France. Hilltop monasteries in Ireland. The ruins of Glastonbury Abbey. I loved hearing every detail. I want to see them too one day. Maybe not the same ones, but ones like them, places with history carved into the stone and ghosts folded into the shadows.

Funny though, now that I think about it... most of the places he talks about are churches. We're agnostic. My parents never raised us with any particular belief. Tobias was the only one who ever seemed curious about faith. Maybe he's found something in it that makes sense to him.

Maybe that's why he changed.

ELLA SET HER PEN down with a sigh, closing her journal with the kind of care most people reserved for secrets. The lunchroom turned study hall buzzed softly with a low murmur of scattered voices, pencils scratching paper, and the occasional clatter of a dropped pen. Overcrowded and overlit, the long tables stretched wall to wall, filled with students in small knots, some buried in books, some whispering about weekend plans, others asleep in folded arms. The drone of distant HVAC blended with the hum of teenage energy, a strange kind of white noise.

Across the table, Sia was staring at her phone, but not reading. Her thumb hovered above the screen, unmoving. Whatever page she was on, it wasn't holding her. Typical. Sia probably finished her homework before homeroom even started. She always did. Ella had always been a little jealous of her best friend's mind, how fast it worked, how nothing seemed to slip through the cracks.

Ella glanced at her journal again, its pages a patchwork of thoughts, notes, half-doodles, and silly crushes. She'd kept it faithfully for over three years. In a way, it helped her stay grounded. A written memory of every version of herself.

Sia stirred beside her, slow, like a sleeper waking from too deep a dream. She blinked, confused, startled almost, then turned to Ella as if suddenly aware they were sitting right next to each other.

There was something in her eyes. Not fear, exactly. More like disorientation. Like she'd forgotten where she was.

Ella smiled gently, voice pitched soft to match the hush around them. "Welcome back."

Sia swallowed, voice quiet. "Hey... Ella?"

"Yeah?"

Sia hesitated, as if chewing on something sharp. "Do you ever have dreams that keep going? Like... you fall asleep the next night, and it picks up where it left off?"

Ella tilted her head. "Not really. Why?"

She tried to keep her voice casual, but the tension in Sia's shoulders had her worried. She thought, briefly, of that awful day, the accident, the one they never talked about. Was this about Mia?

Sia's eyes flicked around the room like she expected someone to be listening. She leaned in close, a whisper brushing Ella's ear.

"I do. Every night. And I can't stop."

Ella didn't say anything at first. Her worry tightened.

"What's it about?" she asked softly.

Sia hesitated. Her fingers fidgeted with the edge of her sleeve. The weight of the moment pressed in between them.

"Promise not to get creeped out or anything?"

Ella turned to face her fully, placing a gentle hand on her shoulder. "Sia, come on. You know me better than that."

Another beat of silence.

Then Sia breathed, deep and shaky.

"Every night when I go to bed... I dream I'm Mia."

Ella's breath caught.

Sia's eyes dropped to the desk, voice a whisper barely audible over the hum of fluorescent lights and muffled conversations.

"And I think she might be in hell."

Chapter 5

Whispers of the Lost

How can you prove whether at this moment we are sleeping, and all our thoughts are a dream; or whether we are awake, and talking to one another in the waking state?

- Plato

THE ROOM AROUND SIA Mason burned once more, the shadows stretching across the walls as if they had lives of their own, moving, twisting, pulsing like sentient things. The light that flickered and churned came from no clear source, yet it painted everything in an eerie, unnatural glow. It wasn't the warm embrace of firelight, nor the steady hum of a lightbulb; it was cold, like the harsh gleam of a moonlit night, with an undercurrent of something darker and more dangerous just beneath the surface.

Sia's bare feet touched metal. Cold, impossibly cold metal. A chill seeped through the soles of her feet, up her legs, and lodged in her chest. It should have been burning hot, after all, this was hell, wasn't it? A place of eternal fire and flame. Yet, the metal beneath her was smooth, slick with an unnatural chill that made her skin crawl in ways she couldn't explain. It was wrong, too wrong. The overwhelming heat of the surroundings only heightened the strangeness of it, as though the rules of this world had been written in a language Sia didn't understand.

She moved through the room, her steps echoing hollowly on the metallic floor, each footfall adding to the eerie rhythm of the furnace-like hum that seemed to permeate the very air. It was the sound of something vast, something ancient, a low and constant growl beneath the surface, like a slumbering beast ready to awaken. The furnace's roar vibrated through her bones, a harsh and unyielding sound that made her heart pound in time with it. The very walls seemed to reverberate with the heat, rippling and twisting as if alive. Waves of heat rolled through the space, the air growing heavy and thick, wrapping around her skin like an oppressive blanket. It was suffocating and yet, somehow, familiar. She had been here before. She would always return to it. The sound of the fire, the crackling of unseen flames, filled the silence like a heartbeat, pulsing, relentless, never-ending.

Sia crept toward the door, though she already knew what lay beyond it. It was always the same. There was no surprise anymore. Her hand gripped the door handle, still cool to the touch despite all the infernal heat surrounding her. Her fingers didn't burn. They never burned. It didn't make sense. She hesitated only a moment before turning the handle, and the dream shifted again, like a riddle slowly revealing its secrets.

The hallway stretched before her once more. The chain-link floor beneath her feet was fragile, shifting with each step, as though the ground itself could give way into the churning pool of infernal fire below at any moment. But it never did. It was as if the universe itself had decided this was where she belonged, here, with the abyss beneath her, and the weight of the world on her shoulders. The sound of the lava below seemed to hum in her bones, as if the earth itself was calling her to step forward into the dark.

She reached the door. No field, no barrier. Just an endless, empty space that only seemed to pull her deeper. And so, Sia stepped forward, the cold of the metal beneath her feet anchoring her to this strange reality. The air thickened as she walked, and as always, there was no escape. She was bound to this place, drawn back to it each night, like a moth to a flame. But the flame never consumed her. No, this place was something else. She was something else here.

The door opened and beyond it, nothing.

Until she stepped through.

The street before her stretched out into the familiar sights of Apple Grove. The quiet was too perfect, like the calm before a storm, as if everything in this place, the world she knew, had been paused, holding its breath.

She was standing at the corner of Main Street, her feet on cool, smooth asphalt that felt oddly foreign beneath her, as if it had no right being here. There were streetlights, casting long shadows over the black pavement, their yellow glow eerily warm against the otherwise cold night. Everything felt out of place, distorted, too crisp, too clean. It wasn't the world she remembered, but it was close enough. The sounds of the night had a muted quality, as though the world had been dipped in gauze.

Then she saw her.

Across the street, standing perfectly still in the muted glow of the lamplights, was a figure that mirrored her. A version of herself, only younger, about twelve years old. Sia's heart hammered in her chest. She'd seen herself in dreams before, but never like this, never so real, so tangible. The girl standing there was not her reflection. No, it was Mia. It had to be.

Her breath caught in her throat. The girl's features were identical to her own, save for the haunted, glassy look in her eyes, the strange emptiness that only grew with time. The eyes that had once been full of life, full of adventure and mischief, now looked distant, searching.

"Mia?" Sia whispered, her voice trembling. She felt like she had stepped into an old memory, one that shouldn't be touched.

Mia didn't respond immediately. She merely stared back at her, unblinking, the silence between them stretching taut. Then, as if finally acknowledging her, Mia took a slow step forward, her movements slow and deliberate.

For a moment, Sia's chest tightened, a wave of warmth sweeping over her. It was a strange comfort, seeing her sister again, even if it was just in a dream. But there was no warmth in Mia's eyes, no recognition, only something colder, more distant.

"Mia? What is this? Where are we? What's going on?" Sia's voice rose in a desperate whisper, her throat tight with a pain she hadn't known she still carried. She took a step forward, each footfall seeming to echo too loudly in the stillness. But Mia didn't move. Didn't even flinch.

Instead, Mia's gaze flicked over her shoulder, as though searching for something beyond Sia. Then she nodded, just once, her movements sharp and deliberate, before her attention turned back to her twin.

Sia followed her gaze, looking over her shoulder as well.

And there he was.

The town drunk. Richard Johnson. Stumbling toward the crosswalk, his movements slow and uncoordinated. He was muttering to himself, not noticing the red headlights that were quickly approaching. Sia's heart skipped a beat, and she opened her mouth to shout, to warn him, but the words caught in her throat.

"No!" She cried out, rushing toward the street, but her body wouldn't move fast enough. Time felt like it slowed to a crawl as she watched Richard cross the street, oblivious to the danger that was barreling toward him. She tried again, her voice frantic, but the man didn't even flinch. He continued on, unaware.

The headlights of the red car were too bright, too close. And then, The screech of tires.

The sickening thud of the car striking the man. The sound of metal crumpling. The body jerking in unnatural angles as he flew over the hood of the car, his legs twisting grotesquely behind him as he rolled onto the pavement.

Sia's breath hitched as she watched, unable to tear her eyes away from the gruesome scene unfolding before her. The man's lifeless body lay in a twisted heap on the ground, his eyes wide open, his mouth agape.

It was over. Just like that.

Sia stood frozen, unable to speak. The seconds stretched, long and heavy, until the sound of the car's engine faded into the distance. All that remained was the echo of the accident and the low hum of the streetlights above.

She barely noticed the clock tower in the distance, its hands frozen on 2:15 AM.

SIA'S EYES FLUTTERED OPEN. The clock beside her bed blinked 2:00 AM in cold blue light. Her mind felt foggy, disoriented, as if she had been yanked from some other world and slammed back into this one. Her breath came in shallow gasps, her chest tight with the remnants of her dream.

She rubbed her eyes, blinking against the dull ache in her temples. The dream had felt too real. She could still feel the metal beneath her feet, still hear the car screeching and crashing into the body on the street. The sickening thud of it echoed in her mind like a pulse, like a beat she couldn't shake.

No, it was just a dream. It had to be. Dreams weren't real.

Yet... as she stared at the clock, the seconds seemed to stretch, each tick of the minute hand sounding louder than the last. Her mind raced with the images she had just witnessed, the town drunk, the accident, Mia's cold eyes, watching from across the street.

Sia pulled the blankets tighter around her, her thoughts spiraling. Could it have been real? Was it possible that she had actually seen the future? No, it was too absurd. Too insane to even consider.

And yet, the vision lingered. The smell of the fire. The faint echo of the furnace-like hum that seemed to pulse through her very veins. The sense of wrongness in the world. It all clung to her like a second skin, unwilling to be shaken off.

Her gaze fell to the picture on her nightstand, two smiling girls, arms around each other, grinning at the camera. The photo was old, three years, the last time Mia had been alive and whole. Sia's fingers itched toward the picture frame, but instead, her gaze lingered on the bracelet Mia had given her. A delicate silver chain with a small crescent moon charm, now tarnished with age, that hung from Sia's wrist. Mia had never worn it. It was Sia's now, something she had never taken off since the day her twin had slipped away. A part of Mia, still with her, still close. The bracelet was the only connection she had left, her anchor, her talisman.

Sia whispered the name, her lips barely moving, "Mia..."

She sat up slowly, the cool night air prickling her skin. The air in her room felt heavy, as though it, too, was waiting for something. She tried to tell herself it was just the weight of the past. Just the ghosts of memories she could never outrun.

But deep down, she knew that it wasn't.

Sia stood from her bed, her legs weak as she moved toward the window. The sight of the quiet street below, with its dark shadows and slumbering houses, gave her no comfort. The quiet seemed too deep, too still. And in the silence, she could hear the faintest echo of her sister's voice.

"Sia, this is real."

The words reverberated through her mind, cutting through the fog. She shook her head. No, this wasn't real. She was still asleep, still lost in the labyrinth of her mind.

But then... she heard it again.

"Sia, this is real."

She froze. The voice was clearer now, more distinct, like it was coming from just behind her, like Mia was standing in the room with her. Sia spun around, but there was no one there. The room was empty, the shadows stretching long across the floor.

Sia's heart pounded in her chest. She felt dizzy, her breath coming faster as the room seemed to close in on her. This wasn't just a dream.

She stumbled back to the bed, sitting down hard, her fingers gripping the edge of the mattress. She wasn't sure what was happening. Was she going mad? Had the pain of losing Mia finally driven her to the edge?

The clock blinked again, 2:15 AM.

And then, she heard the sirens.

Chapter 6
Beneath the Surface

You are not a drop in the ocean, you are an entire ocean in a drop.

Rumi

SIA MOVED THROUGH THE day like a sleepwalker, her mind distant, her body functioning on autopilot. The events of last night still clung to her, thick and suffocating. The street. The car. The dead man. Mia.

Each passing minute was a struggle to keep her composure, to ignore the growing weight of the knowledge that something was terribly wrong. She couldn't explain it. She didn't want to. How could she? It was impossible. But the more she tried to push it away, the more real it felt.

Sia's mind felt distant, the day slipping away in a blur as she moved through the halls like a ghost. The world around her felt disconnected, like everything was happening in slow motion, as though people were living on a different plane. They went on with their daily lives, oblivious to the turmoil that churned inside her.

The man had been killed in a car accident the night before. His death seemed so trivial to everyone else, just another unfortunate event in a small town. But for Sia, it was the culmination of something far darker.

The teenagers barely blinked, their apathy echoing in the silence. Several teachers had shaken their heads, their expressions solemn, but the conversation was brief. No one seemed to care much beyond a passing glance. The man's life was forgotten before it had even truly mattered.

But Sia couldn't shake the feeling of responsibility that clung to her. She had seen it coming. She had known what would happen, and yet she had done nothing.

Sia wandered into American History class, her feet dragging as if the weight of the day was pulling her down. She sat in her usual seat beside Ella, the familiar comfort of her friend a small relief in the midst of the chaos in her mind. Ella sat beside her, offering a playful wink that Sia could barely return. Her friend's innocence and cheer were a stark contrast to the storm brewing inside her.

Ella broke through Sia's trance with a gentle nudge, leaning in close to whisper, "Tobias came home last night. Want to come by and say hi?"

Sia hadn't seen Tobias in nearly four years. The memory of him was distant, faded. She could barely remember what he looked like, just fragments, like a dream on the edge of her mind. Ella had always thought Sia had a soft spot for Tobias, as if the years of distance had turned into something more, a schoolgirl crush she never fully acknowledged.

Sia shook her head, a flicker of discomfort passing over her face. "Not tonight... I didn't sleep well." The words felt hollow, as though she were trying to cover up something bigger she couldn't yet face.

"You never sleep well," Ella said with a knowing tone, lightly tapping Sia's nose. She had always seen through her best friend's defenses, but this time, Sia couldn't bring herself to laugh.

They were interrupted by the drone of their history teacher, Mr. Grayson, who was already looking at them over the top of his glasses, waiting for their attention.

Mr. Grayson surveyed the room, his eyes lingering on them for a moment before his voice cut through the room, breaking the quiet murmur. They were the last ones not paying attention, lost in their own world as everyone else had tuned into the lesson.

Sia shrank back in her seat, feeling the heat of embarrassment rise in her chest. She quickly focused on the front of the room, but her thoughts remained miles away.

"Today, class, we will begin our discussion of immigration over Ellis Island, and how people of different cultures entered our country through New York, and what it means to you as Americans in the state," Mr. Grayson announced, his voice droning on as the rest of the class, predictably, tuned out.

Grayson continued, his voice as monotone as ever, and half the class's eyes glazed over in uniform boredom, the buzz of teenage disinterest hanging in the air.

Now that Grayson had the students in their usual trance, he was free to continue his lecture undisturbed, his words filling the room as Sia's mind wandered once more.

Once again, Sia let her mind drift, unable to focus on anything other than the weight of the night before and the nagging feeling of something just out of reach. She barely noticed as the class ended and the flow of students carried her along towards Study Hall.

The cafeteria was buzzing with noise as usual, students laughing, trays clattering, voices echoing in the high ceilings. Yet, to Sia, it all felt like a dull hum in the background, as if her senses had been muffled by some unseen force. Ella was beside her, talking about something, but Sia didn't hear her words. Her eyes wandered over the room, mindlessly observing the other students as they chattered around their lunch tables.

Nothing seemed out of place.

And yet, everything had changed.

Her thoughts were like a storm she couldn't outrun. A mixture of dread and confusion, of wondering if she had truly seen the future, or if the boundary between dream and reality had been blurred beyond recognition. Every time she tried to focus on something else, Mia's voice seemed to whisper in her ears, as real as if she were standing right there.

"Sia, this is real."

The words clung to her, a thread she couldn't shake. She thought she could hear the tremble in her sister's voice, the desperation she couldn't ignore. Sia's stomach turned, the weight of everything pressing down on her chest. It was like she was carrying something too heavy for her, something that threatened to crush her beneath its reality.

Ella's voice broke through the fog of her thoughts, pulling Sia back to the present.

"Hey, Sia?" Ella asked, her voice gentle but firm, pulling Sia's attention. "You okay?"

Sia blinked, momentarily disoriented. She met Ella's concerned gaze, her best friend's eyes searching hers, filled with a quiet understanding. Sia felt a surge of warmth from that gaze, but also the weight of her own secrets pressing heavier against her chest. She smiled weakly, trying to push the discomfort away.

"Yeah," she answered, though the lie felt like a stone in her mouth. "Just tired. Didn't sleep well."

Ella didn't buy it. But she let it go, the concern not entirely disappearing from her features. Sia was thankful for that. Ella was always like this, soft, perceptive, yet somehow keeping things light, as though she could help carry the burden of the world without even knowing it.

"Alright," Ella said, glancing around the cafeteria. "We should get out of here soon. Are you coming to the Harvest Festival with us tonight? It's going to be fun, you know?"

Sia hesitated. The Harvest Festival. She'd always gone, always participated. But this year, it felt different. Everything felt different. She wasn't sure if she could handle the noise, the crowds, the cheeriness of it all. It felt... hollow.

"I don't know," Sia muttered, her voice distant. "I've got some stuff I need to look into. Some... research."

Ella raised an eyebrow. "Research? What, like in the library?"

Sia's gaze flickered over to the cafeteria windows, watching the sunlight dappling the trees outside. It was as though her mind was already a thousand miles away, trying to piece together the broken puzzle of her dreams. What did they mean? Why now?

"I'll figure it out," she said softly, looking back at her friend. "I just need some time."

The day crawled forward, each moment slipping past Sia in a blur. She tried to focus, tried to drown out the creeping thoughts that had been haunting her since last night. But no matter how hard she tried, her mind always returned to that moment, Mia's face, her eyes, the haunting echo of her voice.

"Sia, this is real."

It wasn't just a dream. Sia was sure of that now. But what did it mean? What was it trying to tell her? She had no answers, only questions that gnawed at her mind, pulling her deeper into the dark corners of confusion.

AT THE END OF the day, when the bell rang and students spilled out into the hallways, Sia felt strangely detached. Everything around her, the chatter, the laughter, the clatter of lockers being slammed shut, seemed far away, as though she were watching life unfold through a veil of glass. She moved through it all without really engaging, her thoughts scattered and distant.

Her footsteps led her outside, the chill of the evening air cutting through her jacket as she crossed the school courtyard. The Harvest Festival was that night, a yearly tradition, and part of her wanted to join in, to pretend that everything was still normal, that life could still be as simple as it once was.

But it wasn't. It hadn't been for a long time.

Ella caught up with her as they neared the entrance. The blonde girl's expression was a mixture of concern and excitement. "Are you sure you don't want to come?" she asked again, her tone light but laced with sincerity.

Sia looked over at her friend, appreciating the effort but knowing it wasn't enough to pull her out of the fog in her mind. "I'm just... not in the mood," Sia replied quietly. "Maybe next year."

Ella hesitated, her brows furrowing. "Alright. But just so you know, Tobias is here, and we're all going to head over together afterward. It's going to be fun. Promise me you won't stay in tonight."

Sia forced a smile, though it didn't reach her eyes. "I'll think about it. Really. I just need to clear my head, you know?"

Ella didn't press further, though Sia could see the concern lingering in her eyes. She gave Sia a quick hug, a soft, comforting embrace that only made Sia feel more alone once it was over. As Ella moved to join the others, Sia stood there for a moment longer, watching her friend go. She wanted to feel the same sense of belonging, the same connection, but all she could feel was a hollowness that seemed to grow with each passing second.

She turned her gaze upward, where the sky was streaked with shades of pink and orange as the sun began to dip below the horizon. The quiet of the evening wrapped around her like a blanket, both comforting and suffocating.

The sirens from the night before echoed again in Sia's mind, cutting through the silence with sharp, jagged edges. The guilt weighed heavily on her chest, a constant pressure she couldn't shake. She had seen it, had known what was coming, and yet she hadn't stopped it. Could she have? Should she have? The questions spiraled inside her, looping endlessly. What if she had tried harder? What if she could have saved him, changed the course of what had happened? But the answer never came, and it left her feeling hollow, more lost than ever.

Her spiraling thoughts were abruptly interrupted by a voice calling her name across the courtyard leading to the student lockers. Sia looked up to see Tobias walking toward her wearing a visitor's pass, his easy smile in place, but there was something else in his eyes, a flicker of concern, or maybe something deeper. It made her pause, a brief hesitation before she allowed herself to meet his gaze.

"You're still here?" he asked, his voice low and teasing, but there was an edge to it, like he was sensing the shift in her mood. His smile softened, his concern slipping through the cracks of his usual lightheartedness. "You always go to the Harvest Festival. What's keeping you this time?"

Sia hesitated, her gaze falling to the pavement as she fought to push the weight of her thoughts aside. The Harvest Festival had always been a source of comfort, a tradition she'd shared with Ella year after year. But this year felt different. She couldn't explain it. The excitement, the pull of the festivities, it all felt distant, like a dream fading at the edges. The thought of being surrounded by noise, by people, by laughter... it felt suffocating. Hollow. Like a piece of her was missing, and no amount of cheer could fill that void.

"I don't know," Sia muttered, her voice faint, as if the words were slipping from her before she could even form them. There was uncertainty in her tone, a tremor she couldn't disguise. The distance between her and everything else felt like a growing chasm, and she wasn't sure how to bridge it. "I've got... things to look into. Some research." It didn't sound convincing, even to her, but it was all she had to offer. She used that to wordlessly excuse herself, leaving Tobias watching her go.

Sia's feet dragged as she made her way to her locker, her mind still reeling from the weight of the day's events. She opened her locker, greeted by the familiar scent of textbooks and paper, small, comforting details that couldn't quiet the storm inside her. The heaviness of her thoughts settled in once again.

Her locker, unlike many, was a reflection of her inner turmoil, unadorned, devoid of the colorful memorabilia that decorated the others. It only held her books and her jacket, which she used to shield herself from the cold air when she ventured outside.

As Sia closed her locker, her eyes caught Marcus Anders standing a few lockers away, his presence somehow commanding her attention. His gaze lingered on her, making her feel as if he were watching more than just her physical movements.

Marcus raised an eyebrow, his playful grin making him seem more approachable than he had any right to be. His locker was just a few down from hers, and though he seemed harmless, Sia couldn't shake the unease that always seemed to follow his gaze.

Just as Sia turned to leave, Marcus called out to her, his voice playful yet insistent. He fell into step beside her, matching her stride with ease, as though it were something he'd done a thousand times before.

Sia quickened her pace, hoping Marcus would take the hint and leave her to her thoughts. But he remained beside her, like a shadow she couldn't shake.

Marcus tried again, his voice a little more hesitant than before. "So... Sia, you into any sports?" His nervousness was palpable, as though he feared the rejection before it even came.

Sia's response was short, blunt, she wasn't in the mood for small talk. "No, I don't like sports." She felt a flicker of guilt at her sharp tone, but it quickly vanished under the weight of her unease.

Marcus, undeterred, pressed on, his tone more upbeat as he tried to steer the conversation into safer waters. "How about TV shows? Got any favorites?"

Sia couldn't help but feel a pang of pity for Marcus, but she knew better than to encourage him. He was trying, but she just didn't have it in her to play along. Her smile was distant, apologetic, but it didn't reach her eyes. She began to leave the school with her bag and her books, umbrella tucked under her arm. Marcus like some kind of lost puppy began to follow her. This was not too unusual as Sia knew Marcus lived only a block away from her.

"Look... Marcus... you're nice and all, but..." Sia trailed off, her gaze flickering to the road ahead, only to pause when she noticed Marcus's attention had drifted, his focus now elsewhere.

There was something unnerving about him, the way he looked at her made her skin crawl. His movements were slow, deliberate, as if he had all the time in the world, and his presence felt far too intense for a simple passerby.

Her gaze followed his, and she froze when she saw a stretch limousine parked down the road. The window was rolled down, and a man inside watched her with a strange intensity, as though he were sizing her up.

When Sia cautiously approached, the man's smile widened into something unsettling, too wide, too knowing. "Are you a local to this town, girl?" he asked, his voice dripping with an unfamiliar, thick accent.

Caught off guard by the strange man's presence, Sia hesitated. Her words came out carefully, her voice steady despite the unease rising in her chest. "Yes, I am. Can I help you?"

The man's smile lingered, unsettlingly so, as he handed her a business card. "I'm Samuel Gomath," he said, his voice silk-smooth, calculated. "Pleasure to meet you, Ms. Mason." His eyes didn't blink, and there was something too calculating in the way he looked at her, a predatory gleam that she didn't yet understand.

Sia took the card, the cold shiver running down her spine again as she read the name. Samuel Gomath. She excused herself, but Marcus's eyes stayed locked on the man in the limousine, his gaze sharp and focused. Sia didn't notice, but his posture had shifted, tense, protective, as if the man's presence had ignited something inside him. His usual easygoing manner was nowhere to be seen.

She excused herself, but Marcus didn't just let her walk away. He followed, his presence heavy behind her, as though he were protecting her from something she couldn't see. Sia didn't notice, but his posture had shifted, tense, protective, as if the man's presence had ignited something inside him. His usual easygoing manner was nowhere to be seen. He was on edge, his jaw tight, eyes narrowed at the man in the car. His hand rested near his pocket, as though readying himself for something. His protection wasn't just for show, he sensed the danger here, though Sia still mistook his actions for a ploy to impress her.

"Creepy." Marcus finally said with a remarkable grasp of insight Sia didn't know he was capable of, "Really creepy."

"Why would you say that?" Sia asked him, hoping for something even more ironic then had already been presented to her. "Seemed like an eccentric old man to me."

"Yeah but..." Marcus rubbed the back of his head, looking at her.

"What, Marcus?"

"How did he know your name? You never gave it to him."

SHE KNEW IT WAS a dream the moment her eyes opened. Had she fallen asleep studying up on what she was experiencing? She had been reading an article on lucid dreaming that seemed promising and then... For a fleeting moment, she thought she might have gone mad. This wasn't the fiery room, the furnace of torment where she'd grown used to waking in. No. This was different.

She sat in a large, comfortable office chair, the kind you'd see in old novels, tucked in the corner of a cozy study. The walls were lined with masks, swords, and clocks, quirky yet refined, the kind of space that felt both welcoming and unsettling in its age. A fireplace crackled softly, its warmth washing over the room. Vinyl records spun lazily on a turntable, the sound crisp yet faint, as the song shifted to something Ella would've called "ancient." The crackling gave way to Bill Kenny's iconic voice as the brassy notes filled the air. The ironic twist was palpable: I Don't Want to Set the World on Fire, the old tune felt strangely fitting, like a dark prophecy.

A voice, gravelly with a hint of a British accent, cut through the room. "They often say a man with the gift of music is a man who's sold his soul, you know." It was oddly melodic, its cadence pulling her attention as her senses sharpened.

She closed her eyes, trying to regain control of her racing thoughts. When she opened them again, her gaze fell to the desk where the figure sat.

At the desk, a man in his late twenties was lounging back in an armchair, his greasy black hair falling haphazardly around his face. His skin was pale, but his sharp features suggested an uncomfortable vitality, one that clung to the room with an unnerving presence. He had the look of someone who was handsome, yes, but only in a way that felt off. His eyes glimmered with something far darker, something lurking beneath the surface. Something ancient.

Sia's voice wavered, but she demanded herself to speak. "Who are you?"

The man let her question hang in the air as he casually lit a cigar, taking a long drag before sitting back even further, his posture too relaxed, too comfortable. He looked at her over the rim of his glasses with an air of knowing. "I go by many names, Sia Mason. But for now, you can call me Mr. Morning."

The name hit her like a cold gust of wind, but she couldn't place why. The man's eyes twinkled with a dangerous amusement as he continued to puff on his cigar, sending thick clouds of smoke into the air.

Sia found herself unnervingly calm in the face of the strange atmosphere. This isn't real, just a dream, she thought. Yet her body responded to him as though it was, tensing with some strange, inexplicable pull.

"Alright, Mr. Morning," she said, her voice gaining steadiness despite the odd calm that seemed to settle over her. "What am I doing here? This isn't really a dream, is it?"

"And how, my dear, do you know this isn't a dream?" His voice, too smooth, almost coaxing. "Isn't it possible that you're merely dreaming the dream of another?"

Sia frowned, biting back a sudden rush of frustration. "I know when I'm dreaming, and this simply isn't one of mine."

He chuckled, a low, rolling sound that left a bitter taste in her mouth. Taking another long drag from the cigar, he leaned back in his chair, clearly amused. "Ah, yes, yes. A good way of seeing it. But who's to say this isn't my dream? Would it be so inconceivable that you might be able to dream the dream of another?"

Sia didn't care for his philosophical musings. The unease in her chest flared into something deeper. "Look... what do you want?" She couldn't keep the edge from creeping into her voice. She didn't like the feel of this place. Something about being here felt like being trapped. "Just get to the point, no more of this double talk."

"To the point, I like that in a woman. No dilly-dallying around for you, eh?" He smirked and ran his hand through his unruly hair, eyes gleaming with that same unsettling familiarity. But when Sia's steely gaze didn't falter, he seemed to understand that the moment of levity had passed.

The man straightened in his chair, shedding the easygoing façade. His expression turned serious, almost business-like. "Very well. I'm here to make you an offer. I can give you back your sister and end your dreams, give you peace, Sia Mason."

Her heart froze at the mention of Mia, the familiar pain tightening around her chest. She couldn't think, couldn't breathe. How was this man, this stranger, talking about Mia?

She barely heard the question spill from her lips, her voice thick with dread. "At what cost?"

His smile didn't waver. "Oh, nothing terrible. Your immortal soul, that's out of the question. For reasons you'll never understand, I already own a part of it. What I want from you is simple: your cooperation. Tomorrow morning, you'll call Samuel Gomath and offer to guide him through town. That's all."

The casual way he said it left her reeling. The idea that he already owned part of her soul wasn't just unsettling, it was terrifying.

"What do you mean you already own part of my soul? Who the hell are you?" Her voice cracked with the stress, and she took a step back, instinctively trying to distance herself from him.

His gaze remained unwavering. "I think you know, Sia Mason."

His eyes burned with a fire too familiar, her fire. The same flames she'd seen in her dreams, the ones that reached up from the blackened floor in that hellish, metal room.

"No," she stammered, her pulse quickening. "I don't."

He leaned forward, his smile now a sinister twist. "Then let me show you." He held up his hand, revealing a rough, calloused palm. On it, a tattoo of an eye stared back at her, a symbol that seemed to pulse with dark energy. As his fingers curled, Sia felt her vision blur. Her very mind seemed to bend, warping in ways she couldn't comprehend.

Sia felt the strange, oppressive heat of the dream envelope her once more. The walls were metallic, too smooth and cold beneath her fingertips, and yet they burned with a heat that seemed to reach into her bones. This was the first time she had crossed this threshold. The door ahead beckoned, opening to an unknown realm, its edges jagged and distorted as if it was a part of some dark reality she wasn't meant to understand.

The moment she stepped through, a strange sense of ownership twisted inside her. This place wasn't hers, not in the way she knew her world, but it was undeniably tied to her. She was drawn here, as though the shadows and the heat were an extension of herself, waiting for her to understand.

The door swung open to reveal the moonlit field, but this time it felt different. There was no sense of peace in this new reality. The air grew thick with tension, the ground beneath her feet like wet ash. The figure that appeared wasn't a knight in shining armor. No, this man felt like a predator stalking his prey, his every movement deliberate, purposeful. His gait was that of someone who knew exactly what he was doing. There was no softness in his eyes, only a cold, calculated intent.

He approached slowly, methodical, his eyes locked onto her with an unsettling focus. The sword he carried gleamed in the pale moonlight, but it wasn't a beacon of protection, it was a harbinger. Its hilt bore a cross, yet it felt like a weapon of execution, the angels etched on the blade seeming to mock her very existence. The sword's weight was immense, yet it felt like it was meant for her, as though it was her fate to face it.

As he neared, Sia's breath caught. His eyes, cold, steel blue, burned with unrelenting fury, rage, and purpose. They were familiar, but not in a way that comforted her. These weren't the eyes of a protector; these were the eyes of someone who had come to end her. The same fire she had seen before, but this time, it wasn't a symbol of some distant, untouchable force. This fire was personal.

A sudden realization hit her like a punch to the gut. Her gasp echoed in the silence, her heart pounding as she finally understood who this man was.

It was Tobias, but not the Tobias she remembered. This version of him wasn't the brother she knew. This was a creature of cold determination, and he was here to finish what he'd started.

CHAPTER 7
Shadows of the Past

"Sweet princess, if through this wicked witch's trick, a spindle should your finger prick... a ray of hope there still may be in this, the gift I give to thee. Not in death, but just in sleep, the fateful prophecy you'll keep. And from this slumber you shall wake, when true love's kiss, the spell shall break."

                    - Merryweather, Sleeping Beauty

THE AIR IN THE winery was thick with the smell of fermenting fruit, berries, apples, and grapes, all blending into a rich scent that seemed to cling to every surface. The Brotherhood Winery was the oldest in America, a place that had survived Prohibition for more reasons than simply dodging the law. Tobias knew it had deeper ties, connections that reached far back into history. For years, the winery had been owned partially by his brother-in-law's family, but the other owner? The one whose identity was kept sealed? Tobias wasn't sure. And the fact that the records were locked away only made his curiosity burn hotter.

It wasn't just about wine. This place, this sprawling, dimly lit structure, was sacred ground. The Church had its hand in everything here, though Tobias wasn't privy to the full story. That part of the history was kept hidden under layers of secrecy, buried deep within the archives. He didn't know why exactly, but he had learned over time that there were things about the winery no one talked about, things he needed to understand.

Tobias walked through the winery's underhalls, his sneakers quiet against the stone floor, the only sound the faint hum of the dim electric lights overhead. The halls were cool, air thick with the musty scent of old oak barrels and damp stone. Rows of casks, some ancient, some barely touched, lined the walls like silent sentinels. He ran a hand over one, its surface smooth but weathered, its markings faded by time. Tobias couldn't help but wonder if the barrels were more than just vessels for wine. What else was stored here, hidden away for centuries? The question gnawed at him.

He wasn't just here for the wine, though. He was here because something felt off. He could feel the eyes of the guards on him as he moved deeper into the winery, shadows creeping along the walls with every step he took. They were following him. Not in a friendly way, but in a way that suggested they were unsure of his intentions, and equally unsure of why they were letting him in. They seemed as though they didn't want him here, but were being forced to let him walk around.

Tobias paused at one of the massive casks, its Holy Trinity symbol barely visible beneath the grime. The cask was larger than he was, towering with an eerie presence. He tapped it lightly with his knuckles, testing its emptiness. "Large cask of sacrament, completely unused?" Tobias asked, his voice low but pointed, casting a sideways glance at the two guards trailing him.

There was a long pause before Baeza, the older of the two guards, answered. His voice was as smooth and practiced as ever, but there was an edge to it, like he was carefully choosing his words. "Ah, not unused, Mr. Archer. The contents of that cask were drained for bottling only two days ago."

Tobias's brow furrowed. That didn't add up. The last sacramental delivery he knew of had been four days ago, not two. His mind quickly ran through the numbers, but his suspicion deepened. The guards knew something they weren't letting on. Why lie about the timing?

Tobias didn't press, not yet. He simply nodded, offering a tight smile before walking past the two guards. They stayed close behind him, moving with an almost predatory grace. The way they watched him, the way they followed his every movement, it felt off. They weren't just security officers. There was something about them, something he couldn't quite place. They moved too fluidly, too carefully, as if they were ready for something he wasn't prepared for. Tobias was used to being watched. It came with the territory of his work. But this felt different. Their eyes didn't just follow him; they were calculating, waiting. Watching him, waiting for him to slip.

The air in the hallway grew thicker, more oppressive. Tobias adjusted his hoodie, pulling it tighter around him as they moved deeper into the winery. He had no intention of letting these guards get under his skin, but he could feel the pressure building. The longer he stayed, the more he knew he was treading in dangerous waters.

"Shall we move on, Mr. Archer?" Baeza's voice snapped him back to the present, and Tobias turned his attention to the guard, forcing himself to mask his unease.

"Lead the way," he replied, trying to keep his tone casual.

Tobias couldn't shake the feeling that he was being watched every step of the way. The heavy presence of the guards lingered behind him, and though their suspicious stares followed his every move, there was something more unsettling. It wasn't them, he knew they were just doing their job, but there was something else in the air. A prickling sensation on the back of his neck, the sense that another pair of eyes, unseen, were locked on him.

Despite their gaze, Tobias moved forward with a steady purpose, his face impassive. If anything, the guards' attention only sharpened his own focus. He had learned long ago to trust his instincts. And right now, his instincts told him there was something terribly wrong about this place.

The winery was far more than it appeared. It had always been surrounded by whispers, of its sacred purpose, its ties to the Church, its long-standing role in preserving sacramental wines. But there was more to it. Tobias was sure of it. Whatever the Church had kept hidden, it was buried here. And the guards, who seemed to have been placed in his path for some unknown reason, weren't the only ones keeping watch.

He glanced over his shoulder, just as the distant hum of the Harvest Festival above reached his ears, the noise of revelers celebrating, laughing, and dancing. Below ground, in this network of dimly lit hallways, the noise seemed muffled, far away. Tobias moved cautiously, knowing that the shadows here felt thick enough to swallow him whole. But it wasn't the darkness that bothered him. It was the oppressive feeling that something was wrong.

A quick glance to the side told him the guards were still there, trailing him just out of view. But it wasn't them that made the hairs on his neck stand on end.

The sense of being followed was growing stronger.

Shaking it off, Tobias pushed forward. He knew this part of the winery like the back of his hand. He had been here countless times, moving through its forgotten, unmarked corners, inspecting its barrels and casks for anything suspicious. But this time was different. This time, something was waiting for him. And he couldn't shake the feeling that it had been here far longer than he had.

His eyes fell on the massive cask ahead, marked with the Holy Trinity symbol. It stood taller than any normal barrel, a sacred relic of sorts, but something about it caught his attention. He stopped, studying it from a distance. Something felt off.

He approached the cask slowly, his mind racing. The guards' footsteps echoed behind him, but it wasn't them he was focused on. No, the closer he got to the cask, the stronger the feeling of being watched intensified. His heartbeat quickened as if something within the cask itself had stirred, acknowledging his presence. He wasn't sure what it was, but it felt like a silent warning, something had been disturbed, and it wasn't just the guards.

Tobias reached the cask and knocked against its surface, listening for the faintest of sounds. Empty. He had known it was empty. But the way the guards had answered his earlier question about its contents felt off. They'd claimed it had been emptied just days ago for bottling. But Tobias knew better. The delivery schedule didn't match. The last shipment of sacrament wine had gone out days earlier. So why was the cask so freshly drained? Why was there no wine inside?

His suspicions only deepened, the sense of being watched intensifying. Tobias made a mental note to come back to this spot later. Something wasn't right with this cask. The entire situation felt wrong, like a puzzle with missing pieces, and he couldn't afford to leave it unsolved.

He moved away from the cask, but his thoughts were already planning his next steps. He couldn't just walk away now. There were too many questions, too many things hidden in the dark corners of this winery. But as he slipped out of the hallway and began to head toward the service door he had noticed earlier, the unsettling sensation grew stronger. It was like a pulse, a faint echo in the back of his mind. Someone, or something, was following him. Watching him.

Tobias paused for a moment, his eyes scanning the shadows. His hand instinctively reached for the dagger under his hoodie. The feeling of unease, of being hunted, was growing. And though the guards were still a few steps behind him, he knew the real threat wasn't them. There was something else here, something that had been watching him from the moment he set foot inside.

Tobias wasn't sure who, or what, it was. But he knew this: it wasn't human.

The creature didn't hesitate.

The moment Tobias's eyes locked with the glowing red orbs of the creature, the air between them thickened, oppressive and suffocating. It wasn't the usual bloodlust Tobias had felt when facing dangerous beings, it wasn't even fear. No, it was something deeper, darker. The creature radiated a sense of purpose, its form exuding an unnatural calm as it took a slow, deliberate step forward.

Tobias didn't wait to find out what would happen next. He lunged to the side, his body instinctively reacting before his mind had fully caught up. He hit the stone floor with a roll, pushing off the ground and springing to his feet in a fluid motion.

His hand reached for the retractable knife hidden up his sleeve. He was fast, faster than the average human, but he knew that wouldn't be enough. The creature was far faster.

The creature let out a low hiss, its bat-like wings flapping once, sending a gust of wind through the room that knocked Tobias off balance. He staggered but recovered quickly, turning just in time to see the creature's talon reaching for him. It was fast, unnaturally so, and the claws gleamed like black obsidian in the dim light.

Tobias slashed with the knife, but the creature was already retreating into the shadows before his blade could connect. It was toying with him, moving with an unsettling grace, its wings stretching wide as it flitted from one corner of the room to the other, like an impossible shadow.

Tobias's pulse raced, his senses sharpening as the seconds ticked by. He needed to think fast, but the weight of the situation pressed down on him. The room, this hidden chamber, wasn't just a place of ritual. It was a cage. The walls were lined with relics and old forgotten tools, things that had been left behind by those who once practiced dark rites in this very place.

He darted around the room, desperately searching for something to use, but it was like the creature knew his every move. Each time he tried to circle around the altar, the creature was already there, waiting.

And then he heard it, the unmistakable sound of something cracking underfoot.

A small piece of stone. Tobias's mind seized on it. The room was falling apart, the structure weakened with age. He needed to force the creature into a mistake, to create an opening.

Tobias backed toward the door, his mind working in overdrive. The creature followed, its eyes never leaving him, but its movements were becoming more erratic, more panicked. It was playing with him, but Tobias knew he had no time to waste. This thing wasn't just a creature, it was a warning.

He swiped the spade-shaped knife at the air again, just to keep the creature distracted. It lunged for him, but this time, Tobias was ready. He dropped to the ground, rolling beneath the creature's claws as it struck the stone wall behind him. A powerful tremor shook the chamber, sending dust falling from the ceiling.

Tobias knew this was his chance.

With a burst of strength, he pushed himself to his feet and dashed toward the altar, grabbing the nearest object he could find. It was a heavy, rusted chain. Without hesitation, he wrapped it around his arm and swung it toward the creature's wings, aiming for the thin, delicate membrane. The creature screeched in surprise as the chain wrapped around its wing, binding it in place.

For a moment, the creature was trapped. Tobias didn't waste it. He dove for the door, scrambling as quickly as he could. He could feel the heat of the creature's breath on his back as he made it into the hallway, just barely escaping the swing of its claws. The creature roared in fury, but Tobias kept running.

He knew the winery's halls well, but this was different. The sound of pursuit followed him, unrelenting, constant. He had a head start, but for how long? The creature was fast, and it knew the territory just as well as he did.

His heart pounded in his chest as he navigated the twisting corridors, seeking the exit. The walls around him seemed to close in, the floor beneath him shaking with the creature's fury. Tobias didn't know how much longer he could outrun it.

He pushed open a door at the end of the hallway, his breath ragged, and sprinted out into the open air of the winery's grounds. The sounds of the Harvest Festival were still going strong, but now they felt distant, muffled by the adrenaline rushing through his veins.

Tobias didn't slow down. He couldn't afford to. He had to get to the car, get out of there, before the creature found its way out of the cellar. The creature wouldn't stop. It wouldn't rest until it had him, and whatever else it had been sent for.

His steps were swift, echoing through the wine-soaked night, but in the back of his mind, a new realization was forming. This was no random attack. The creature was guarding something. Something in that winery, something he had stumbled upon.

But what was it? And who else was involved in this dark conspiracy?

The answers were just beyond his reach, but he was getting closer.

And he had no intention of stopping until he had them.

Tobias didn't stop running. His mind raced as he darted through the winery's grounds, trying to put as much distance between himself and the creature as he could. The wind cut across his face, its cold bite grounding him, reminding him that he was still alive. The rustling of the trees and the noise from the festival up ahead felt surreal, like a distant memory he wasn't quite a part of anymore.

His heart was pounding, adrenaline coursing through him as he reached the side of the building, his fingers grasping the cold metal of the door handle. He yanked it open, practically throwing himself inside.

The air in the winery felt stale, thick with the scent of old oak barrels and fermented grapes. But it was the creeping sensation of being watched that unsettled him most.

He paused at the door, listening. The faint sound of footsteps echoed in the distance, steady, deliberate. They were following him, but not in the way he expected. The guards? Or was it the creature? His gut told him it wasn't the guards.

Tobias wasn't a paranoid man by nature, but something about this felt off. He wasn't just being watched by the creature; he was being hunted, observed, analyzed.

He moved swiftly through the back halls, the corridors twisting like a labyrinth, unfamiliar even to him. The flickering lights overhead seemed almost intentionally dim, casting long shadows that played tricks on his eyes. He wasn't just dealing with a creature. Something much larger was at play here.

The door at the far end of the hallway creaked open in front of him, and Tobias stepped into the hidden room, the walls lined with long-forgotten relics and tools, each more obscure than the last. The room felt ancient, its purpose far beyond any mortal understanding. The air was thick, the silence almost too perfect.

But the silence was broken by the unmistakable sound of slow, measured footsteps. He wasn't alone.

Tobias's hand moved instinctively to the small silvered dagger tucked under his hoodie, the weight of it familiar and reassuring. The blade had seen him through many encounters before, a reliable tool for close-quarters defense. But he knew, deep down, that it wouldn't be enough for whatever was waiting for him in the shadows.

The man didn't step forward; he simply stood there, as though waiting for something to happen. The atmosphere around them thickened, the air charged with a tension that made the room feel smaller.

Tobias didn't waste time with words. He knew better than to speak in these situations. His instincts kicked in, and in one fluid motion, he lunged toward the man. The dagger flashed through the air, aimed at the figure's throat, but the man wasn't where Tobias had expected him to be.

He sidestepped, effortlessly.

Tobias's feet hit the floor with a hard thud, but he didn't miss a beat. He spun around, ready for the next move, but the man was already gone. The room felt colder now, emptier, as if the very air had drained out.

Tobias stiffened, his pulse quickening. He wasn't sure what he was dealing with, this man wasn't human, and he knew it. But there was no time to waste. Tobias advanced, his focus sharp as a blade.

He could feel it now, the oppressive weight of something ancient closing in on him. Whatever this man was, Tobias was sure it wasn't the real threat. The air felt charged with malevolent energy. His hand gripped the hilt of his dagger tighter, his knuckles turning white.

The man's voice echoed through the room. "You've come too far, Tobias."

The words hit Tobias like a physical blow, as if something had shifted in the very fabric of the space around him. He gritted his teeth, stepping forward and slashing out with the dagger. But this time, the man didn't move, he didn't have to.

There was a sharp, sickening crack. The blade shattered, its silvered edge snapping off with a clean cut. Tobias's hand stung as the dagger broke in his grip. He stared at the jagged remnants, the familiar weight of the blade now gone. The man had anticipated that.

Tobias's eyes flicked back up, but the figure was already gone. There was no time to wonder how or why, he needed to act.

The sound of footsteps in the distance echoed louder now, growing more persistent. Tobias glanced at the broken remnants of his dagger, the sense of urgency pressing down on him. The creature, the true enemy, was still out there, somewhere, and he couldn't waste any more time here.

He moved toward the exit, carefully and silently, but the feeling of being followed never quite left. It wasn't just the guards. No, this was something much more dangerous. Something much more insidious.

Tobias pushed open the door and slipped into the shadows of the winery grounds, barely making a sound. He needed to find answers, and fast. But as he reached the trees, a strange sense of unease began to settle in his gut. He wasn't sure if it was the broken dagger or the feeling that something far more dangerous was watching him from the darkness, but Tobias was certain of one thing: he wasn't going to leave here the same.

CHAPTER 8
The Templar's Burden

Some secrets are meant to stay secret forever.
Liane Moriarty

TOBIAS CAREFULLY STEPPED BACK into the shadows of the winery, his heart pounding from the encounter with the creature, his dagger now useless in his hand. The fire had been quick to spread, a dangerous omen that followed him as he fled the burning remnants of the ancient beast. Yet the strange sense of familiarity from the confrontation gnawed at him, something about that creature's form, the manner in which it had fought, it was... different. Not a demon, but something older, something connected to the land, the myths. Something that might have been guarding the secrets of Dobahold long before anyone knew what they were.

The echoes of the battle still rang in his ears, the claws scraping across the stone floor, the powerful wings beating against the confines of the cellar. He had done what he could, leaving the creature unconscious, but still very much alive. The priests were too keen on keeping things quiet, keeping their sacred grounds secure. The fact that he couldn't understand why these creatures were here, why they were so protective of a simple entrance to some forgotten place, it bothered him deeply.

He didn't have time to dwell on it now.

Tobias reached into the folds of his hoodie, his fingers brushing the cold, metal object hidden beneath the fabric. He pulled out the silver knife, his backup, the one he trusted to keep him safe when his larger weapons failed. There was no room for mistakes. Whatever was hidden in this winery, whatever danger lay ahead, Tobias wasn't sure yet, but it wasn't just about finding it anymore. It was about surviving it.

The sound of the winery's heavy doors creaking open echoed through the dim passageways, followed by the soft footsteps of guards that patrolled the halls. Tobias pressed himself into the stone wall, his back flat against it, blending into the shadows. He felt the vibrations of approaching footsteps before the voices became clearer.

"Is it all contained?" Baeza's voice was sharp, always commanding. Tobias winced at the tone. It wasn't a friendly one, nor one that hid much suspicion.

"Yes, sir. It seems like the fire's under control," came the reply from the other guard. But there was hesitation in the words, something that didn't sit well with Tobias.

He strained to hear, his pulse racing. What was the real nature of this place? And why did he feel the unrelenting gaze of someone, or something, watching him? It wasn't just the guards. There was something else in the winery, something that had been following him ever since he stepped foot inside.

Tobias' hand rested on the hilt of his silvered knife as he moved carefully forward, avoiding the guards' path. He slipped past a hallway corner, his footsteps light, barely audible against the hard floors of the winery. The fire had burned in the wrong direction, and he knew he needed to get back to the cellar to retrieve the cask, to understand its true nature. There was something wrong about the way the cask had opened, a hidden passage behind it. Something old, far too old.

THE AIR WAS THICK with the scent of fresh apples and roasting corn, the familiar warmth of the Harvest Festival wrapping around Ella like a cozy blanket. The usual hum of laughter, music, and the occasional shout of victory from a game booth filled the air. Families, friends, and kids ran about in excitement, creating an atmosphere of chaotic joy. The evening sun hung low in the sky, casting long shadows that added a touch of magic to the otherwise normal fall evening.

Ella, always at the heart of things, was busy behind the game booth, managing the ping pong ball toss. She smiled as a young child, no more than five, let out a cheer after landing the ball in the jar. Her family had contributed heavily to the festival each year, and this year was no different. As much as she enjoyed helping out, she couldn't shake the feeling that something wasn't quite right. It had been gnawing at her for a whole day, ever since Sia had backed out on coming to the festival.

"Hey, Ella, you okay?" Marcus asked, his voice cutting through her thoughts. She turned to find him standing nearby, his arms crossed and an expression of concern on his face. She hadn't realized he'd been watching her.

"I'm fine," Ella said quickly, forcing a smile. "Just... thinking about Sia."

"You know, you've been worried about her a lot lately," Marcus said, his voice low. "She's been acting... weird."

Ella nodded, but didn't respond right away. "I don't know," she said softly. "I think she's just... struggling. You know? Ever since Mia..." Ella let the sentence trail off, the weight of the name hanging in the air between them. Marcus nodded, his expression softening.

"I just hope she's okay," Ella added, her voice cracking slightly. "I want to help her, but I don't know how."

Marcus paused for a moment before speaking again, his tone thoughtful. "She's not the only one who's struggling, you know. I think we all are. But sometimes, people have to face their demons alone."

Ella met his gaze, her brow furrowed. "Yeah, but sometimes they don't have to face them alone. And I'm not going to let her."

At that moment, a figure appeared at the corner of her vision. It was Sia, walking toward the booth with a quiet expression on her face, despite saying she wasn't coming. Ella's heart gave a small leap of relief. "Well, look at that, she came after all."

Marcus noticed the same thing, raising an eyebrow. "Yeah, she ca me... but it's like pulling teeth with her. I bet she didn't want to, but she did because, " He hesitated, his voice lowering slightly. "I think I know why she showed up after all. Yesterday, that creepy guy in the limo? The one who knew her name?"

Ella's stomach churned. "What about him?"

Marcus leaned in, his voice dropping even lower as he glanced around to make sure no one else was listening. "Sia didn't tell you? Well, yesterday, he pulled up beside us while we were walking home. Just... out of nowhere, and asked if she was a local. Then, he said her name. He knew her name, Ella. Like, he'd been watching her for a while. And I know she didn't tell you about it, because she wouldn't." He sighed, shaking his head. "It's just creepy, right? I mean, how did he even know her?"

Ella's stomach turned with unease. "Sia didn't tell me about that... but... why didn't she say anything?" She wondered aloud.

Marcus shifted uncomfortably, a nervous glance flicking to where Sia was approaching. "I think she's just trying to keep it together, you know? But something about that guy's presence, it felt off. And I'm sure Sia feels the same way, even if she's not saying anything."

Ella nodded, feeling a sudden coldness in the pit of her stomach. "That's... not okay. She should have told me. She shouldn't have had to handle this alone."

"I'll be honest with you, Ella," Marcus said, his voice softer now, "I don't like that guy. He's too... polished, too smooth. Like he's hiding something."

Ella took a breath and nodded. "I'll talk to her. She needs to be safe. We need to figure out what this guy's deal is."

Without wasting another second, she turned to walk toward Sia, who had stopped near the trees again. She didn't know what she was going to say yet, but she knew she couldn't let her friend slip away again. As she neared him however, so did someone else, stepping out of the trees by the winery was none other than Tobias, his hood over his head, coat looking a little crispier than it had been when he'd left the house that morning.

Sia froze when she saw Tobias.

It felt like a sudden punch to the gut, that familiar figure standing in front of her, so out of place in the peaceful setting of the Harvest Festival. He wasn't the same as the Tobias she had known as a child, the one she had shared stories and secrets with. No, this Tobias, the one standing here now, was a man who had come from a different world, and his presence here, in this moment, felt like an intrusion.

Before yesterday, she hadn't seen him in years. Not really. Not since that night, that horrible night when everything changed. Not since Mia died. The memory of that night was a sharp pain in her chest, but it was nothing compared to the flash of a vision that had come to her just a few nights ago. Tobias, his face set in cold determination, raising a sword above her, about to strike.

A scream echoed in her mind, and the reality of the situation hit her like a flood. Tobias... could he be the one? Was he the one who was supposed to kill her? Was he the one in her nightmare?

Her breath hitched, and she took an involuntary step back. Her pulse quickened, her heart hammering against her ribs. The air seemed to grow heavier, thicker, as if the ground beneath her was about to give way. She couldn't shake the feeling that she was looking at a stranger, someone she couldn't trust, someone she didn't know.

Ella must have noticed, because she immediately turned to Sia, her expression softening, a hint of concern flickering in her eyes. "Sia? You okay?" Ella's voice was calm, trying to ground her, but Sia's thoughts were spinning.

Tobias, for his part, seemed unaware of the effect he was having on her. He stood there, arms crossed, his expression unreadable. He hadn't changed, not really. Still that same boyish face, the same tousled blonde hair that fell into his eyes, the same quiet confidence that came from years of being the older sibling, the one people expected to have the answers.

But the memories of him were slipping away, replaced with the terror of the vision. Her vision. Was that really him? Was that the truth of the future, or was it some twisted trick? A sudden wave of nausea washed over her, and she could feel the knot in her stomach tightening.

"Is something wrong?" Ella's voice broke through her haze, concern thick in her words. She was still watching her closely, her gaze flicking between Sia and Tobias.

Sia swallowed hard, trying to clear the fog in her mind. "I... I don't know." She could feel the tension in her voice, the uncertainty creeping in.

Tobias seemed oblivious to the storm brewing in her chest, his lips curling into a small, almost amused smile as he approached them. "I didn't mean to scare you, Sia," he said, his voice warm, though there was something about it that made her skin prickle. He wasn't even aware, was he? Didn't he see the fear in her eyes, the way she was practically trembling? Didn't he understand how his presence alone was enough to stir up every possible nightmare she'd been hiding?

Ella, ever the diplomat, didn't seem to notice the shift in the air. She chuckled lightly, trying to defuse the tension. "You've changed, Tobias," she said, teasing lightly. "Still the same old troublemaker, huh?"

But Tobias's smile faltered for a moment as he looked directly at Sia. The weight of his gaze settled like a physical thing. "I'm sorry," he said, voice suddenly softer, almost like he was speaking to her alone, and the rest of the world had faded away. "I didn't mean to..."

The words trailed off, and Sia felt her heart skip a beat. She took a step back, the words in her vision from the other night echoing in her ears: He's going to kill you. Tobias's face hovered in her mind like a shadow, not the Tobias she remembered, but something far more dangerous. Something she didn't know. Something that scared her more than anything.

"I, " She stopped herself, shaking her head as the words got caught in her throat. Her hand instinctively reached for the necklace Mia had given her, the one with the moon charm. The cold metal under her fingers grounded her, but the unease in her chest only seemed to grow.

Ella watched her closely, concern flashing in her eyes. "Sia, what's going on? You're shaking."

"I'm fine," Sia muttered, forcing a smile, though it didn't reach her eyes. The tension in her body was palpable, and she knew Ella could see it. Hell, even Tobias seemed to notice now, his brows knitting together in confusion.

But the vision still wouldn't leave her mind. The sword. The fire in Tobias's eyes. It had to be a mistake, didn't it? No, it couldn't be. It was real. It was going to happen.

Tobias stepped closer, and Sia instinctively took another step back. "I don't mean to make you uncomfortable," he said quietly, his voice so calm it made her skin crawl. "But... I think we need to talk."

Sia's pulse roared in her ears, and she glanced at Ella, silently pleading for her to say something, to break the tension that was threatening to crack the world open. But Ella was staring at her, clearly unsettled, as though she were seeing her friend for the first time.

Tobias's presence here, after everything she'd learned, was too much. It was too much for Sia to handle right now. Not like this. Not with everything else swirling in her mind.

She turned on her heel and bolted, not even waiting for a response from either of them.

She couldn't do it. She couldn't face him. Not now. Not after everything she'd seen.

Ella called after her, but Sia didn't look back. She couldn't. Not with Tobias standing there, so close to her, so close to the nightmare she couldn't escape.

Tobias stood a little closer to Ella, his expression softened with the weight of everything he hadn't told her. Around them, the festival continued in full swing, the sounds of laughter, chatter, and carnival games filling the air. The bright lights from the booths illuminated the evening, creating a warm, festive atmosphere that clashed with the conversation happening between the two siblings.

Children ran past them, pulling at their parents' hands, while the clink of metal coins dropped into machines echoed nearby. The aroma of caramel apples and roasting corn filled the air, a stark contrast to the tension that sat heavy on Tobias' chest. The chaos of the crowd was both comforting and suffocating, the world around them unaware of the storm brewing just beneath the surface.

Ella's voice broke through his thoughts as she spoke again, her gaze still focused on the trees where Sia had disappeared. "I don't know what to do, Tobias. She's shutting us all out... but I can't just stand by and watch her fall apart. Not when I know she needs help."

Tobias glanced at her, his mind racing. She was right, of course. Sia did need help. But he wasn't sure if she'd accept it from anyone, let alone him. Still, he knew that if anyone could reach her, it was Ella. She had always been the one with the ability to get through to people, to break down the walls they built around themselves.

But Tobias was beginning to realize that helping Sia wouldn't be enough. Not anymore. Not with everything that was coming. He couldn't do this alone.

He hesitated, looking around at the throngs of festival-goers who seemed oblivious to the weight of his thoughts. The noise, the clamor, the joy, they all felt so distant. How could anyone have fun when the world was on the edge of something darker?

Ella noticed the distant look in his eyes and took a step closer, lowering her voice. "What's wrong?"

"I'm starting to realize that I can't do this alone," Tobias murmured, his voice so quiet that only Ella could hear it over the clamor of the festival. "And I think you're the only one I can trust with this. I need to tell you everything, Ella. Everything about what's really going on, about why I'm here... why I can't just leave."

Ella's brows furrowed, confusion flashing across her face. "What are you talking about, Tobias?"

He looked around them again, the weight of the festival's noise against his quiet words like a surreal backdrop to the secret life he was about to unfold for her. The crowd's laughter, the sound of game booths operating, the distant music, all of it felt unreal compared to the gravity of what was building between them.

His gaze softened as he met her eyes. "I'm not just here because I care about you and Sia. I'm here because there's something bigger, something you don't know yet. And I can't do this without you. I don't know how to explain it, but I need you to understand... I need your help."

Ella stared at him, her mind racing. Tobias wasn't the type to confide in anyone, let alone her. He wasn't the type to share anything that wasn't strictly necessary. And the tension in his words, the way his posture had stiffened... this was serious.

"You're scaring me, Tobias," she whispered, her tone quiet but filled with concern. She hated seeing him like this. "What are you talking about?"

Tobias exhaled a breath he hadn't realized he'd been holding. His voice dropped even further, his words so quiet it was as if he were speaking directly to her soul. "There's a war coming. A war that's already started. I've been part of something... bigger than you could imagine. And I need you in it. I need you to understand. You're the only one I can trust with this. You've always been there for me. Always."

Ella's heart pounded in her chest. "What are you saying? What do you mean you need me?"

He took a step back, running a hand through his hair, a conflicted expression in his eyes. The tension between them stretched thin, as if the weight of his confession was too much for him to bear. "I need you to understand the truth, Ella. The truth about me, about what I'm really here for. I'm not just some guy who came back to visit. I'm here because it's my mission, because there's something I have to stop. And... and I need you to be ready for what's coming. Because you'll be a part of it, whether you want to be or not."

Ella looked around, her mind still reeling from the sudden intensity of Tobias' words. The festival continued unabated, the noise of the crowd a stark contrast to the quiet, urgent conversation they were having. She felt small in the middle of it all, caught between the life she knew and the one Tobias was trying to pull her into.

"I don't know what to say," she admitted, her voice thick with uncertainty.

Tobias gave her a soft, apologetic smile. "I know it's a lot to take in. But you're the only one I can trust with this. Please, Ella. Please, let me explain."

Ella stood there for a moment, her mind turning over his words. She had always known there was more to Tobias, more to his life than he let on. But this... this was different. This wasn't just about family. This was something else entirely.

Finally, she nodded, a hesitant but firm decision in her eyes. "Okay. I'll listen. I'll help. Just... please don't shut me out again. You're my brother, Tobias. You're the only family I've got."

Tobias' expression softened, and for the first time in what felt like ages, he let his guard down completely. "Thank you," he whispered.

And as the noise of the festival continued around them, a new understanding passed between them. No matter what was coming, they would face it together.

The distant sound of laughter and the bright music from the festival seemed to fade as Tobias turned his focus inward. He stood silently for a moment, the weight of his mission pressing down on him. The world around him, the joy and lightheartedness, felt like a distant echo. He could feel the tension building, and it wasn't just because of his secrets. It was because of the greater truth that had been knocking at the door of his conscience for so long now.

Ella stood in front of him, her expression a mixture of confusion and curiosity, but her loyalty was unwavering. He had expected more resistance, more questioning, but there was something in her gaze now, something that told him she was ready to understand. Ready to know what had been left unsaid for so long.

He exhaled deeply, standing tall despite the weight that had settled on his shoulders. He had known this moment would come, and now it had. The time to protect Ella from the truth had passed. She had to know, and she would understand, he would make sure of it.

"I'm part of the Templars," Tobias finally said, his voice steady but heavy with meaning. "The Knights Templar, the order that's been guarding the world's secrets for centuries. We're more than just warriors; we're keepers of the balance. Keepers of the line between what's human and what's not. And right now... right now, we're in the middle of something that could tear it all apart."

Ella blinked, trying to process the words, but the more he spoke, the clearer it became. Tobias wasn't just a man with a secret life. He was part of something ancient, something far bigger than she had ever imagined.

He met her eyes, the intensity in his gaze only adding to the weight of his words. "For years, I've been hunting creatures, beasts that cross into this world from places we can't see. Demons, monsters, whatever you want to call them. They exist, and they've always existed. But lately, something's changed. The balance is shifting, and there's a war coming. I can't explain everything just yet, but I need you to trust me when I say this: we're being watched."

Ella's breath caught in her throat. "Watched? By who?"

"By them," Tobias answered simply. "By the very creatures we've been hunting. And I don't think they're working alone. There's someone, something, behind it all."

He ran a hand through his hair, frustration growing as he thought about how little he actually knew. "I've been tracking something, a force of darkness that's been pulling the strings. I thought it was just one creature, just one of the demons we've dealt with before. But no, there's something more. Something older. The Templars are keeping an eye on it, but we've been too busy with the smaller threats to notice the bigger picture."

Ella's eyes softened with concern, but she still didn't speak. She was listening now, her gaze steady, her hand reaching for his. He hadn't expected her to believe it all at once, but he needed her to understand. He needed her to believe him.

"I've been sent here for a reason," Tobias continued, his voice softer now. "To stop whatever's coming, before it's too late. To stop the things that could destroy everything we know, everything we love." He met her eyes. "But I can't do this alone."

Ella's face darkened as she nodded slowly, taking in his words. "You need me to help. But how? What can I possibly do?"

Tobias exhaled, his shoulders sinking as he felt the full weight of it all. He had hoped to shield her from the reality of his mission, but there was no choice now. "I don't know if you can help, not yet. But I do know that you'll be in danger whether you're involved or not. The Templars... we're spread thin. Our numbers are few, and the threat is growing."

Ella took a deep breath, stepping closer to him. "You said the Templars have been guarding the world's secrets. What does that even mean? What are we really fighting against?"

He hesitated. The question had always been harder to answer than he wanted to admit. What were they fighting against? Creatures? Evil? Or something even darker than that?

"It means we're fighting against things you can't even imagine," Tobias replied quietly. "It's not just demons or monsters. It's the things that have been hiding in the shadows for centuries, things that could break the barrier between the worlds and flood this one with chaos. We're trying to prevent that from happening. But the truth is, it's all bigger than any of us."

Ella stood there in silence for a long moment, processing it all. The weight of the festival's noise, the games, and the laughter around them, seemed so distant now. The joy and lightness of the evening felt false, like a stage set for a play, where everyone pretended things were okay. Ella wanted to scream, to lash out at the sudden heaviness of Tobias's words. But she didn't. She stood, steadying herself, knowing that she had to face the reality of what Tobias had just told her.

"So... where do we go from here?" Ella finally asked, her voice steady but laced with uncertainty.

Tobias turned, his gaze sweeping across the field of festivity. He couldn't pretend to be part of this world anymore. There was too much at stake.

"We move forward," Tobias said, his voice steady but filled with unspoken urgency. "And I need you with me, Ella. But only if you're ready to face what's coming. I can't do this without you."

CHAPTER 9

Carrying the Blessed Home

"There may be those on earth who dress better or eat better, but those who enjoy the peace of God sleeps better."

- Thomas Holdcraft

TOBIAS AND ELLA PULLED up to St. Luke's Church, a quiet stone edifice that loomed like a guardian at the edge of town. The heavy, weathered stones seemed to absorb the last rays of the fading sun, casting long, angular shadows that crept along the worn path leading to the entrance. The church stood apart from the rest of the town, as if untouched by time. In the distance, the boisterous hum of the Harvest Festival spilled from the fairgrounds, but here, a profound silence reigned. It was a silence that felt heavy, pregnant with secrets.

The air around the church was thick with the scent of incense, a faint trace of something sweet and smoky, that mingled with the lingering fragrance of the apples and roasted corn from the festival. Tobias's car sat in the nearly empty parking lot, parked under the tall, gnarled oak tree that towered over the front of the church. The only other signs of life came from the faint rustle of leaves in the breeze and the muted sounds of far-off laughter and music.

Ella glanced at Tobias, sensing the weight of something pressing down on him. His eyes were narrowed, a flicker of something both tense and determined behind his usually calm exterior. She didn't know what it was, but she knew that whatever secret he was about to share had been eating away at him for a long time.

He turned toward her as he pulled the keys from the ignition, his voice low, his tone serious. "I think, Ella, it's time I showed you what I've been doing with my life since I left home."

Ella felt a tightness in her chest, the same uneasy feeling she'd had for years whenever Tobias was around, but especially now, when she knew he was about to unveil something he'd kept hidden for so long. She had always suspected there was more to him than the serious, detached man he presented. She had even joked with Sia that Tobias could be a secret agent, something mysterious and dangerous, yet she never thought she'd be facing the truth behind those suspicions.

She took a breath, her fingers lingering on the door handle. "Alright, Toby. Show me."

Tobias didn't hesitate, opening the door for her with a quiet, almost formal gesture. As she stepped out into the fading light, he placed a hand on her back, guiding her toward the church's imposing entrance. The large, red wooden doors were freshly painted, the deep crimson a stark contrast against the stone façade. She couldn't help but notice that the doors were too grand, too deliberate in their design, nothing about this place was casual.

"This might say St. Luke's out front, but this place was once called Catheois en Broda," Tobias began, his voice quieter now, the weight of his words heavy. "It's a local... base, you could call it. A base for the Church."

Ella raised an eyebrow, her curiosity piqued. "Base? For what?"

Tobias led her toward the doors, pushing them open with ease, the cool air of the church's interior rushing to greet them. "The world isn't exactly what you think, Ella. The Church isn't just a religion. It's a nation. And like any nation, it has an army. An army that fights against forces that aren't from this world."

Ella's heart stuttered in her chest. She'd heard stories of knights and holy warriors, but this felt... different. Her mind couldn't quite reconcile the images of saints and prayers with the idea of an actual army, one tasked with fighting things beyond human comprehension.

As they stepped into the grand, darkened foyer, the heavy wooden doors closed softly behind them. The stone floors were cold beneath her feet, the air thick with the fragrance of waxed candles and incense, the scent mixing with something older, earthy, ancient. The light from the stained glass windows, depicting scenes from the crucifixion and resurrection, seemed to shimmer unnaturally, casting fractured pools of colored light on the stone walls. The faint sound of a bell, muffled by the walls, reverberated in the air like the call to a distant battle.

To either side of them, rows of prayer candles flickered in steady rhythm, their soft flames casting dancing shadows across the stone, like watchful eyes in the dark. The pews sat empty and unused, their red cushions still pristine under the careful architecture, as if the space had been frozen in time.

Ella's breath caught in her throat as Tobias led her farther into the heart of the church. The altar was directly ahead, bathed in golden light from the large, arched windows at the back of the room. But it wasn't the altar that drew her gaze, it was the massive, intricately designed stained-glass window behind it. The image depicted a crusader, draped in white armor, wielding a silvered sword, a symbol of purity and might. The knight's eyes were stern, fierce, and unwavering.

"That window," Tobias said, his voice tinged with reverence, "it's always been my favorite. A knight, holding the Blade of Truth. The Archangel Gabriel's feather is said to be imbedded in the sword."

Ella looked at her brother, his expression unreadable. "A knight? So you're telling me you're... part of an army?"

Tobias let out a slow breath, the seriousness of his words thickening the air. "Not just an army. We're called Paladins, warriors of God, soldiers of the Church. The term Templar is often used for the entire Order. But the Paladins, the twelve of us... we're different."

Ella stopped in her tracks, her mind struggling to catch up with his words. "So, you're telling me you're a... crusader?"

Tobias's lips tightened, and he nodded. "Yes, but we're not what you think. This is real. We fight against the forces of Hell, not just in the physical world, but in the spiritual. Our mission is to defend humanity, protect the innocent, and destroy the corrupt, those who consort with dark powers."

Ella blinked, her mind trying to digest the enormity of what he was saying. "So, you're telling me you work for the Pope?"

He nodded again, his eyes never leaving her face. "Exactly. I was recruited after high school. At first, I wanted to be a priest. But they saw potential in me, potential that was better suited for a... different calling. A calling to fight against the forces of darkness."

Ella could barely process his words. This wasn't the Tobias she knew. Her brother was a man of deep faith, but this... this was something far beyond anything she'd ever imagined. "Why are you telling me this now?" she finally asked, her voice cracking slightly.

Tobias turned to her, his expression softening but still full of that same quiet intensity. "Because soon, Ella, the lines between the world we know and the world we're fighting will blur. Soon, the walls that separate us from the forces of Hell will crumble. I need you to understand what's coming. I need you to be ready."

Ella shook her head, her mind swimming with disbelief. But Tobias's gaze never wavered. "Are you asking me to join this... army?" she whispered, her voice trembling slightly.

Tobias took a long breath, his eyes firm. "Yes, and to learn how to defend yourself. To fight. You don't have to believe everything I've said right now, but you need to trust me. Trust your heart. You'll learn soon enough that this world is much darker than we've been led to believe."

As they stepped further into the heart of St. Luke's, the weight of the church's atmosphere settled around them. The dim, flickering candlelight reflected off the walls, casting long shadows that seemed to whisper of hidden secrets. The air was thick with the smell of aged wood, wax, and incense, something ancient and sacred. The faint smell of lavender lingered, so deeply ingrained in the church that it felt as though the very walls exhaled the scent, infused with prayer and devotion over centuries.

Ella followed Tobias toward the center of the sanctuary, her footsteps muffled by the plush red carpeting that ran down the aisles. Each step echoed in the stillness, the faint hum of a distant chant somehow reverberating through the space, though no one else was present. It felt like they were the only two people in the world, walking in a space where time stood still, a place suspended between earth and heaven. The sense of age in the church, of history buried beneath the dust of centuries, was palpable. This place wasn't just a house of worship, it was something older, more esoteric.

Tobias's voice broke the quiet as he led her to the altar, his words heavy with the weight of secrets long kept. "The Church isn't just a faith, Ella. It's a living, breathing force, a nation that has survived through millennia. And like any nation, it has an army. But the forces we fight against are not earthly powers. They're far darker."

Ella stopped short, looking up at him, her brow furrowing in confusion. "Darker than what?" she asked, her voice soft, still processing his words.

Tobias took a deep breath, his eyes scanning the shadows in the far corners of the room before meeting her gaze. "Hell itself," he said plainly, the words hanging heavy in the air. His voice dropped even lower, as though speaking too loudly might bring down the walls around them. "The enemy of the Church is not another country, not terrorists, and not politics. The true enemy is the very thing the Church has spent centuries keeping at bay. Demons. Fallen angels. And those who choose to consort with them."

Ella blinked, trying to make sense of what he was saying. This was beyond anything she'd expected, beyond anything she'd ever imagined. She could see the conviction in his eyes, the absolute belief that everything he was saying was true, but she had trouble reconciling that belief with the world she knew. "Are you serious?" she asked, her voice tremulous, barely above a whisper. "You're telling me there are actual... demons?"

Tobias nodded, his face hardening with a seriousness that made her stomach twist. "I am. And I'm not the only one who fights them. The Paladins are the Church's warriors, its secret defenders, and I'm one of them. We were chosen not just for our faith, but for our ability to fight in a way that's... beyond normal human capacity. We wield the power of God's wrath, and we protect the world from what lies in the dark."

He paused, letting the silence stretch out between them, filled only by the faint hum of an unseen choir, distant yet tangible in the sacred space. The stained-glass windows, each one depicting scenes from the Bible, cast colorful beams of light across the stone floor, giving the church a surreal, almost otherworldly glow. The knight depicted in the massive window behind the altar seemed to come to life in the flickering light, the sword in his hand gleaming like a beacon in the dark.

"The Church isn't just a faith, Ella," Tobias continued, "it's a battle. And I've been chosen to fight on the frontlines."

Ella looked at him, her mind racing. She'd always known Tobias as serious, distant, but never as someone who was caught up in something this... grand. She had no idea how to process it. "But... why are you telling me this?" she asked, her voice barely above a whisper.

He exhaled slowly, as though the words were hard for him to say. "Because soon, everything you know will be challenged. The lines between our world and theirs, their world of darkness and evil, will blur. I need you to understand what's coming. I need you to be ready."

Ella felt a tightness in her chest. She wanted to reject it, to turn away from this reality he was presenting, but she couldn't. The conviction in his voice, the fire in his eyes, it was impossible to ignore. "You want me to join your... army? To fight demons?" she asked, her voice barely audible as she stared up at him.

Tobias smiled grimly. "Yes. And you need to be ready to fight. The world is changing, Ella, and soon, you won't be able to pretend you don't see the monsters anymore."

Ella took a deep breath, trying to calm her nerves. "What... what do I have to do?" she asked, her voice shaky but determined. She was scared, scared of the unknown, scared of the power Tobias wielded, and scared of what it all meant for her. But the look in his eyes, the way he held himself like a soldier preparing for battle, it drew her in. She couldn't turn her back on him, on this.

Tobias's expression softened, the warrior in him giving way to the brother she'd always known. "For now, nothing. Just understand that this is real, and you're going to need to accept it. It's not about believing in everything I say right now. It's about trusting me, and trusting yourself."

Ella nodded slowly, the weight of the decision already heavy on her shoulders. She couldn't back away from this, not now. "Okay," she said quietly, her voice firming with resolve. "Teach me."

Tobias smiled softly, and for a moment, Ella could see the exhaustion in his eyes. He reached into his coat and pulled out a small, intricately carved wooden box. "I was going to wait for a more... formal time, but we don't have the luxury of that. I need to begin your training now."

He opened the box, revealing a small, silver pendant inside. It was a cross, but it was unlike any she'd ever seen before, more ornate, more detailed, as if it had been forged for a specific purpose. Tobias took it out and handed it to her, his fingers brushing hers for a moment longer than necessary.

"This is your first step," he said. "The Pendant of Saint Michael. It will guide you when you're ready to fight, and it will protect you when you're not."

Ella took the pendant, feeling its weight in her hand. It wasn't heavy, but it felt powerful, almost as though it had a pulse of its own. She looked up at Tobias, her resolve solidifying. She didn't understand everything, but she knew one thing for sure: her life was never going to be the same again.

Tobias led Ella to the side of the church, away from the looming altar and the solemn stillness that surrounded them. The noise from the festival was faint but still detectable, as though the world beyond the stone walls was carrying on as usual. But here, in this quiet, hidden corner, the air seemed thicker, heavier. This was where secrets were kept, where the walls seemed to hold stories too dangerous for the light of day.

Tobias stopped and turned to face her, his expression tight. "I need you to understand something about my past, Ella," he said softly, his voice steady but laced with a quiet pain. He placed a hand on the cold stone wall beside him, leaning slightly against it as though the weight of what he was about to reveal could send him crumbling to the floor.

Ella looked up at him, her heart heavy with the weight of his words. "What's going on, Toby? What do you mean by all of this? The Templars, the army, how does it all fit together? You've always been the strong one, the one who could handle anything. But this... this feels like something else."

Tobias exhaled, the deep breath rattling in his chest. He pulled away from the wall, taking a step back as he looked out toward the festival lights flickering beyond the church grounds. "It's because I haven't been able to handle it, not really. Not since that night. The night Mia died."

The words hit Ella like a blow to the chest, and she stepped back instinctively. It had been years since that night, but the memory of it still haunted them both, pulling them back to the most painful moment of their lives. Tobias's eyes darkened as he spoke, the weight of guilt and loss clear in his gaze. "You know how it happened. I was the one driving when the truck came at us. I couldn't save her. Mia... she was gone before the ambulance even arrived."

Ella's throat tightened as she listened, her eyes welling up with unshed tears. "Toby..." she whispered, reaching out instinctively to place a hand on his arm. "You couldn't have known."

"I should have known," he said, his voice growing colder. "I should have done more. I was supposed to protect her. Instead, I failed."

He turned away, his fists clenched at his sides. "After that night, I couldn't just sit idly by anymore. I couldn't just keep pretending that the world was this nice, safe place. I had to do something. That's when the Church found me. They saw something in me that I didn't even know was there."

Ella's eyes narrowed. "So, this is all about... guilt? You're doing this for redemption?"

Tobias's gaze snapped to hers, a faint flicker of something darker in his eyes. "It's not just guilt. It's more than that. It's about protecting the world from the darkness Mia never had a chance to see. It's about fighting against everything that threatens people like her, people like you." He paused, his voice lowering, becoming more personal. "It's about making sure the things that took her away... don't take anyone else."

Ella took a breath, her heart racing as she tried to absorb what he was saying. "But why me, Toby? Why are you telling me all of this now?"

Tobias turned back to face the church, his jaw tightening. "Because you're the only one I trust. The only one who can help me. And because I need you to understand what's coming. You're not just my sister anymore. You're part of this. Part of this fight."

Ella's breath caught in her throat as he spoke, the weight of his words pressing down on her chest. "What do you mean? I'm not a fighter. I don't know anything about demons or... whatever it is you're dealing with."

He smiled faintly, his eyes softening for a moment. "I know. But that's what I'm for. To teach you. To help you become strong enough to stand beside me when the time comes." He looked at her, his gaze intense. "The forces we fight aren't just monsters. They're something worse. They can hide behind anything, people, places, even our own fears."

Tobias took a step closer, lowering his voice to a near whisper. "You've already seen a glimpse of it. This isn't just about monsters under the bed. This is real, Ella. The fight we're about to face isn't just for our world, it's for the next one too."

Ella's eyes widened as she processed his words. "And you want me to fight in this war? After everything you've told me... how can I just accept it?"

Tobias stepped back, his posture firm, a hint of pride in his voice. "Because you're stronger than you think. I know you don't believe it now, but you're ready, Ella. You've always been ready."

Ella looked at him, her heart hammering in her chest. She couldn't deny the fear gnawing at her. But she also couldn't deny the pull to stand by him. She had always trusted Tobias, and now, more than ever, she needed to understand what he was fighting for, and what she was meant to do in this strange new world he was showing her.

Tobias gave a slight smile, but there was a gravity to it. "For now, though, we have to start somewhere. I'm not asking you to be a warrior right this moment, Ella. But you need to learn to protect yourself. That's the first step."

Ella blinked, taken aback. "What? You mean... you're going to teach me to fight?"

"Not fight, yet," Tobias said with a soft chuckle. "Right now, you're just going to learn how to defend yourself. One step at a time. But you're going to need to know how to wield a sword at some point. The rest will come later. But for now, we'll start with some basics."

She frowned, still trying to wrap her mind around what he was saying. "And I'm just supposed to... what? Start swinging a sword around?"

Tobias's smile turned serious again. "The sword isn't the only thing you'll need to learn how to control. You'll need to learn how to control your focus, your will, and your strength. The physical part is just the surface. The real fight begins within. And I'll help you get there."

Ella looked at him, still uncertain but willing to follow him for now. It wasn't that she believed everything he said, it was that she couldn't let him face this alone. And if there was a chance to protect herself, to be able to stand beside him when the time came, then she had no choice but to try.

Tobias placed a hand on her shoulder, his expression softening. "You'll be ready, Ella. I know it."

TOBIAS STEPPED BACK AND took a deep breath, his eyes scanning the quiet church courtyard. The festival's noise still echoed faintly in the distance, a reminder of the world outside, where life went on in its merry chaos. Here, in the sanctuary of the Templar's hidden world, the air felt different. Charged. Purposeful. Ella felt a shiver run down her spine as Tobias turned to her, his serious demeanor returning.

"Alright, Ella. This is where it starts," he said, his voice clipped, like a commander giving orders. "This won't be easy. You'll want to quit, but I need you to stay focused. You're going to learn how to defend yourself. No more running, no more waiting."

Ella swallowed, trying to keep the unease from showing on her face. She had expected something different, maybe a history lesson or some kind of deep, spiritual revelation about the Templars. But instead, here she was, standing in a deserted courtyard, about to wield a weapon. A sword. Her heart pounded at the thought, her hand sweating as it instinctively clutched the smooth wooden stick Tobias had handed her.

"First lesson," Tobias said, lowering his stance as he gripped his own practice weapon. "A sword isn't just for fighting. It's an extension of your body. Your focus, your intent, all of it is channeled through the blade. If you don't control your mind, you'll never control your sword. And if you can't control that, you won't survive."

Ella watched as Tobias moved into a ready position, his grip firm but relaxed. He was right. She had no idea how to even hold a sword properly. Her fingers trembled around the wooden stick, and she shifted uncomfortably on her feet.

Tobias gave her a small nod. "It's simple. You follow through. Keep your movements sharp, and don't waste energy. Now, show me what you've got."

Ella took a breath and lifted the stick in front of her, trying to mimic the position Tobias had taken. She wasn't sure what she was doing, but she figured that at least this way, she'd look the part.

"Don't overthink it," Tobias said, his voice more encouraging now. "Move, feel the stick, feel the weight. Let your body dictate the movement, not your mind."

Ella moved cautiously at first, unsure of herself. She swung harder, more determined, but Tobias blocked her again, his movements smooth and fluid. He barely seemed to put any effort into it.

"Again," Tobias said, his tone calm, but firm. "You need to stay grounded. Don't let yourself get thrown off by the first failure."

Ella scowled, determined not to let Tobias see her frustration. She had always prided herself on being competent in everything she did, but now? She felt clumsy. Awkward. The sword was heavy, the movements unnatural. Still, she tried again.

This time, she approached with more confidence. She swung harder, more determined, but Tobias blocked her again, his movements smooth and fluid. He barely seemed to put any effort into it.

"You're relying too much on force," Tobias observed, lowering his practice blade. "Force won't get you far. It's about control. Your focus should be on precision, not power."

Ella nodded, her mind racing as she tried to digest his words. Every part of her wanted to give up. To step back and walk away. But she couldn't. Not when she knew how much this mattered.

"I know this is hard," Tobias said softly, seeing her frustration. "But you have to learn. There's no room for hesitation when it comes to this. People's lives are at stake. My life is at stake. The people I protect are counting on me, and if you're going to fight at my side, you have to be ready."

Ella felt a knot tighten in her stomach. "I didn't ask for this, Tobias," she muttered, her voice low.

"I know you didn't," he said, his expression softening slightly. "But you're here now. And I'm not going to let you get hurt because you weren't prepared."

He motioned for her to try again. "This isn't just about sword fighting. It's about learning to trust yourself. To trust your instincts. It'll take time, but you've got it in you."

Ella inhaled sharply and squared her shoulders. She couldn't let Tobias down. Not now. Not ever. Slowly, she raised the wooden sword again, this time with more control, more thought. She swung again, this time with purpose.

Tobias blocked the strike effortlessly once more, but there was something different in her approach. Her movements were more controlled, less frantic. He gave her a small nod of approval. "That's it. You're getting there."

But Ella knew it wasn't enough. Not yet. She was still far from where she needed to be. Still too unsure, too raw. But it was a start. And a start, for now, was enough.

As she stepped back, wiping the sweat from her brow, Tobias's eyes hardened with resolve. "We'll continue tomorrow. There's no time to waste. Every day you spend training is another day you're closer to being ready. But we don't have much time. We're running out of it, Ella."

Ella's breath caught in her throat. Something in his voice struck a chord deep inside her, a gut-wrenching feeling that told her the clock was ticking faster than she realized. Something was coming, and she was about to be part of it.

Tobias stepped toward her, his face serious, but there was an underlying tenderness there. "Are you ready for this?"

Ella hesitated for just a moment, but then she met his gaze, nodding firmly. "I'm ready."

Tobias gave a curt nod in return, his expression unreadable. "Good. Tomorrow, we begin in earnest. We train until you're ready. Until then, rest. You'll need your strength."

As he turned to leave the courtyard, Ella stood there, her mind racing with everything he had just said. There was no turning back now. Whatever was coming, she had to be prepared.

And as the distant sounds of the festival faded into the night, she knew that the true battle, her battle, had only just begun.

CHAPTER 10
Warriors Within and Without

A knight is sworn to valor, His heart knows only virtue, His blade defends the helpless, His might upholds the weak, His word speaks only truth, His wrath undoes the wicked.

Charles Edward Pogue, Dragonheart

THE NEXT DAY CAME faster than Ella expected. The sky was overcast, a muted gray stretching over the town as the sounds of the Harvest Festival echoed in the distance. For most people, it was just another day of celebration, but for Ella, the weight of her brother's words hung over her like a storm cloud.

She found herself standing in the same courtyard again, where Tobias had left her the night before. The cobblestones beneath her boots felt cold, and the air seemed thicker today, more charged. The anticipation was tangible.

Tobias stood across from her, his expression unreadable as always, but there was something in his stance that spoke of determination. A silent promise that today, he would push her harder. She could see it in the tightness of his jaw, the way he held himself steady despite the chaos of the world outside this little hidden corner of the Church.

"Ready?" Tobias's voice broke through her thoughts, his tone flat but expectant.

Ella nodded, trying to ignore the creeping doubt gnawing at her insides. She was trying to focus, trying to understand what he had been telling her. But her mind kept going back to what he had said about the Templars. The world wasn't as she knew it. There were real demons. Warlocks. Dark forces. And somewhere in all of it, she was supposed to fight.

She glanced at the wooden sword Tobias had handed her. It felt heavier than it had the day before. Maybe it was because she now understood that it wasn't just a piece of training equipment, it was the first step in a long, terrifying road.

Tobias motioned for her to take her stance, and she did, holding the sword awkwardly in front of her. She could already feel the weight of it. She wasn't sure what she was doing, or even why she was doing it, but she couldn't back out now. Not after everything Tobias had told her. Not after the way he'd looked at her, like he was already preparing her for something she wasn't ready for.

"Focus," Tobias said, his eyes narrowing as he watched her. "Don't think too much. Move with intention. Like this."

Before she could react, Tobias moved forward in a blur of motion, his own practice sword coming down swiftly to knock hers aside. Ella barely had time to adjust, stumbling back as the force of his strike left her off-balance. Her heart raced, and her hands tightened around the wooden hilt.

"Don't think you can just swing it around and hope it works. If you're going to fight, you need to anticipate every move before it happens," Tobias said, his voice steady, as though he was lecturing her in combat, not pushing her to survive.

Ella wiped the sweat off her brow, trying to keep up. She wasn't sure how long they had been at this, an hour, maybe two. The sun had risen higher, and the faint sounds of the festival were still carrying through the air, but it felt like another world altogether here. She couldn't stop to rest. Not yet.

"Again," Tobias ordered, moving back into his stance.

Ella stepped forward again, more determined this time. She swung her sword in a wide arc, focusing all her attention on the strike. But Tobias was faster, his sword blocking hers with ease. He didn't even break a sweat.

"You're thinking too much," Tobias said. "You're moving like you're waiting for something to happen. You need to be in the moment. This isn't just about you, it's about everything around you. It's about your opponent's next move, your environment, and your own body. You're not just swinging a sword. You're becoming one with it. With your surroundings."

Ella paused, her breath coming in ragged gasps. She wiped her face with the back of her hand and tried to shake the frustration out of her bones. She didn't know how to do this. She didn't know how to fight. The thought hit her like a ton of bricks, and she froze for a moment. Tobias noticed, and his expression hardened, though his voice remained calm.

"Are you ready for this?" he asked, eyes piercing into hers. "Because it won't be easy. And it will hurt. But you can't let that stop you. You have to face it. Whatever comes next, you face it. Head on."

Ella stood there for a moment, her heart pounding. She could feel the weight of his words, and the pressure of the world beyond this courtyard closing in on her. Everything was changing. Every choice, every move she made from here on out would bring her closer to the reality of what was coming.

"I'm ready," she said, though her voice barely rose above a whisper.

As soon as she said it, something inside her clicked. It was subtle at first, a sense of clarity, like an instinct awakening deep within her. She felt it in the way her body moved, the way her muscles knew just where to go, even if her mind had no clue.

It was the same feeling Tobias had had all those years ago when he first picked up a sword, a strange, almost natural instinct. An ability that ran in their blood, a force they couldn't fully explain, but one that was undeniable.

Tobias, watching her, took a step back. There was a flicker of recognition in his eyes, as if he had seen something in her that he hadn't expected. The change was subtle, but it was there.

"Good," Tobias said, nodding. "You're starting to get it. But we'll need to keep pushing. There's a lot you still need to learn before you're ready to fight at my side."

Ella nodded, determined. She wasn't sure what this meant, or how she could fight against what was coming, but there was something in her that had just awakened, something primal that was ready to face the unknown.

She lifted the sword again, her grip steadying. There was no turning back. The path ahead was unclear, but Ella felt something deep within her telling her she was more than ready to face it.

The day stretched on, with the soft hum of the world beyond the courtyard barely reaching the two of them. The secluded church grounds felt far removed from the noisy bustle of the Harvest Festival just a few miles away. Here, the air was still, heavy with the scent of blooming roses and the earthy smell of freshly turned soil in the well-maintained garden. It was peaceful in a way that contrasted sharply with the weight of the decisions Tobias and Ella were facing.

Ella stood in the courtyard, her feet shifting on the cool stone beneath her, sword in hand. The surrounding statues of saints, carved in stoic poses, seemed to watch over them, their stone eyes unblinking. The manicured garden stretched out behind them, a patchwork of colors from the flowerbeds, pinks, purples, and whites, setting a tranquil, almost ethereal backdrop. The silence of the space was only broken by the occasional soft flutter of wings from the small birds that nestled in the trees above.

As she swung the sword, the weight of it settled in her hands. The blade felt both awkward and natural, a strange extension of herself. Tobias moved around her, his eyes sharp, his body poised in the calm, controlled stance of someone who had spent years perfecting this art.

"You're thinking too much again," Tobias said, his voice cutting through her thoughts, the sound of his footsteps barely audible over the hum of the wind. His voice was calm, but firm, he wasn't just her brother now. He was a teacher, an instructor, pushing her further than she thought she could go.

Ella looked up, letting out a breath she hadn't realized she'd been holding. "I don't know if I can do this, Toby," she admitted quietly, her gaze flicking to the statues that lined the edges of the courtyard. "This isn't me. I'm not meant to be a warrior. I'm not like you."

Tobias paused, his expression unreadable as he watched her. For a moment, the only sounds were the distant calls of priests and nuns walking in and out of the church, tending to the quiet corners of the garden. Their world was vastly different from Ella's, filled with prayers, devotion, and a kind of calm certainty that she was just beginning to understand.

"You're wrong about that," Tobias replied softly, his voice breaking the stillness. "You might not see it now, but this is in your blood. The instinct to fight, to defend, it's something we're born with. Our family has always had it, Ella. I didn't choose this life, but it was always in me, waiting."

Ella shifted uncomfortably, the weight of the sword now feeling more like a burden than a weapon. "But I'm not you, Toby. I'm not... trained like you."

"No," Tobias agreed, his voice low and steady, "you're not. But that's why I'm here. To help you find your way."

He stepped toward her, his eyes flicking toward the small stone fountain in the middle of the courtyard, its waters splashing softly, mingling with the sound of wind through the trees. "You're already stronger than you think," he continued, "and it's not just about physical strength. It's about knowing when to act and when to hold back. I can see that in you. It's in your eyes. You don't think I see it, but I do."

Ella wasn't sure what to make of his words, but as she looked up at the serene faces of the saints, their stone features set in eternal prayer, she felt a strange sense of peace in the quiet of the space. The tension in her shoulders eased slightly, though the weight of her doubts still clung to her.

She looked at Tobias, her gaze steady now, and took a deep breath. "Alright. I'll trust you."

Tobias smiled, nodding once in approval. "That's all I need, Ella. Now, let's try again."

As the sun dipped lower in the sky, casting long, golden shadows across the courtyard, Ella picked up her sword again. She wasn't sure if she was ready for what was ahead. But in the silence of the church grounds, with the sacred statues watching over them and the distant hum of the world beyond, she took the first step toward something she couldn't yet understand.

The sound of Tobias's blade slicing through the air, as he moved gracefully around her, was the only thing that kept her grounded. She would keep going. Even if it terrified her. Even if she wasn't sure she could do this.

The sun had fully set by the time Tobias and Ella finished their training for the day. The courtyard was now bathed in the soft glow of the moon, casting long, quiet shadows against the statues and the stone walls of the church. The nuns had retired for the evening, their footsteps echoing softly as they disappeared into the chapel. The priests had already begun to prepare for evening prayers, their chants echoing faintly through the church, blending with the stillness of the night.

Ella's arms were sore, the muscles in her shoulders and back protesting after hours of practice, but she stood tall. Tobias had pushed her hard, testing her reflexes, her speed, her ability to anticipate every move. It had been exhausting, and at times, frustrating. But now, as she caught her breath, she could feel something shifting within her, a sense of purpose, however faint. The warrior's instinct Tobias spoke of was slowly awakening.

"You've improved," Tobias said, his voice light with approval. He lowered his practice sword and wiped the sweat from his brow, watching his sister with a grin. "I mean, wow. You're picking this up faster than I expected. You're a natural at this."

Ella glanced at the sword in her hand, its wooden form far lighter than the real thing, but still heavy in her hands. "I don't feel like I've improved," she admitted, rubbing the back of her neck, sore from the effort. "It's all so... overwhelming. It doesn't feel real, Toby. I'm not sure I can do this."

Tobias tilted his head, studying her with a gaze full of warmth. He grinned and stepped forward. "What did I tell you? The key is not to think about it too much. You're doing great. Trust yourself. Trust what you can do. You've got the instincts, you've got the heart. That's the most important thing. Everything else will follow."

Ella bit her lip, frustration clouding her thoughts. "But what if I'm not good enough?" She met his eyes, her voice quiet. "What if I can't keep up? What if I'm not... like you?"

Tobias smiled at her reassuringly, a softness in his eyes that she hadn't seen in a while. He placed a hand on her shoulder, steadying her. "Hey, you're not supposed to be like me, Ella. You don't have to be like me. I'm not asking you to be a perfect soldier, just to keep going. You've already got what it takes. Just one step at a time."

Her brow furrowed, doubt still lingering in her eyes. "But I'm scared, Toby. I'm scared of what's coming... scared that I won't be able to handle it."

Tobias placed his sword down and turned to face her fully. "You're going to handle it, because you've got something that will make you stronger than any fear. You've got the will to protect what matters. That's all anyone needs to get through what's ahead."

Ella stood still, absorbing his words. The silence of the courtyard felt heavier now, the weight of the world settling over her shoulders as she realized the true gravity of Tobias's mission, and how it was becoming hers as well.

Tobias offered her a small, wry smile, trying to lighten the moment. "Look, I know it's a lot to take in, but you've got the heart of a warrior. That's something people can't teach you. You're already on your way."

Ella swallowed hard, nodding slowly. "I'll try."

"That's all I can ask," Tobias said with a soft chuckle. He gave her a small nudge. "And remember, this isn't about being perfect, it's about giving it your best. No one expects you to be flawless. You just have to keep going."

Ella sighed, feeling a little lighter. "Alright, Toby. I'll keep going."

Tobias nodded, his expression more serious now. "Good. Because things are going to get tough. We don't have time to waste. You'll need every ounce of this warrior spirit if we're going to protect everyone we care about."

The moonlight reflected off the stone walls of the courtyard, casting long shadows across the ground. Ella felt the weight of his words settle into her bones, the sense of urgency tugging at her chest. She wasn't sure what was coming, or how she would handle it, but she knew one thing for certain.

Her life was no longer the same. And neither was Tobias's.

The path ahead was dark, uncertain, and fraught with danger, but for the first time, Ella felt the stirrings of something deeper within herself, a strength she hadn't known she had, rising to meet the challenge.

The evening had fully set in, and the church courtyard, once bathed in sunlight, was now cloaked in shadows. The air was cooler, and a soft breeze stirred the trees, carrying the scent of the distant harvest festival. The sound of distant laughter and music faintly reached the courtyard, but it felt worlds away from the conversation taking place in the stillness of the garden.

Tobias and Ella stood in the center of the open space, the moonlight casting long shadows across the stone tiles at their feet. The ancient statues of saints seemed to watch over them, their stone faces forever frozen in prayer, offering silent support in this moment of transition.

Ella stood a few paces away from Tobias, her fingers gently gripping the hilt of the wooden sword, the weight of it now a little less foreign to her. She had learned more than she realized in the last few hours, each swing of the practice sword pushing her further from the girl she had been.

She glanced up at Tobias, who was watching her carefully. His eyes weren't just filled with the professional, almost clinical concern of a trainer anymore; there was something deeper there, something personal.

Tobias cleared his throat, breaking the silence that had stretched between them. "Ella, I know I've pushed you hard today. But the truth is, we're running out of time. I don't know what's coming, but I know it's coming fast."

Ella looked at him, her brow furrowing. "What do you mean, Toby? What's coming?"

Tobias hesitated, the weight of the question pulling him into a deeper contemplation. His usual confidence seemed to waver, just for a moment. He didn't know how much he should tell her, but he knew that if he was going to ask her to take this path, she needed to understand the gravity of what lay ahead.

"The truth is, Ella, I don't have all the answers. What I do know is that there's a war going on, and we're right in the middle of it. It's not just physical, there's a spiritual side to it too. It's not just demons and warlocks. The forces of Hell are moving, and we have to move faster than them. The Church has trained me, and now it's time for me to train you."

He stepped closer to her, lowering his voice so only she could hear. "I've been to the front lines, Ella. I've seen things, things that you can't even imagine. But it's not just me now. It's you too. You're part of this fight now, whether you like it or not."

Ella swallowed, the weight of his words heavy on her chest. "So... what do we do?"

Tobias placed a hand on her shoulder, his touch warm, grounding her. "We prepare. We get stronger. You're going to need everything we've worked on today, and more. The Templars are a network, and we're part of it. But right now, our focus is on what's coming for us.

You'll need to learn not just how to defend yourself, but how to fight for others."

Ella nodded slowly, the weight of his words settling deeper within her. She didn't have a full grasp of what was coming, but she could see now that Tobias wasn't just trying to protect her, he was preparing her for something much bigger. Something dangerous.

Tobias continued, his voice a little softer now, yet more resolute. "You'll need to trust in the training, Ella. The way forward will be full of danger. You'll feel fear, doubt, maybe even regret. But you can't let that stop you. Not when people are depending on you."

Ella met his gaze, her chest tightening. "I don't know if I'm ready for this. I don't know if I can do what you're asking."

"I'm not asking you to be perfect," Tobias said, his voice firm but full of understanding. "I'm asking you to trust in yourself. In your instincts. This isn't about being the best. It's about being there when it matters."

Ella stood still, her heart pounding. She had spent so long trying to avoid the weight of the world around her. But now, it was impossible to ignore. She was in this, whether she wanted to be or not.

"What if I fail?" she asked, her voice barely above a whisper.

Tobias' expression softened. "You won't fail. Not if you keep pushing. And if you stumble? We'll help you get back up."

A moment of silence passed between them, the only sounds now the distant hum of the festival. Ella thought of the warmth, the laughter, the feeling of normalcy that had seemed so far away from this world of swords and Templars and ancient battles. It felt like another life.

"Alright," Ella said quietly, finding a newfound resolve deep within herself. "I'm in. I'll do whatever it takes."

Tobias smiled, his eyes filled with pride and something else, something akin to relief. "Good. Because whatever comes next, we face it together. As a team."

The wind shifted again, a soft breeze stirring the flowers in the garden, and for a moment, Ella almost felt like she could breathe again. The road ahead was dark, but with Tobias at her side, perhaps she could find the strength to face it.

As the moon rose higher in the sky, Tobias took a step back, offering her a nod. "Rest now. We'll train again tomorrow."

Ella smiled faintly, feeling the weight of the night pressing in on her. But there was something new inside her now, something that had been sparked by Tobias' words, something that would carry her through the trials ahead.

Tomorrow would be a new day. And she was ready to face it.

CHAPTER 11
Another Stranger Me

Side by side or miles apart, siblings will always be connected by heart.

Anonymous

SIA STARED INTO THE mirror, the reflection that met her eyes a pale shadow of who she used to be. The radio played softly in the background, DJ Sal's voice crackling through the static, but it was nothing more than noise, a distant hum to fill the silence she couldn't escape.

"Hey, you're listening to WBGH, and we're calling out to all you cats who were at the Harvest Festival yesterday! Was that fire crazy or what!? Well, good news, the festival is still going on, so you volunteers, get down here and join me and all our guests. I'll be here all day taking your requests and giving out free t-shirts!"

Her eyes never left her reflection as the words of the DJ faded into the background. She saw herself, yes, but it was someone she didn't recognize. Her once-bright eyes now seemed tired, hollow, the dark circles beneath them a constant reminder of the sleepless nights. She had been living in a fog for so long now, where even the simplest things felt heavy.

Mia would've teased her about it, maybe told her she looked like a ghost, maybe even suggested they switch places again, just for fun. Mia had always been the more playful one, the one who could make people laugh even in the darkest times. The two of them had been inseparable, twins in every sense, as alike as night and day. But now, Mia was gone, and Sia was left with this gaping hole in her chest.

A lump rose in Sia's throat, but she forced it down. She had no tears left to cry. It wasn't that she didn't miss Mia, she missed her with every part of herself. It was that the pain had become so familiar, like an ache that never fully healed. Losing a sibling wasn't a wound you could bandage up, it was a scar that became part of who you were. A piece of you was forever missing, and it was something you had to learn to live with.

As she stood there, staring at the girl in the mirror who was supposed to be her, she wondered: would Mia have looked like this? Would she have had the same tired eyes, the same heaviness in her chest? Would she have carried the same burden of grief, silently living with a loss so profound it couldn't be put into words?

Mia had always been the one to lighten the mood, to remind Sia of the beauty in life, even when things seemed darkest. But now, on this day, Sia was left to wonder if she'd ever be able to live without that shadow of loss following her. The world moved on, but the pain didn't. It stayed with her, carved into her soul, a constant reminder that some losses never truly fade.

The thought made her breath catch in her throat. It was her birthday today, but it was Mia's too. And Mia wasn't here. Mia would never grow older, never have the chance to experience all the things they'd dreamed about. Today wasn't just about her, it was about Mia, too. And somehow, that made the day feel even heavier.

Her reflection seemed to mock her, this broken version of herself, the one that no longer felt complete. She couldn't help but imagine that if Mia were still alive, she wouldn't look like this. She'd be vibrant, full of life, like she always had been. But the truth was, Mia was gone. And no matter how much she wished she could change it, nothing would bring her back.

Sia sighed, her breath unsteady, and reached for her hair tie, pulling it back into a simple ponytail. She went through the motions of getting dressed, her hands moving on autopilot. When her fingers brushed against her wrist, she paused for a moment. She felt the cool metal of the bracelet Mia had given her, the moon charm still hanging there, a quiet symbol of the bond they had shared. It was a gift Mia had given her when they were younger, something to wear every day to

remind each other that no matter what, they were always connected. Even though Mia was gone, that bracelet was the one piece of
her that Sia could still hold onto.

She tightened the bracelet, her thumb brushing over the moon,
and then adjusted the smock over her clothes. She was going to the
festival, but not before doing something she felt was long overdue.
She'd been selfish these last few years, letting her parents worry
about her and fret over her mental wellbeing while at the same time
knowing full well she could control her own emotions. Her guilt for
that was immense. She headed down the oak-finished steps into the
living room, where her parents looked up from watching the news.

Sia sat between her parents on the couch, the air in the room
thick with unsaid words. The low hum of the television was still in
the background, but it faded into the noise as she shifted closer to
her mother. For a moment, she was just a daughter again, a daughter
in need of comfort, something she hadn't allowed herself to feel in
years. She wrapped her arms around her mother and buried her face
in her lap, letting out a long, shaky breath.

Her mother froze at first, her arms not knowing whether to
embrace or stay still. After a moment of hesitation, Mrs. Mason
wrapped her arms around Sia, her touch soft and warm, the comfort
of a mother's embrace that Sia had been denying herself for so long.
It felt like coming home, like stepping into the safety of a place that
had always been there, always available, but that she had avoided
out of shame.

Sia had always felt like she needed to protect her parents from
her pain. Since Mia's death, it had been as if they all carried separate burdens, and the weight of her own grief was something she
couldn't share. It was easier, she thought, to keep the facade up, to
shield them from the storm inside her. But here, in this moment,
that wall between them started to crack.

"I'm sorry, Mom," Sia whispered, her voice trembling, "I
should've been better... I shouldn't have kept this from you."

Mrs. Mason stroked Sia's hair, a gentle, soothing motion, like she
had done countless times when Sia was younger. The words seemed
to weigh heavily on her, but she said nothing. She didn't need to.
The silence was enough for Sia to feel the love, the acceptance she
hadn't allowed herself to feel in so long.

Peter Mason, who had been sitting silently beside them, watched his wife and daughter with a mixture of concern and sorrow. He knew his daughter's struggles all too well, yet he hadn't known how to help. He had hoped, perhaps naively, that she would eventually find a way to heal on her own. He didn't know how to fix it, and that uncertainty had left him distant. But now, watching his daughter break down in her mother's arms, he understood how much he had failed her.

He glanced at his wife and mouthed, Should we tell her yet?

Mrs. Mason shook her head gently. It was too soon, too heavy a burden to put on their daughter's shoulders today. This day wasn't just any day. Today, of all days, Sia needed them to be her parents, not just guardians of a tragic secret. Today was supposed to be about Mia, but it wasn't the time to burden Sia with something that could shatter what little peace she had found.

Mr. Mason gave a slight nod, but the weight of their shared knowledge still hung heavy between them. Sia wasn't ready yet. Not today.

"Is everything alright, dear?" Mrs. Mason asked softly, her voice a low hum of concern as she smoothed the hair from Sia's face. The tenderness in her voice made Sia's heart clench with guilt, guilt for having kept them in the dark, guilt for not allowing them to be there for her.

Sia looked up, her eyes red-rimmed from the tears she hadn't even realized she'd shed. She bit her lower lip, her mind racing. How could she explain the nightmares? How could she tell them about Mr. Morning and Gomath? The idea of their worry, of being institutionalized, locked away in some sterile place where she would be considered a "crazy person", was enough to freeze her thoughts. They had already lost one child. She couldn't bear the thought of them thinking they might lose her too.

"I'm fine... I've just had trouble sleeping," she said, the words tasting bitter on her tongue.

Peter and Mariah exchanged a brief, wordless glance. They both knew there was more to it than that, but for now, they said nothing. It was clear that Sia wasn't ready to share what was truly going on in her mind, and neither of them wanted to push her too hard. They wanted to be there for her, but they didn't know how to bridge the distance that had formed between them.

Peter sighed and mussed Sia's hair, a small, affectionate gesture that spoke volumes. "Tonight, after you get home, we should all have a talk. Maybe we can help, dear."

Sia nodded, trying to smile through the cracks in her heart. She wasn't sure how much help they could really offer, but the comfort of having her parents there, even if they didn't understand everything, was a balm she hadn't realized she needed.

As Sia finally released her mother and stood, her feet felt heavy. It wasn't that she was afraid of the festival or anything, it was just... today, the weight of the world felt particularly heavy on her shoulders. And though she had always known that no matter how many years passed, Mia would always be a part of her, today, the emptiness felt more pronounced.

She had a promise to keep, though. She had to go to the festival, to see it through, to try to honor Mia's memory. As she turned toward the door, her fingers lightly brushed over the bracelet that Mia had given her. The moon charm felt cold against her skin, a soft reminder of the bond they shared, even in death. A small part of Sia, in the depths of her heart, wished Mia could have been there, walking beside her through all the pain.

But Mia wasn't there. She was gone.

Sia stepped out the door, determined, despite the crushing weight of the loss, to take the first step forward. Mia was gone, but Sia had to live, for both of them.

SIA WALKED THROUGH THE streets of the town, her steps heavy as the world around her buzzed with the excitement of the Harvest Festival. The air was thick with the smell of roasted meats, caramel apples, and the crisp fall air. The sounds of laughter, children's voices, and the clinking of game booths all blended into a backdrop that should have felt festive, but instead, felt like hollow noise in Sia's ears.

As she passed the brightly colored tents and stalls, she couldn't help but notice how everything seemed to move in a blur. People smiled, waved, and called out greetings to one another, but none of it seemed to reach her. The memories of her twin sister haunted her today more than ever. Mia's absence was a void that seemed to stretch across the entire festival.

Sia found herself walking aimlessly toward the game booths, where she spotted Ella, Marcus, and Eric in the midst of their usual duties. The two boys were chatting animatedly, but their physical presence couldn't be more different.

Marcus towered over the crowd, his broad, muscular frame casting a shadow on everything around him. Tall and strong, with a solid build that had always made him stand out, he looked like he belonged on a sports field or in a gym, not behind a game booth. His broad shoulders and thick arms rippled with strength, the kind that came from hours spent in the weight room. Despite his imposing stature, there was a warmth in his easy smile, one that made it clear he wasn't the typical "jock."

He wasn't exactly shy, but there was a softness to him that balanced out his athleticism. The type of guy who always had a joke on hand, but who could still walk the line between confident and kind. Sia had always known Marcus to be a little bit of both, a goofball and a gentle giant. His dark eyes sparkled with mischief whenever he cracked a joke, and they held an underlying sincerity that made him easy to like.

Eric, on the other hand, stood a few feet away from Marcus, a tall and lanky figure with dark hair that fell slightly into his eyes. His wiry frame gave off a mischievous energy, always a little too quick to make a sarcastic remark or crack a joke, especially when the tension was too thick for comfort. His clothes, a bit too loose and always unbuttoned at the collar, gave him the air of someone who didn't take things too seriously, unless, of course, you made him. But the gleam in his sharp, light-colored eyes suggested there was a lot more going on behind that snarky exterior than he let on.

As Sia approached, she could hear their laughter. Marcus had just said something funny, and Eric had thrown his head back, laughing loudly, completely carefree. Their usual back-and-forth was like a performance that they'd perfected over the years, with Marcus being the one to deliver the punchlines while Eric played the exaggerated straight man, always acting as if Marcus's jokes were the funniest thing he'd ever heard.

Sia felt herself drawn toward them, but as soon as Ella noticed her, her expression softened. "Sia! You made it!" Ella called out, practically bounding over to her. She wrapped her arms around her in a hug, her smile bright and welcoming, as always.

Sia returned the hug, her arms feeling stiff at first, but then she let herself relax, if only for a moment. The comfort of her best friend's embrace was soothing, but it didn't quiet the gnawing ache in her chest.

"I promised I'd come," Sia muttered, forcing a smile. "I just... needed a bit of time."

Ella gave her a knowing look, then stepped back, her eyes scanning Sia carefully. "You okay?" she asked softly, her voice quieter now.

Sia nodded, not trusting herself to speak. It was easier to lie and say she was fine, even though the truth was anything but fine. The moment Ella pulled away, she felt the weight of her emotions trying to come back in full force, but she fought it. Not here. Not now.

Marcus, who had been watching from the sidelines, grinned and walked over with Eric. "Look who finally decided to show up," he teased, though his tone was gentle. The grin that usually made him seem a little cocky, now felt warm, like he was genuinely happy to see her.

Sia forced another smile. "Yeah, well, someone had to run the booth while you guys had fun." She shot him a playful wink, trying to distract herself from the heaviness of her thoughts.

Eric, who was leaning against the booth, raised an eyebrow as he tossed a ball into a bucket. He was grinning, his sharp features animated by his usual playful energy. "It's about time. We were beginning to think you were going to skip out on us altogether."

Sia shrugged, but there was a flicker of something in her eyes, a shadow of doubt and uncertainty that only Ella seemed to catch. Ella, sensing that Sia wasn't completely herself, gently pulled her to the side.

"What's really going on, Sia?" Ella asked, her voice low but firm. "You've been distant for weeks now. What's happening?"

Sia froze, her eyes dropping to the ground. How could she explain everything? The nightmares, the visions of Tobias, the man in her dreams who seemed to be playing a twisted game with her mind. She couldn't burden Ella with that, not now.

"It's nothing," she said quietly, brushing her off. "Just... I've been thinking a lot, that's all."

Ella didn't seem convinced, but she let the topic drop, opting instead to change the subject. "Well, we've got a whole day of fun ahead of us. I want you to at least try to enjoy yourself a little, alright?"

Sia hesitated, feeling the weight of the conversation sitting uncomfortably between them. She wanted to enjoy herself. She really did. But the tension in her chest, the constant worry gnawing at her insides, it made it nearly impossible to relax. Still, she nodded, offering a small smile. "Yeah, I'll try."

But as the afternoon dragged on, Sia's thoughts continued to spiral. The festival was just a distraction, a temporary reprieve from the darkness she could feel lurking at the edges of her mind. She found herself absentmindedly wandering from booth to booth, not really participating in any of the activities, just going through the motions. The laughter of the crowd felt distant, muffled.

It was then that her gaze caught on something, or rather, someone. Across the field, standing by one of the more secluded booths, she saw a figure she hadn't expected to see today.

Tobias.

Her heart skipped a beat. He stood there, talking to someone she didn't recognize, his tall figure imposing even from across the crowd. Sia's breath hitched, and for a moment, she couldn't move. Her mind went back to the vision from her dream, the one where he stood over her, sword in hand. The memory felt so vivid, so real, it made her stomach twist.

Why was he here? What did he want?

Before she could even process the question, he turned, his sharp eyes locking onto hers from across the field. For a long moment, they just stared at one another, the noise of the festival fading into the background. Tobias's gaze was intense, unreadable, as if he was sizing her up in that quiet way of his. Then, without a word, he turned and walked away, disappearing into the crowd.

Sia's breath came in shallow gasps, her heart racing as she stood frozen, her mind spinning with confusion. What was that? Why had he been looking at her like that? Was it her imagination? Or was he somehow connected to the nightmares that haunted her every night?

"Everything okay?" Ella's voice cut through her thoughts, her concerned eyes studying Sia's face.

Sia blinked and shook her head. "Yeah... just, just a little tired."

Ella didn't seem convinced, but she didn't press. She simply took Sia's arm and led her back toward the game booths, her bright, welcoming smile never faltering.

Sia tried to focus on the festival, on her friends, but her thoughts kept returning to Tobias. To the strange, uncomfortable feeling that settled in her chest every time he was near. What was it about him that made everything feel so off?

As the afternoon wore on, the festival seemed to lose its color for Sia. The laughter, the games, the playful banter, it all became a distant hum, like background noise to a world she could no longer touch. She watched Ella interact with Marcus and Eric, both of them full of life, cracking jokes and making sure everyone was having fun. But Sia felt like she was stuck, caught in a loop where her body moved, but her mind was far away.

She hadn't been able to shake the memory of Tobias. She kept replaying that strange moment when their eyes locked across the crowd. There was something in the way he looked at her, something that made her skin crawl. It wasn't just the vision of him standing over her, sword in hand. It was more than that. There was something in his presence that unsettled her, like a memory not quite fully formed, but lurking just beneath the surface.

Her mind drifted back to her conversation with her parents earlier. The guilt had been gnawing at her for weeks, the weight of her silence pressing down on her chest. She had been keeping secrets from them, dreams, visions, whispers in the night. She had told herself that they didn't need to know, that it was better to keep her worries locked inside. But today, something felt different.

"I'm fine," she had said to her mother, but it wasn't true. She wasn't fine, and that fact was becoming harder to ignore.

Sia's gaze shifted to the center of the festival, where people were gathered around a stage, listening to a local band play. The music drifted through the air, filling the empty spaces between her thoughts.

The soft beat, the strumming of guitars, it was a welcome distraction, but it didn't erase the unease that was tightening around her heart.

She couldn't help but glance back toward the edge of the field where Tobias had been standing. For a moment, she thought she saw him again, this time talking to someone else. But when she blinked, he was gone. Had she imagined it? She couldn't tell anymore.

A hand brushed her shoulder, and she turned to find Eric standing next to her, his face unusually serious. "You alright, Sia?" he asked, his usual playful tone replaced by something softer, more concerned.

She nodded quickly, forcing a smile. "Yeah, just... tired."

Eric didn't buy it. His sharp blue eyes searched her face, and for a moment, Sia felt like he was peering straight through her, as if he could see the tangled mess of emotions she was trying to hide. "You sure? You've been quiet all day. You're not usually like this."

Sia swallowed, the lump in her throat making it harder to speak. "I just... I don't feel like myself. I haven't for a while."

Eric's expression softened, and he put a hand on her arm, a rare gesture of comfort from him. "You know you can talk to us, right? Ella, Marcus, me... we're all here for you."

Sia looked at him, surprised by the sincerity in his voice. Eric, the jokester, the one who always had something to say, was showing a side of himself she rarely saw. For a moment, it made her want to open up to him, to tell him everything. But the words stuck in her throat, heavy and unspoken.

"I know," she murmured, looking away from his intense gaze. "But it's... complicated. I don't even know where to start."

Eric gave her a small nod, understanding without needing further explanation. He didn't press her for answers, but his presence was a quiet comfort nonetheless. He stayed by her side for a few moments, just watching the festival around them in silence.

The sound of a loud cheer broke their quiet moment, and Sia's attention was pulled back to the booth where Marcus and Ella were running the prize games. The kids were laughing, tossing ping pong balls into jars, and the atmosphere seemed to shift back into something lighter. But even as Sia's eyes followed the movement of the crowd, the weight of the moment still lingered inside her.

As if on cue, Ella appeared beside them, her arms raised in excitement. "Sia! Eric! Marcus is having a meltdown over there, you need to come help!"

Sia smiled, the momentary distraction lifting some of the weight from her shoulders. She turned to Eric, her lips curving into a small but genuine smile. "You heard her. Let's go save Marcus from himself."

The three of them walked back toward the booth, the sounds of the festival picking up again around them. Marcus was indeed standing near the prize table, surrounded by a small crowd of eager kids, but he was looking flustered and panicked as he fumbled with a jar of tickets.

"What's going on?" Sia asked, raising an eyebrow as she approached.

Marcus turned to her, a sheepish grin spreading across his face. "I... uh... might've miscalculated the number of tickets needed for the game. Long story short, I'm drowning in prizes and tickets and don't know how to keep up with it all."

Sia couldn't help but laugh, and the sound of it was like a weight being lifted from her chest. There was something comforting about the simplicity of this moment, the carefree nature of Marcus's clumsy panic. It was a reminder of normalcy, something she desperately needed in a world that felt like it was spinning out of control.

"Alright, alright," Sia said, stepping in to help. "Let me show you how it's done."

And for the next few hours, as the sun sank lower in the sky and the festival continued in full swing, Sia managed to lose herself in the rhythm of the games and the laughter of her friends. For the first time in what felt like forever, she allowed herself to feel a little bit of joy.

But even as she smiled and joked with Marcus and Ella, the nagging feeling at the back of her mind remained. Something was coming. She could feel it in her bones, and the visions, the dreams, they only confirmed it.

She didn't know what it was, or when it would come, but she knew that soon, everything would change again.

The evening wore on, and the Harvest Festival's energy seemed to swell with every passing minute. The crowd grew thicker, the lights brighter, and the music louder, blending together into an almost dizzying swirl of activity. As Sia and her friends helped with the booths and games, the laughter and voices of others felt like a distant hum to her, like she was in a bubble, observing from the outside.

Marcus, Eric, and Ella were all caught up in the excitement, their banter and laughter blending into the atmosphere of the festival, but Sia couldn't shake the uneasy feeling that had settled deep within her. She tried to focus on the games, on helping the kids, but her thoughts kept drifting back to the unsettling images from her dreams.

She couldn't stop thinking about Tobias. The more she tried to push him out of her mind, the more his image seemed to haunt her, flickering in and out of her thoughts like a shadow at the corner of her vision. She couldn't ignore the fact that he was different, there was something about him that didn't sit right, and that unsettled her even more.

Just then, as Sia helped a young girl toss a ball into a jar, she felt a presence at her side. Her heart skipped a beat, and she turned instinctively to look.

It was him.

Mr. Morning.

The man from her dreams.

His presence seemed to distort the air around him, and suddenly, the noise of the festival, the music, the chatter, the laughter, faded as though it was being muffled by a thick fog. The sounds slowed down, like a record being turned down to a low hum. The flashing lights of the carnival rides became distant, muted. Time itself seemed to hold its breath. The world around her paused, just for that moment, as if everything was happening out of sync with the presence of this man.

He stood at the edge of the booth, watching her with an unnerving intensity. His grin was wide, too wide, stretching across his face like a mask. And yet, it wasn't the smile of someone who was happy, it was the smile of someone who knew something that you didn't.

Sia felt a chill race down her spine. Her body froze, and for a brief, breathless moment, she could do nothing but stare back at him, caught in the grip of his gaze.

"Ms. Mason," he said, his voice smooth and dark, like velvet wrapped around a blade. "It's so good to see you again. I must say, I've been keeping a rather keen eye on you."

The words settled into her chest like cold stones, and she couldn't find her voice. The world around her was strangely still, as if the seconds themselves had been suspended, the bustling festival locked away in another dimension while she was trapped in this suffocating moment.

"What do you want?" she finally managed to croak, her voice thick with unease.

Mr. Morning chuckled, the sound dark and hollow. "Oh, I think you already know, Sia. I'm here for you. Just as I've always been."

The words hit her like a punch, and her blood ran cold. Always been? What did that mean? What was he talking about?

Before she could say another word, he stepped back, as though satisfied with her reaction, and disappeared into the crowd as suddenly as he had appeared. The world around her began to shift back into its usual rhythm, the noise rushing back to fill the space around her, but the unease, the chill, still lingered in the air.

The voice of the DJ crackled over the loudspeaker once more, announcing some new event or game, but Sia couldn't pay attention to any of it. She had to get out of there. She had to breathe.

"I'll be right back," Sia muttered to no one in particular, her voice barely above a whisper. Without waiting for an answer, she turned and walked briskly away from the booth.

As she stepped away from the noise, the festival sounds growing quieter in the distance, Sia felt a hand on her shoulder.

"Hey, where are you going?" It was Ella, her voice full of concern.

Sia turned, forcing a tight-lipped smile. "Just... getting some air. I'll be right back."

Ella studied her for a moment, her expression softening. She nodded, though Sia could tell she was still worried. "Alright, but don't go too far. You're scaring me, Sia."

Sia nodded and quickly walked away before Ella could say anything else, not wanting to explain what had just happened, not wanting to share her terror. She knew if she told Ella about Mr. Morning, Ella would think she was losing her mind. It was all too much, even for Sia to understand.

She wandered further into the trees near the festival grounds, seeking the quiet and solitude that always seemed to soothe her when the world became too overwhelming. The rustling of leaves in the gentle breeze was the only sound that accompanied her as she moved deeper into the woods, until she found a small clearing by a creek. She sank down onto the ground, her legs folding beneath her as she rested her head in her hands.

What does he want from me?

The question circled in her mind, growing louder with every passing second. The visions, the nightmares, the strange man who seemed to know things about her that no one should know. She felt like she was losing herself, like she was caught in some terrible, otherworldly game.

And the worst part was, she didn't know how to escape it.

Chapter 12

Shadows Gather

Fear has two meanings: Forget Everything And Run
or Face Everything And Rise. The choice is yours.

Zig Ziglar

THE EVENING AIR WAS crisp, the soft murmur of the distant festival
sounds muffled by the dense trees surrounding the clearing. Sia barely
noticed the coolness of the evening seeping into her skin as she sat on
the moss-covered ground, her mind still reeling from the unsettling
encounter with Mr. Morning. Her breath came in shallow gasps as she
tried to steady herself, her heart pounding in her chest like a drumbeat.
The world seemed too loud, too bright, and yet in this small patch of
forest, it was almost too quiet.

She shut her eyes for a moment, pressing her palms against them
as if to erase the images of his face, his smile, the chilling words. But
no matter how hard she tried, they wouldn't go away. His presence
lingered like a shadow, stretching into the corners of her thoughts.

What was he? Who was he?

She couldn't answer, but a gnawing feeling in her gut told her that
she was in far deeper than she had ever realized.

A snap of a twig broke through her thoughts, and her body went
stiff. Instantly, her hand moved to her pocket, where she had tucked
away a small knife, a habit she had picked up over the years when the
world seemed to be closing in around her. The sound was small, barely
audible, but in the stillness of the woods, it was as loud as a clap of
thunder.

Her eyes darted around the clearing, scanning the shadows.

Nothing.

But the feeling... the feeling of being watched didn't dissipate. It was there, thick and suffocating, hanging in the air like a heavy mist. She wasn't alone.

A rustle from behind, followed by the soft crunch of leaves. Sia's breath hitched. She slowly rose to her feet, moving as silently as she could manage, every muscle tense and coiled, ready to spring into action if necessary. Her eyes scanned the trees again. There was nothing.

She was far enough into the woods now that the sounds of the festival, the laughter, the music, the chatter of excited voices, had faded into nothing more than a distant hum, as if the world of lighthearted noise had simply evaporated. In its place, the sharp creak of branches and the swish of leaves underfoot seemed unnaturally loud, echoing in her ears, amplifying her sense of isolation. She wasn't sure which was worse, the silence or the growing sense that she was being hunted.

Her breath quickened again, panic rising in her chest. Then, as if her body had been waiting for it, a soft crunch of leaves underfoot broke the stillness. This time, it was closer. Much closer.

A shadow.

There, just on the edge of her vision, a hulking form moving between the trees, barely visible through the darkness. It was fast. Too fast.

Sia's heart raced. She forced herself to move forward, her feet stumbling over roots and branches as she broke into a run. Her legs burned with the effort, but the adrenaline spurred her onward. She had to get away.

The sound of the figure's pursuit grew louder, closer, the crunching of leaves and the rustle of branches getting more distinct. Sia's pulse thudded in her ears, drowning out the other sounds of the forest. She pushed herself harder, the night air biting at her skin as her breath came in ragged gasps. Her feet thudded heavily on the forest floor, each step carrying her further away from the safety of the festival.

Then, a new sound, something familiar, yet distant, began to filter through the trees, faint at first, like the soft murmur of wind through the branches. The low rumble of voices. The rhythmic clinking of game booths, distant laughter, the soft strains of music. It was the festival, just barely audible now. A sign. She was running in the right direction.

But there was still something behind her, and it was closing in. She pushed herself harder, her mind screaming for her to get out of the woods. She couldn't see the figure, but she could feel it. Its presence was like a shadow, ever-present, looming just out of her reach, but always too close. The air around her seemed to grow colder, the feeling of being pursued sharper than ever. She didn't dare look back, she didn't have to. The growing sounds of the festival were enough of a beacon. She was getting closer.

Her legs began to ache, but she forced herself to keep moving, the noise of the woods fading as the sounds of life returned to her ears. She was almost there. Almost out. The night air seemed to grow lighter as the festival sounds grew louder, until finally, the trees began to thin out, and she could see the light from the festival lanterns flickering through the branches.

Sia burst out of the tree line, her feet slamming onto solid ground, and she immediately slowed, coming to a panting halt just as the sounds of the festival rushed back into her senses. The music, the chatter, the warmth of the crowd, it was all there. She had made it.

But she didn't feel safe.

She didn't feel free.

She looked around, searching the crowd, her breath still ragged as she took in the faces of people laughing, talking, living, oblivious to the nightmare she had just escaped. The figure, the shadow, it had been so close. She could still feel its presence, like a phantom pressing in on her mind.

She took a shaky step toward the lights of the festival, but a voice interrupted her thoughts, breaking through the fog of terror that clouded her mind.

"Sia?"

It was Ella's voice. She was here. She was safe.

Sia slouched up against a tree, with company present she no longer felt the eyes on her. Ella seemed to somehow scare away whatever had been stalking her... or maybe it really had just been a trick of her imagination. Seeing Sia's state, Ella moved over and sat down beside her under the tree.

The moonlight filtered softly through the trees, casting long shadows on the ground as Sia sat quietly beside Ella. The sounds of the festival had grown faint, drowned out by the rustling of leaves and the distant call of night birds. It was here, in the quiet of the woods, that Sia had finally allowed herself to feel the weight of her emotions, to face the overwhelming truth that had been haunting her.

Ella, ever the patient friend, had given her the space to collect herself. For a long time, neither of them spoke. The only sound between them was the soft rustling of Sia's hair in the breeze, and the distant hum of the festivities, now a mere memory.

It was Ella who broke the silence first, her voice gentle, as though not wanting to disturb the fragile moment. "Sia... you've been so quiet lately. I know something's been going on, and I've been waiting for you to talk to me. I just want to help."

Sia shifted uncomfortably, her fingers twisting around the hem of her jacket. She stared at the ground for a moment, her thoughts racing. Her chest tightened with the weight of all she had been holding in, the truth that she had kept buried deep for so long.

"I don't know where to start," Sia confessed, her voice barely above a whisper. The words felt like a weight, heavy and raw, but they needed to be said. "It's just... everything's so messed up, Ella. I'm scared."

Ella's gaze softened, and she reached out to squeeze Sia's hand. "I'm here, Sia. Whatever it is, I'm here for you."

Sia swallowed hard, the lump in her throat making it difficult to speak. "It's the dreams," she said, finally looking up at Ella, her eyes filled with a mix of fear and sorrow. "They're not just dreams. They feel real. I... I see things that happen before they actually do. Like, I saw that man get hit by the car. I saw it before it happened, and I didn't do anything."

Ella's heart sank as she listened to her best friend's words. She had known Sia had been struggling, but hearing the depth of it, the pain, made her want to do more, to fix everything.

"Those dreams," Sia continued, her voice trembling, "they've been happening for years now. But lately, it's gotten worse. I see Mia, Ella. She's there, in my dreams, like... like she's still with me. But she's not just there, she's trapped, and I can't do anything to help her. And then there's him... Mr. Morning. He's part of it. I don't know what he wants, but he's connected to everything."

Ella's mind raced, the weight of Sia's words crashing over her. She couldn't fully comprehend everything Sia was saying, but she could hear the truth in her voice, the fear that was so raw it made Ella's heart ache.

"Wait... Mr. Morning?" Ella asked, her voice rising in confusion. "Who is he? What's going on with him?"

Sia looked away, her eyes distant as if trying to make sense of the chaotic mess in her mind. "I don't know. He showed up in my dreams. He said he wanted something, something from me. And then there's that man, Samuel Gomath. He works for him, I think. I don't understand it, Ella. I don't know what's real anymore."

Ella's mind spun as she tried to process it all. She had always known Sia to be strong, but the cracks were beginning to show, and they were too deep to ignore. Sia had been carrying this burden alone for so long, and Ella had missed the signs. She had no idea how much pain her best friend was in.

"Maybe it's not all just a dream," Ella said slowly, trying to make sense of the impossible. "Maybe there's more to this. Maybe... Maybe Mr. Morning is real, and he's connected to something we don't understand yet."

Sia shook her head, a tear slipping down her cheek. "I don't know. But I can feel him. He's always there, watching me. And I'm scared, Ella. I'm scared for Mia, for myself, for everyone. I don't know what to do."

Ella's heart broke for her friend. She had never seen Sia so vulnerable, so lost. It was as though a part of her had been taken away with Mia's death, and now, that part was trying to come back, only to haunt her.

"We'll figure it out, Sia," Ella said, her voice firm with resolve. "You're not alone in this. I'll help you. Whatever it takes."

Sia gave her a shaky smile, but there was no mistaking the exhaustion in her eyes. "I'm sorry, Ella. I never wanted to burden you with all this. You've got your own life to live. I didn't want to drag you into my mess."

Ella shook her head quickly, her grip tightening on Sia's hand. "No, don't say that. We're best friends. That means we help each other, no matter what. I don't care how messy things get. I'll be with you, every step of the way."

As Sia allowed herself to finally lean on Ella, she was dimly aware of Marcus and Eric, who had been standing at the edge of the clearing, quietly observing. Their presence, though they hadn't interrupted, offered an unspoken form of support, a safety net around her in the form of their quiet concern.

Marcus, ever the silent giant, had his arms crossed, his usual easygoing demeanor replaced by a seriousness that Sia wasn't used to seeing in him. He met her eyes with a nod, as though silently acknowledging her struggle. His dark eyes were somber now, filled with understanding.

Eric, on the other hand, shifted his weight back and forth on his heels. His usual joking face was gone, replaced by a rare intensity. His light blue eyes, usually playful and mischievous, were now focused. He wasn't smiling.

"I'm sorry, Sia," Marcus finally spoke, his voice low. "We didn't know. If you need anything... we're here for you too, okay?"

Eric chimed in, his tone less playful than usual, "We got your back, always."

Sia's breath hitched slightly, her emotions overwhelming her. "Thanks," she whispered, wiping her eyes. "I just... I didn't want to be a burden. But I don't think I can do this alone."

"You're not alone," Ella said firmly, pulling Sia into a tight hug once more. "Not anymore."

And for the first time in years, Sia allowed herself to fully believe it.

After spending a little bit more time relaxing, Ella suddenly recalled that they had all abandoned the game booth and left to check on it, Eric accompanied her as if escorting, a wise precaution when the girls were afraid they were being stalked. Marcus quietly wondered to himself if Ella and Eric would be alright running the stand on their own he walked back with Sia at a slower pace. Soon they came upon a gentle creek.

The air was cooler by the creek, the gentle trickle of water from the small stream adding a peaceful sound to the silence between Marcus and Sia. They'd walked deeper into the woods, away from the loud festival noise, until it was just the two of them. The world around them felt distant, as though the night was pulling them into another realm altogether. Sia had stopped at a rock bed overlooking the water, her expression distant, lost in her thoughts.

Marcus lingered nearby, standing a few feet away, watching her closely. He knew she was hurting. He could smell the salt from her tears, feel the exhaustion hanging over her like a heavy blanket. She didn't know it, but the woods had always called to him, always welcomed him with a sense of belonging that had nothing to do with human reason. He found comfort in the way the earth seemed to hum beneath his feet, but right now, it was the girl sitting by the water that held his attention.

He had followed her here, not out of duty, but because he couldn't shake the feeling that she needed someone to be there. He'd been told not to get too attached, to keep his distance, but Sia... Sia felt different. He knew her scent, knew it like he knew the forest, earthy, wild, and familiar. It was strange how easily he had memorized the scent of her skin, her hair, her breath. For some reason, it didn't feel wrong, even though he had been avoiding these feelings for a long time. She always thought he was interested in Ella, but that wasn't true. The truth was, he was drawn to her, to Sia, and he couldn't deny it anymore.

He sat beside her now, not too close but close enough to show that he was there. She was asleep, her head tilted back against the rock as the exhaustion from the night before took its toll. Marcus could see the tear streaks on her cheeks, and something tugged at his heart. Quietly, he reached out, brushing her hair from her face, wiping away the moisture from her skin. She didn't stir, not even a little.

"Come on, Sia," he whispered, his voice barely a murmur over the soft sound of the creek. "You deserve some peace. If only for a little while."

Marcus leaned back against the rock, his head resting on his hands as he watched the water flow by. He wasn't sure why he'd stayed. Maybe because he couldn't let her be alone right now. Maybe because his instincts were telling him to stay close, and his instincts had never been wrong. The forest felt like it was pulling at him, but here, with Sia beside him, he didn't mind.

For the first time in what felt like forever, he let his guard down. His thoughts wandered back to when they had first met, when she was still the shy, nervous girl, always hiding behind Ella's light. He had never quite known how to reach her, how to tell her that he had always admired her quiet strength. It was only after everything had happened, the accident, the loss, and the way she seemed to carry the weight of the world on her shoulders, that he realized just how much he cared for her.

He didn't know how long he stayed there, just listening to the water and watching the moonlight play on the trees, but eventually, she stirred. Her eyes fluttered open, and for a moment, she seemed confused, her gaze scanning the area before landing on him. Marcus smiled softly, trying to hide the nervousness that bloomed in his chest. He had never been good at this, the talking part, the connection part, but here, in the quiet of the woods, it felt... easier.

"More nightmares, Sia?" he asked, his voice gentle, though he couldn't completely hide the concern in his tone.

She blinked, clearly disoriented. It took a moment for her to process where she was and who was beside her, but when she did, she sat up straight, her eyes wide with the realization that she had fallen asleep. Her first instinct was to move away from him, but she stopped when she saw him holding her bag in his lap.

"I... I'm sorry," she murmured, her voice shaky. "I didn't mean to... fall asleep on you."

Marcus chuckled softly, though there was a trace of nervousness in his laugh. "You didn't. You needed it. You've been running on fumes for way too long." He handed her the bag, and when she took it, his fingers brushed hers, a spark of something unspoken passing between them. He hoped she didn't notice, but he couldn't deny it. His pulse quickened every time they made contact.

Sia didn't say anything at first. She just looked at him, searching his face for something, for a sign. She probably thought he was being too kind, too understanding, but the truth was, he couldn't let her down, not when she needed him so much. He could feel it in his bones, in his instincts, that she was caught in something bigger than both of them. And whatever it was, he had to help her, even if she never fully understood why.

"You don't have to apologize," he added softly. "I'm not going anywhere."

For a long moment, Sia just stared at him, as if weighing his words. Then, her shoulders slumped in relief, and she sighed. "I don't know why I keep doing this... hiding away from everyone." Her voice cracked slightly as she spoke, and Marcus's heart ached at the rawness of it.

"You're not hiding from me, Sia," he said, his voice firm but gentle. "You don't have to. Whatever this is, whatever you're going through, you don't have to go it alone."

Sia's eyes flickered up to his, and for a brief second, he saw something in her eyes, something softer than the guarded mask she usually wore. But then, just as quickly, it was gone, replaced by that same defensive look. She wasn't ready, and Marcus didn't push her. He knew better than to force her to open up before she was ready.

As the moment passed, the air between them settled, but Marcus couldn't shake the feeling that something was different now, that they had crossed a line. He didn't know what that meant, didn't know where this connection would lead, but he knew one thing for sure: He was staying with her, no matter what.

SHE HAD SLIPPED AWAY again, perhaps because he was so comforting. The dream came swiftly, unbidden, as it always did. The field stretched endlessly before her, the wind teasing her hair and the grass. She was wearing the gown again, the one that always felt wrong, yet it was the only thing that ever felt familiar in these dreams. The trees around the field looked like the ones near the winery, dark and looming as they swayed in the night air.

A voice broke the silence, familiar yet distant. "You shouldn't depend too much on what these dreams show you, Sia."

She whipped around, her heart thudding in her chest as she saw her sister standing before her. Mia.

"Sia," Mia said, her expression serious, her eyes piercing. "You're not alone in this. I came to warn you. We don't have much time."

The words sent a jolt of fear through Sia's chest. Her twin, standing there, alive in the dream. How could it be real?

CHAPTER 13

Calm in the Storm

It is only in sorrow bad weather masters us; in joy we face the storm and defy it.

Amelia Barr

THE AIR WAS THICK with the scent of wet earth and moss, the creek's gentle trickle a soothing backdrop. Sia's mind, however, was far from calm as she sat on a rock bed, knees pulled up to her chest, watching the water flow beneath her feet. The silence of the woods wrapped around her like a heavy blanket, muting the distant sounds of the festival.

Marcus sat beside her, giving her space but staying close enough to offer silent comfort. He observed her for a moment, taking in her troubled expression, the tears that still stained her cheeks. She hadn't said much, but she didn't need to. Everything about her was raw, and he could see it in the way she avoided his gaze, like the weight of the world had found its place on her shoulders. He hesitated but ultimately wiped away her tears, unsure if he had the right, but knowing it was the only thing he could do to help.

He sat quietly beside her, letting the peace of the creek's flow soak in, trying to calm his own restless thoughts. There was so much going on, so much more than he could explain. There was Sia, the girl he'd known for years, but lately, she seemed more lost, more untethered from the world than before. And then there was his own turmoil, the odd connection he felt toward her, the way his senses heightened around her. He'd never told her, of course. She always assumed he was enamored with Ella, and he let her think that. She didn't need to know the truth, didn't need to know that something about her kept pulling him back, that it wasn't just the fact that she was Ella's best friend. No, it was deeper than that. He could smell it. He could feel it. There was something in her scent, in the way she moved, that drew him in. Something primal. Something in his blood told him that there was more to Sia than met the eye.

Marcus leaned back, letting his gaze wander to the sky as dusk began to settle in. He was grateful for the stillness, for the time to think. He didn't need anyone's approval, but he found himself wishing he could speak to Sia, wish he could share what was bothering him. He was starting to feel that he'd have to, soon.

But he wasn't ready yet. Not with her. Not with his secret.

He kept his thoughts to himself, allowing Sia the space she needed to gather herself. Slowly, he felt her relax, her breathing becoming slower, deeper. He couldn't help but smile faintly as he noticed how she had begun to drift, her exhaustion overwhelming her. She hadn't slept properly in years, he knew that. He also knew that, despite his protective instincts, he couldn't do everything for her. She was strong. She would get through this.

She was starting to sleep. And for once, Marcus wasn't going to wake her.

THE DREAM PULLED HER down like a rushing tide, washing over her as the familiar landscape unfolded. She found herself in a vast, empty field, the wind stirring the tall grass around her. It felt cold, welcoming in its embrace. It always did, but it was an odd kind of cold, one she had become all too familiar with. She looked around, finding herself in the same gown as before, the one she had been wearing when she'd first encountered the man with the sword.

She took a slow breath, feeling her heart pound in her chest as she stepped forward, the grass brushing against her legs. She felt like a foreigner in her own skin.

And then, she heard it, the voice, the one that felt so familiar and yet so strange.

"You shouldn't depend too much on what these dreams show you, Sia."

Sia's breath caught as she spun around. She blinked rapidly, disbelieving. The voice belonged to a figure standing just ahead of her, and as she focused, the world around her seemed to fade to a dull hum.

Mia.

It had to be Mia.

Her twin, the one she had lost so many years ago. The one who had been ripped away from her in the blink of an eye. Mia stood before her, looking just as she had in life, beautiful, with that mischievous smile tugging at her lips, her eyes still gleaming with the same fire that had never been extinguished, even in death.

"Mia?" Sia choked out, her voice cracking. She stumbled forward, unable to stop herself. "How? You're... dead..."

Mia didn't move at first, just stood there, her eyes soft but serious. "I am," she said, her voice gentle. "But that's not what's important right now, Sia. Death is just a new kind of beginning. And you'll learn that soon enough."

Tears sprang to Sia's eyes as she approached, her hands trembling as she reached for Mia. This time, there would be no running away, no pretending she wasn't there. This time, she was going to embrace her twin.

The moment they touched, Sia's heart broke all over again. The emptiness inside her that had festered for so long flooded out. She squeezed Mia tightly, letting the sensation of her presence fill her to the brim, and for just a moment, she felt whole again.

But Mia pulled away, gently but firmly. "Another time, Sia," she whispered, her voice now tinged with urgency. "Right now, you need to listen to me."

Sia nodded, her breath ragged. "I'm listening."

Mia's gaze sharpened, her expression hardening. "Something is coming for you, Sia. And the dreams you've been having, they're both warnings and hints at what you will need to survive. You may think Morning is bad, but he's just the icing on the cake. Something worse is coming. That's the true threat. You need to be careful."

Sia swallowed hard, trying to wrap her mind around the weight of Mia's words. "Mia... how are you here in my dreams? Are you really real?"

"I'm real enough," Mia said, her voice steady. "I'm dead, yes. But when I died, I was taken to Hell. Morning knows I'm not supposed to be there. He's holding me to get to you. You can't let him use me to get to you."

Sia's heart plummeted. "Mia, I, "

But Mia held up a hand, shaking her head. "We don't have much time, Sia. You need to trust your friends. All of them."

Sia's confusion deepened. "My friends?" She started to speak but was interrupted by the sound of something shifting in the air behind Mia.

A clawed hand tore through the dark sky and reached for her twin, and Sia gasped in horror as Mia turned to run. "Mia, no!" she screamed.

But Mia didn't look back. "Sia!" she called over her shoulder, her voice distant. "You have to remember, trust your friends. ALL of them!"

"Mia!" Sia cried, but her twin was already disappearing into the night.

The dream shattered like glass, and everything went black.

SIA'S BODY JERKED AWAKE with a gasp, her breath ragged and her heart pounding in her chest. She sat up quickly, her hands flying to her face, as if to make sure she was still in the real world. The sky was darkening, the sun having long since dipped below the horizon. She glanced around, realizing she was still sitting by the creek, with Marcus beside her.

Marcus, too, started at her sudden movement. He leaned forward, concern written all over his face. "More nightmares, Sia?"

Sia's head whipped toward him, startled. As the dream's vividness began to fade, her reality settled in around her. She could feel the cool air of the evening, hear the soft rustle of leaves.

She glanced at Marcus, her mind still reeling from the vision. He had been there, but not just physically. The way he had stayed with her, the way he hadn't left her side, something about it made her feel... safe.

She quickly looked down at her clothes, her skin prickling with the unease of being so vulnerable. She was alone with him, in a moment of weakness, and that made her uncomfortable. But Marcus hadn't crossed any boundaries, hadn't overstepped. He had been kind, and Sia couldn't ignore that.

"Why? Want to know how crazy I am?" she asked, her voice raw.

Marcus met her eyes, and for the first time, there was no jest in his voice. "No... Sia. I'm sorry. I don't want you to think I doubt you. I heard what you said. I believe you."

Sia studied him for a long moment, and then, reluctantly, she nodded. "Alright. Apology accepted."

Marcus smiled at her, relief washing over him. He looked down at her bag, which was sitting next to him, and handed it back to her. "It's no problem, Sia."

They stood up together, and as Marcus reached out to offer his hand, Sia hesitated only a moment before accepting it. Together, they began to walk back toward the fairgrounds, unaware of the pair of glowing eyes that watched them from the trees above. Nightfall was coming.

The silence of the woods hung around them like a heavy cloak, broken only by the distant rustling of leaves and the soft gurgle of the creek. As they sat there together, the fading light of the festival a distant hum, Marcus glanced at Sia, taking in the way she seemed so much more at ease here. The strain that had been so evident earlier in the day seemed to have loosened just a little.

He still couldn't shake the memory of the way she had looked at him when he found her, her tear-streaked face, the confusion in her eyes, the weight of whatever she was carrying pressing down on her shoulders. But now, as she sat there beside him, her gaze softened and distant, he saw something different. For the first time in what felt like ages, she wasn't retreating into herself. She wasn't pushing everyone away. She was... here. Present.

They had said little since they sat down. It was enough just to be in each other's company, a simple, quiet kind of companionship that felt almost like a respite from everything else. Marcus let out a soft sigh, his eyes drifting to the horizon where the last sliver of sun dipped beneath the trees. His hand, still resting on the ground beside him, brushed against Sia's as she adjusted her position. She didn't pull away. It was such a small gesture, but to him, it felt significant.

"I'm sorry about all the craziness," Marcus said after a moment, his voice low. "I didn't mean to push you earlier. I was just trying to... I don't know, lighten the mood, maybe."

Sia glanced at him, her eyes still a little puffy from crying, but there was a flicker of something softer there now. "I get it," she replied quietly, her voice carrying a depth of understanding that surprised Marcus. "It's just... I've been holding everything in for so long, and... and sometimes it's hard to let people in."

He nodded, though he wasn't entirely sure if she was talking about him, or about everything else that had been haunting her. Either way, he could tell it wasn't easy for her to talk about it. Hell, it wasn't easy for him, either. But there was something about Sia, about the way she tried so hard to be strong, even when she didn't need to be, that made him want to fight harder for her.

"I know what you mean," Marcus said after a beat, meeting her gaze. "You're not the only one who keeps things inside. I've spent most of my life just... pretending to be the goofy, carefree guy because it was easier than dealing with anything else. But when it's just the two of us, when it's you and me... I don't know, Sia, I feel like I can actually be myself."

Sia smiled, just a little. It wasn't much, but it was something. It was a start.

She shifted closer, her shoulder brushing his lightly. It felt natural. The cool night air surrounding them seemed to fade as their connection, however quiet, grew. They had both been running from things, for so long. But sitting here, together, they weren't running anymore.

"Thanks," she murmured, the gratitude in her voice not entirely hidden. "For being here. For not... pushing me away."

"I'd never push you away," Marcus said, his voice firm but gentle. "Not now, not ever."

There was a brief pause as they sat in companionable silence, the sounds of the festival still faintly drifting in from a distance. The world felt distant and muted, as if the two of them were suspended in a quiet bubble, untouched by the chaos of the world outside. It was as if the night had wrapped them in a blanket of calm, shielding them from everything else.

But deep inside, Marcus knew the peace was fleeting. The sense of foreboding still lingered, just beneath the surface. He couldn't shake the feeling that something was coming, that whatever had been hunting them, whatever force had been watching from the shadows, was drawing nearer.

Still, in that moment, all he could do was focus on the girl beside him, on the way her presence soothed the chaos inside him, on the way the evening light made her seem almost ethereal in the dimming twilight. And for once, he allowed himself to forget about the looming threat. For once, he could just be here with her.

After a long moment, Sia broke the silence, her voice small but steady. "We should probably head back. Ella and Eric are probably wondering where we went."

Marcus nodded, though he didn't immediately stand. He took a final look at the quiet woods around them, and then, reluctantly, pushed himself to his feet. "Yeah, they're probably going crazy wondering if we're lost in the woods."

Sia stood up as well, brushing the dirt off her jeans. She didn't seem quite as weighed down as before, though he knew it wasn't all gone. It never really would be. But for now, he was content to walk beside her, to know that for this moment, they were in this together.

They turned and began walking back toward the festival, the sounds growing louder as they neared the booths and crowds. It felt like they were stepping back into reality, back into the world that had seemed so far away only moments ago.

But as they walked, Marcus kept his attention on Sia. He still unsure of everything, of his own feelings, of the danger lurking ahead, of the strange connection he was starting to feel with her. But one thing was certain: he wouldn't let her face whatever was coming alone.

They reached the edge of the festival grounds, the lights flickering like beacons in the night. They passed by the game booths, where the laughter of children and the clink of carnival games filled the air. It all felt so... ordinary. So out of place, in a way. But Marcus could only push the thoughts aside for now.

For tonight, at least, they were safe. And maybe, just maybe, that would be enough.

CHAPTER 14

Turn the Page

In the middle of the journey of our life I came to myself within a dark wood where the straight way was lost.

Dante Alighieri

NIGHT WAS GENTLY DESCENDING over the festival grounds, signaling the closure of the colorful merchant stalls and lively game tables, though the festivities themselves seemed far from over. Golden lights strung across tents began glowing warmly in the gathering twilight, while the rich scent of bonfire smoke and freshly prepared festival food drifted invitingly through the cool evening air. Laughter mingled with distant strains of music, creating a lively yet intimate atmosphere.

Sia felt her heartbeat quicken as she and Marcus approached behind the game tents, their fingers intertwined. Her hand was warm in his gentle grip, comforting yet exhilarating, a feeling she wasn't quite sure how to handle. Ella's scandalous grin pierced her thoughts, instantly flooding her cheeks with heat. Self-consciousness surged, and she instinctively pulled her hand free from Marcus's grasp as though burned.

Marcus chuckled softly, a faint but genuine warmth in his eyes as he looked at Sia, seeming both amused and understanding of her embarrassment. Without another word, he turned away casually to help Eric dismantle the pavilion tent. Watching him go, Sia felt a curious mix of relief and disappointment. She exhaled, regaining her composure before joining Ella to pack up the carnival games, carefully stacking bottles, cards, and other prizes into crates.

Ella's eyes sparkled mischievously as they worked side by side. "So, you and Marcus, huh?"

"It's not what you think," Sia quickly countered, feeling heat spread across her face again.

"Right," Ella teased lightly, nudging her friend's shoulder. "I think it's exactly what I think. And about time, too."

Before Sia could protest further, Eric's voice interrupted from across the grounds, inviting them to join him and Marcus to watch the bands perform deeper into the winery, where teenagers were already gathering around bright bonfires. Ella's enthusiastic nod drew a reluctant sigh from Sia, prompting an amused grin from her friend.

"You realize," Sia said pointedly, grabbing a crate a bit too firmly, "that if you disappear with Eric, I'm stuck with Marcus for the evening."

Ella tilted her head, a playful gleam in her eyes. "And the problem is...?"

Sia crossed her arms defensively, forcing herself to look stern. "You aren't seriously setting me up with that pervert, are you?"

Ella's laughter bubbled up, genuine and infectious. "Pervert? Really? That's new. Care to share how exactly he earned that title?"

Sia hesitated, remembering the warmth of waking next to Marcus, how safe and right it had felt before embarrassment quickly overtook her. Unwilling to voice this thought aloud, she quickly redirected the conversation. "Let's just finish loading these if you're determined to drag me along on this impromptu double date."

Ella smiled, raising an eyebrow as she picked up another crate, voice lightly teasing. "Oh, no one ever said anything about a date, Sia, though clearly, it's on your mind."

Sia groaned softly, knowing she'd lost the battle, but unable to entirely suppress a tiny, secretive smile of her own.

BEYOND THE VIBRANT LIGHTS and cheerful sounds of the festival, deeper shadows gathered unseen, stirring with a primal, bestial hunger that twisted and writhed within the darkness. An unnatural stillness cloaked the outskirts, cold and unsettling, in sharp contrast to the warmth and merriment nearby.

Something monstrous and sinister watched ravenously from the shadows, taking the shape of the dog it had devoured, its form rippling and shifting like dense, viscous ink given life. Crimson eyes glowed dimly, fierce and primal, pulsating with a savage, insatiable patience. It reveled in the lingering, sweet taste of mortal flesh, memories of previous feasts intensifying its yearning. A hellish appetite gnawed relentlessly within it, amplified by promises whispered from beyond the mortal plane by the Morning One.

Tonight it would feed again, its feral hunger unbearable, sharpened into a feverish, consuming obsession. The girl's scent was close, delicate, pure, irresistible. All it needed was for her to stray beyond the fragile barrier of festival lights into the waiting embrace of darkness, and the promised feast would finally begin.

AS THE GROUP CROSSED the increasingly quiet festival grounds toward the storage trailer, an unnatural chill prickled their skin, the friendly atmosphere abruptly turning tense and foreboding. Sia shivered involuntarily, the sudden dread wrapping around her like an icy blanket. A vision, swift and terrifying, flashed vividly in her mind, dark, ferocious hounds lunging violently at Marcus and Eric.

Instinct surged through her, urgent and unstoppable. She shoved Eric aside roughly just as a monstrous shadow dog leapt from the darkness, narrowly missing him. It landed heavily, snarling viciously, its smoky form coalescing into a tangible threat with eyes burning a malevolent crimson.

Marcus reacted instantly, his movements unnaturally swift and precise. As another beast lunged at him, his arm blurred with super-human speed, slamming the creature down and dispelling it momentarily into smoky wisps. Eric stumbled back, eyes briefly flickering an unnatural icy blue, quickly dismissed by Sia as a trick of her panicked mind.

More shadowy beasts poured from the darkness, encircling them with hungry growls. Sia's heart pounded frantically, adrenaline sharpening her senses. Without hesitation, she seized Ella's hand and pulled her friend into a frantic run toward the cover of the forest, guided by an instinctive awareness of danger near the festival bonfires.

Behind them, Marcus's human appearance flickered unsettlingly. Silver-blue scales shimmered briefly across his skin, sharp black claws emerging from his fingertips as he stood protectively beside Eric. Eric raised a hand to the earth, speaking words of ancient power in a voice resonant with strength and authority, "CALCULO ERUMPANT!" The ground exploded upward violently, crushing several dark creatures beneath its stone fury.

Yet more beasts lunged from the shadows, their crimson eyes glowing fiercely. Marcus spun fluidly, dispatching two more creatures with rapid slashes of his clawed hands. Eric braced himself again, sweat dripping from his brow as he shouted another incantation, sending jagged stones hurtling at the charging hounds.

"Impressed or terrified, Sia would definitely have questions," Eric muttered breathlessly, eyes wide with amazement and fear as the final beast dissolved into black smoke.

Marcus growled deeply, voice heavy and barely human now, his form shimmering ominously. "Questions later, survival first."

DEEP WITHIN THE SHADOWED woods, Ella suddenly pulled Sia into a clearing, releasing a piercing, familiar whistle, a signal from their childhood games. Sia stumbled to a halt, heart hammering as Tobias emerged silently from the shadows, his presence imposing yet reassuring. The moonlight gleamed upon him, illuminating the striking image of the sword he held aloft, its blade shimmering with an ethereal, golden glow.

Fear gripped Sia, memories of terrifying dreams surging forward, visions of Tobias menacingly wielding a blade against her. She hesitated, panic clawing at her throat, until Tobias surged past her in one swift motion, his sword slicing through a shadowy hound that instantly dissipated into nothingness. Relief warred fiercely with confusion in Sia's chest.

Tobias turned, his eyes intense and focused. "Ella, get Sia to the car. Arm yourselves, do not engage unless absolutely necessary."

Ella nodded, pulling Sia onward. Tobias stood firm, blade glowing brighter as he prepared for the onslaught of shadow creatures spilling into the clearing. He moved with breathtaking grace and deadly precision, a warrior fully revealed. His sword danced through the air, cutting effortlessly through monstrous forms that erupted into clouds of smoke upon contact, the air ringing with his whispered incantations.

As Ella tugged her away, Sia struggled internally, the world she knew fracturing rapidly. Tobias, a protector? Her dreams had betrayed her, and yet here was undeniable reality. Monsters, magic, and heroes hidden among them. All her certainties shattered as she fled, leaving Tobias to stand defiantly against the darkness.

Reaching the old Volkswagen parked near the edge of the forest, Ella frantically broke into the vehicle, grasping a silver sword just as a dark tendril lashed out, grazing her skin. She cried out, stumbling backward, the blade trembling in her grip. Sia's eyes widened in horror as Ella's skin rapidly turned an ashen gray, veins darkening visibly beneath her skin. Her friend's usually vibrant eyes filled with a crimson glow, terrifying and alien.

"Ella?" Sia whispered, her voice shaking with panic. She reached out instinctively, then pulled her hand back, feeling an unnatural heat radiating from her friend.

Ella's body stiffened, muscles twitching violently as if struggling against an unseen force. Her gaze snapped toward Sia, expression contorting into one of sinister hunger mixed with anguish. With a guttural cry, Ella surged forward, grabbing Sia tightly and pulling the cold silver blade dangerously close to her throat.

"Ella! Please stop!" Sia gasped desperately, heart hammering painfully. Fear and disbelief crashed through her mind, her vision blurred by tears of panic and helplessness.

A harsh, distorted voice tore from Ella's lips, inhuman and filled with malicious intent. "Guardian, surrender the girl, or watch your sister perish."

Tobias's jaw clenched, his stance rigid, eyes blazing with determination and agony. "Let her go," he demanded forcefully, though anguish crept into his voice. His sword glowed fiercely, illuminating the darkened clearing in defiance.

Before the shadowy presence could respond, a sudden rush of heat and light erupted from above. Marcus descended swiftly from the sky, wings outstretched, releasing torrents of fire that incinerated the surrounding shadows. Ella's grip loosened as she collapsed, darkness fleeing her eyes. Tobias fell to his knees, drained from the battle, his sword's glow fading slowly into the quiet night.

Sia dropped to her friend's side, shaking uncontrollably, overwhelmed by shock and relief. She cradled Ella gently, tears streaming down her face, praying desperately for the nightmare to end.

Across the festival grounds, amidst the eerie glow of distant bonfires and the crackling whispers of embers, Eric stood alone, heart pounding as he faced Gomath, the sinister mage commanding the shadowy beasts. Gomath stepped forward casually, his elderly appearance masking a chilling, predatory confidence. His eyes, sharp and calculating behind thin spectacles, burned with cruel amusement. He took a leisurely drag from a cigarette, exhaling smoke tinged faintly red, his gaze fixed mockingly upon Eric.

"I must admit, I underestimated you," Gomath drawled, voice dripping with contemptuous admiration. "A Mage and a Dragon defending the girl, such unexpected obstacles. Why risk so much for one mortal life?"

Eric steadied himself, feeling the immense weight of Gomath's presence pressing upon him like a suffocating darkness. Yet despite his fear, anger surged within him, fueling his courage. "Because some things matter more than power," he retorted sharply, hands clenched tightly, drawing pure flames from the surrounding bonfires into a radiant, blazing orb. The air around him vibrated, filled with the clean, resonant hum of natural fire.

Gomath chuckled darkly, the sound low and guttural, echoing oddly as if coming from something monstrous beneath his human guise. He extinguished his cigarette casually between his fingertips, blackened claws briefly visible beneath the illusion of his human form. "Power is the only thing that matters, boy. You could be powerful, more powerful than your pathetic Order of Blue ever dreamed." He extended a twisted hand, a flame dark as midnight erupting from his palm with a disturbing, crackling hiss. "Join me. Abandon these futile morals. The girl could even be yours when we're finished."

Eric's stomach twisted in disgust, revulsion surging alongside his resolve. Visions of Sia's trusting smile flooded his mind, strengthening his determination. "You think I'd ever become like you? Sell my soul for hollow power?" he spat defiantly. "Never."

With a fierce shout, Eric hurled the gathered flames toward Gomath, the brilliant inferno surging forward, burning with purity and purpose. Gomath unleashed his shadowy fire simultaneously, a corrupted torrent of black flames wreathed in dark-red sparks. The two opposing magics collided violently with an explosive thunderclap, creating a vortex of blistering heat and searing darkness. The ground shook violently beneath their feet, accompanied by the deafening roar of conflicting elemental forces.

Gomath's calm facade fractured further as his shadowy flames surged wildly, dark smoke curling around him, briefly revealing grotesque, horned shapes and shadowed wings that flickered and writhed behind his true form. His eyes glowed a malevolent red, mouth twisting into a snarl filled with sharp, predatory teeth.

Sweat streamed down Eric's face, muscles trembling as he channeled more of the pure, natural fire drawn from the bonfires, pushing the darkness steadily back. He cried out defiantly, his flames growing brighter, their warmth a direct reflection of his inner strength and integrity. Gomath's confidence faltered visibly as the infernal darkness weakened against Eric's unwavering resolve.

Their explosive struggle illuminated the night sky, a fierce testament to the purity of Eric's courage and the corrupted depths of Gomath's ruthless determination.

Amid the fading chaos and lingering echoes of magical conflict, Sia cradled Ella gently, heart still racing but gradually steadying as silence descended over the clearing. Around them, the air felt thick and charged, residual energy from the fierce battle still lingering, yet gradually dissipating into a calm, almost serene quiet.

Sia slowly lifted her eyes, absorbing the scene before her, breath catching in awe at the impossible reality unfolding clearly before her. Marcus stood nearby, his massive draconic form imposing yet comforting, scales shimmering under moonlight and starlight alike. His wings were partially extended, catching the light in a mesmerizing display, powerful yet graceful, a creature straight from the myths she had never dared to believe in.

Beside her, Tobias rose slowly, gripping the hilt of his now softly glowing sword, the warrior in him evident in every line of his posture.

His eyes were weary yet resolute, reflecting the depth of his silent burden and unwavering courage. His very presence radiated quiet strength and reassurance, a stark contrast to the frightening figure of her dreams.

In that powerful moment of stillness, Sia felt the boundaries of her reality shift irrevocably. Her mind raced through the visions she'd seen, the dangers she'd narrowly escaped, and the truth now undeniably present. Magic was real. Monsters existed, and her friends, people she had trusted and loved, were far more extraordinary than she had ever imagined. Her world, once familiar and comfortably mundane, had expanded wildly, beautifully, and terrifyingly beyond her previous comprehension.

Tears blurred her vision briefly, a mixture of relief, awe, and overwhelming gratitude. She squeezed Ella's hand softly, grateful beyond words for her friend's survival. She looked again at Marcus, the warmth in his reptilian eyes surprisingly comforting, and at Tobias, steadfast and protective despite his evident exhaustion.

A gentle peace settled over her as clarity blossomed fully within her heart: the dreams had not been warnings alone, but revelations of truths hidden just beneath the surface. Tonight marked not an end, but a beginning, an opening of her eyes to a new world filled with peril and wonder.

For the first time, Sia truly understood that her dreams had been only the beginning.

CHAPTER 15

Skalds and Shadows

All of us, at some moment, have had a vision of our existence as something unique, untransferable and very precious. This revelation almost always takes place during adolescence.

Octavio Paz

THE GRANITE-WALLED SITTING ROOM was quiet, the kind of quiet that came after truths had been spoken but not yet understood.

Sia sat on a bench near the hearth, her hands curled around a cup that had long gone cold. The tea had tasted earthy and strange, like herbs steeped in memory rather than water. It grounded her, just enough to keep her present. The low fire before her crackled gently, throwing soft light against the smoothed stone. Every corner of this chamber had been carved with deliberation, not brute force. Bookshelves lined the far wall. Scrolls rested in alcoves. The chairs were worn but polished, the air clean and faintly perfumed with dry herbs and coal. This place hadn't been hewn by monsters, it had been built. Built by people who valued knowledge and silence.

Across from her, Tobias leaned against the arm of a carved wooden chair, sharpening a blade with the slow patience of someone who had nothing left to say. At the other end of the room, Eric stood, arms folded, watching the fire with the stillness of a man who had been part of this world for far too long.

They were all quiet, but not because there was nothing to say.

Because there was too much.

Sia finally broke the silence, her voice softer than she meant it to be. "So all of this... dragons, demons, gods... it's all real."

Tobias glanced up at her. "It's been real for a long time."

Her fingers tightened around the cup. "And you never told me."

"You weren't ready," Eric said from across the room. He didn't look at her when he spoke. "Your parents didn't want you caught in it. They thought you could live free of it all."

He paused, his gaze distant. "After Mia... after we lost her, they changed. It broke something in them. They thought shielding you was the only way to protect what little they had left. Throwing you into this world, into demons and blades and divine magic, it would've felt like letting go of both daughters. So they clung to hope instead. Maybe too tightly."

"They were wrong," she said quietly. "I was never free of it. I just didn't know what had already claimed me."

Eric sighed, stepping toward her. "Because your bloodline doesn't get to be free of this. Not really. You were born into the middle of a war older than anything you've read in a book."

Tobias sheathed his knife and spoke quietly. "We tried to spare you. Ella too. But fate doesn't care who's protected. It cares who's useful."

Sia stared into the fire, the flames dancing like whispers just out of reach. The walls around her didn't close in, they watched. There was something about this place that made every spoken word feel recorded, like the stone itself remembered.

"So what now? I'm just supposed to catch up? Learn all of this overnight?"

"No," Eric said gently. "But you can start now. And you're not starting alone."

There was a pause, long and heavy.

Sia looked between the two men, Tobias, Ella's older brother, who had long acted like a protective shadow in her life, and Eric, Marcus's mage friend, more known for his crooked smile than his wisdom. They weren't her family by blood, but they were standing with her now. Both had walked this path in silence while she'd been kept in a world that wasn't real. And now that curtain had been torn down with fire and blood.

"I want the truth," she said. "All of it. No more riddles. No more hiding behind 'you're not ready yet.' I've walked through dreams and shadows. I've seen what's coming. And I'm done being the last to know."

The quiet crack of the fire filled the room again.

Tobias met her eyes, and for the first time, there was no mask of sarcasm or stone-faced silence. Only a weary kind of pride.

"Alright," he said. "Then let's begin."

Eric was the first to speak. He sat on the arm of a nearby bench, arms still crossed, but his expression had softened with the kind of weariness only time could carve.

"There's no clean way to explain all of it," he said. "Because magic, real magic, isn't a straight line. It doesn't play by simple rules."

Sia remained quiet, her fingers still wrapped around the cooling tea. She didn't interrupt. Not this time.

"The world's old," Eric went on. "Older than the stories you heard growing up. And it's layered. There's the world everyone sees, the mundane, the explainable. And then there's what lives underneath it. The things that used to rule this place, long before humans made nations and named gods. Dragons. Spirits. Shadowkin. Entities that remember the first flame and the first fall."

Tobias leaned forward slightly, elbows on his knees. "Dobahold was built to guard the boundary between those layers. It's not just a haven for dragons. It's a watchtower. The last one left, probably."

Sia raised her eyes. "Then why hide it? Why keep any of it from me?"

"Because it's dangerous," Tobias said flatly. "You saw what happened. One spell, one slip, and you're bleeding in a mall fighting something out of hell. The people down here, they're warriors. Mages. Wyrmbloods. You weren't trained for any of that."

"She was born into it, though," Eric added, looking at Sia. "Your mother was one of the strongest wielders we'd ever seen. Not just in raw power, but in how she understood the Dreaming. Her bond to it was deep, primal. And your father? He wasn't just a scholar. He studied the old bloodlines, the way magic nests inside certain families."

Sia blinked. "They never told me any of this."

"Because they were trying to live," Eric said. "Not fight. Not hunt. They left the old war behind to raise you. That was the deal."

Eric's voice lowered, almost reverent. "But when Mia died, " he paused, correcting himself, ", when she was lost in that crash... it was like a chasm opened beneath the whole plan. One twin gone, the other left behind. Half a prophecy cut off mid-sentence."

He looked at her, serious now. "The community didn't take it lightly. A pairing like that only comes along once in an era. Magic twins. One soul born in two bodies. To lose one... it shook people. Shook Dobahold. Some feared you'd collapse, others feared you'd explode. Either way, no one knew what that kind of loss would do to someone born with that kind of destiny."

Tobias crossed his arms and added, "It made your parents clamp down even harder. They were already scared. That made them desperate."

Eric nodded. "That's why they didn't train you. That's why they tried to make you normal. Safer to hope the world forgot you than to risk fate remembering."

Sia sat still for a long time after they finished speaking, her cup forgotten beside her. The fire in the hearth had dimmed, now more ember than flame, casting slow-moving shadows across the smooth granite walls. The world felt quieter than it had any right to be.

"So... that's it," she finally said. "I'm the echo of a war my mother barely escaped. Born into a prophecy I didn't ask for. And Mia, if she really is gone, then what does that make me? Half of something that never had a chance to be whole?"

Neither man answered right away.

Eric shifted first, his gaze softening. "It makes you you, Sia. Not a weapon. Not a prophecy in boots. Just you. The fact that you care about what it means, that you're not shrugging it off or turning it into some grand crusade, that matters."

Tobias snorted, though it wasn't unkind. "You think too much."

Sia glanced at him. "What else am I supposed to do? I don't have a sword. I barely have control over my magic. And now you're all looking at me like I'm supposed to be the keystone holding back the apocalypse."

"You don't need to be," Tobias said simply. "You're not a hero yet. You're just someone who lived. That's more than most people get. And it's enough to start."

The fire cracked softly, sending a single, bright ember up the flue.

"I used to think magic was... beautiful," Sia said. "Like art. Something that could make things better."

"It still can," Eric said. "But it's also dangerous. Terrifying, even. Real magic isn't about fireworks or glowing glyphs. It's about power. And power always asks questions."

"Like what?" she asked.

Eric gave a faint, tired smile. "Like whether the person holding it will use it to heal... or to burn the world down."

Sia didn't answer right away. Her gaze drifted to her hand, resting on her thigh. She curled her fingers slightly, imagining the glow she'd summoned earlier. It hadn't felt like fire. It had felt like memory. Like a thousand lives whispering all at once.

She wasn't just born into something.

She was becoming something.

And that, more than anything, scared her.

A firm knock echoed from the hallway door, sharp and deliberate. The sound rang out through the stone room like a signal. The three of them turned, silence falling over the chamber once again.

Something waited beyond that door.

CHAPTER 16
Where Dragons Wait

There are no strangers here; Only friends you haven't yet met.

William Butler Yeats

THE KNOCK ECHOED LIKE a drumbeat in stone, each strike bouncing across the vaulted ceiling like a warning.

Tobias opened the door slowly, half-expecting trouble. Instead, it was one of the younger keepers of Dobahold, a boy barely older than Sia, wearing layered robes marked with silvery thread. His boots scraped the polished stone with a sharp skrrt as he shifted nervously.

"Lord Domingo requests your presence," the boy said with a small bow. "He asks that you come at once."

Eric leaned back in his chair and groaned. "Fantastic. Nothing good ever starts with a summons 'at once.'"

Sia stood, her legs still stiff from sitting so long. The stone beneath her feet felt cool even through her boots, a reminder that this place, this entire world, was not hers. Her thoughts were still tangled in everything she'd just learned, about her mother, about Mia, about the destiny she was never meant to escape. But movement helped. Action gave her something to hold onto.

Ella hadn't stirred since they'd carried her into the infirmary. The healers said she'd be okay, eventually. Sia tried not to think about the blood, the way Ella had collapsed into her arms like a broken blade.

Instead, she followed Tobias and Eric out into the winding halls of Dobahold.

The corridors here felt older, deeper. Less sanctuary, more strong-hold. The torches burned with soft, smokeless flame that crack-led faintly like whispering voices. Between the arches, etched reliefs danced in the flicker, dragons soaring, cities burning, stars falling in spirals. The scent of incense and old parchment filled the air, a dry warmth like breathing in forgotten oaths.

They passed what looked like an old gathering hall, its high, vaulted ceiling painted with constellations that didn't match anything in the surface sky. One wall was dominated by a tapestry depicting a great serpent coiled around a mountain, its eyes stitched with real gemstone chips that caught the light as they moved. Down a narrower corri-dor, Sia glimpsed a massive door bound in old dragonbone and iron, guarded by two silent figures in blackened armor.

"This place is huge," she murmured.

"Dobahold goes deeper than most know," Tobias said. "The drag-ons built it long before most of the world above had names."

Eric glanced over his shoulder. "Some say it was never built at all. Just uncovered. Like it was waiting for the right hands to claim it."

Sia frowned at that, but said nothing. The idea of something an-cient waiting beneath her feet felt less like comfort and more like prophecy breathing down her neck.

They turned down another corridor, this one lined with obsidian statues, warriors, scholars, even children, each one with a dragon's shadow carved looming behind them. The symbolism wasn't subtle. You didn't walk alone in Dobahold. Not even in death.

And for the first time, Sia wondered if she truly belonged here, or if she was just walking deeper into someone else's legend.

Eric slowed as they passed one of the child statues, his usual smirk fading into something softer, more distant. He stopped completely, one hand brushing the base of the plinth like it was sacred.

"His name was Richard," Eric said quietly. "My older brother. He didn't even live long enough to earn his first change. He was twelve when the monsters came. We were supposed to be safe behind the old wards, but that night... nothing held."

Tobias paused a few steps ahead but didn't speak.

Sia turned toward Eric, startled by the weight in his voice.

"He wanted to be a dragon more than anything," Eric continued. "Would've been brilliant at it. Had a temper like wildfire, but he cared. Too much, maybe. He died protecting me."

He stepped back, straightened, and forced a grin that didn't quite reach his eyes. "Haven't felt like laughing much in this corridor since."

Then he turned and kept walking, leaving silence in his wake.

At the end of the corridor, a set of double doors awaited them, carved with intertwining dragon motifs and inlaid with veins of glowing crystal that pulsed faintly with magic. Two sentries stood at either side, their armor marked with the sigils of the old wyrmguard, eyes following the trio with practiced stillness.

One of the guards stepped forward and gave a sharp nod before pushing the door inward with a deep groan of stone and metal.

Warm light spilled from within, tinted gold by hanging lanterns that burned with smokeless flame. The room beyond was wide and circular, ringed with ancient stone columns and lined in high-backed chairs, empty now, save for the single figure seated at the far end.

Lord Domingo.

He was dressed in layered robes of deep navy and silver, embroidered with curling script that shimmered like starlight. But beneath the regal outer layer, the fabric parted just enough at the knees to reveal faded jeans and a pair of well-worn sneakers. A plain black t-shirt peeked out from under the robe's folds, stamped with the cracked logo of a decades-old rock band.

His long white hair had been bound back in a thick braid, but his eyes were sharp and clear as ever, eyes that seemed to see through the chamber and into the marrow of anyone who entered.

"Come in," he said, his voice low but commanding. "There is much to discuss."

Tobias stepped in first, giving the old man a respectful nod. Eric followed, hands stuffed into his coat pockets like he was resisting the urge to touch everything. Sia lingered at the threshold for a breath longer, the strange tension in the room crawling along her skin like a static charge.

"Sit, if you'd like," Domingo said, gesturing toward the curved bench across from him. "Or stand. I don't mind either way."

They took their places, with Sia settling between the two men. The chamber was quiet save for the hum of enchantments running through the pillars. Despite its grandeur, it didn't feel like a throne room, it felt like a crossroads.

"I heard about what happened at the mall," Domingo began, steepling his fingers. "About Ella. And the shadows. And Sia."

His gaze landed on her with full weight, not unkind, but heavy. "You stepped into a truth most are never ready for. And you walked out of it still standing."

"I nearly didn't," Sia replied, voice low. "Ella took the worst of it."

Domingo nodded. "She bought you time. And in that time, you awakened something. Whether you meant to or not."

Sia felt her shoulders tense. "You mean magic?"

"I mean something older," Domingo said. "Something buried. Magic is only the echo. What you heard, what you felt, was the first sound."

Sia blinked. "That's not ominous at all."

Eric smirked faintly. "And here I thought I was the dramatic one."

Domingo allowed himself the ghost of a smile. "You've taken your first step, Sia Mason. But there is a reason the world was kept from you, and why it will not stay hidden much longer."

Domingo's gaze swept over them again. "The shadows that came for you were not acting blindly. They knew who you were. What you are."

Sia's stomach tightened. "You're saying I was the target."

"Precisely. And they were sent by one who has stalked our kind for generations. He goes by many names, but here and now, he is known in your world as Mr. Morning."

Eric's posture stiffened. "That name's been whispered for months. Even in the mage circles. Always attached to something going missing."

"In the tongue of demons," Domingo said, "his true name is Gomath. A sorcerer of the old blood, twisted by time and pact. He was once a man of power, but now he is something far worse: a mage turned predator, sustained by deals struck in the dark."

Tobias crossed his arms. "You think he's the one who took Mia."

"I do not merely think," Domingo replied, voice like stone cracking under pressure. "I know. Mia was taken, not in body alone, but in soul. Gomath does not kill without purpose. He needed her alive to unmake her, to turn her into something obedient. Corrupted. Controlled."

Sia's breath caught. Her knees nearly gave out, and she had to steady herself on the edge of a nearby stone bench. "She's alive?"

Domingo nodded solemnly. "In some form, yes. Twisted, perhaps. Enchained. But not gone. Not yet."

Eric stepped closer, his voice unusually serious. "That's why the shadows have your scent. He's not done with your family, Sia. Not by a long shot."

"Because you are the balance undone," Domingo said. "The twin who remained. The echo without its voice. He wants to see what you become without your other half, or worse, what he can forge you into before you find her again."

Sia stood frozen for a long moment, the weight of it all bearing down like stone pressing on her chest. The silence in the chamber seemed to lean in.

"No," she whispered.

Domingo tilted his head slightly. "No?"

"I'm not some chosen savior. I'm not... destined," she said, louder now, though her voice trembled. "This wasn't supposed to be me. I didn't ask for this. I didn't want any of it."

Eric opened his mouth as if to speak, but Tobias raised a hand to stop him.

"I just want my life back," Sia continued, her voice cracking. "I want to be normal. To wake up and not feel like I'm being hunted by things that shouldn't even exist."

Her hands trembled now. "Mia was the strong one. If she's still alive, then maybe she's the one he wants. Maybe I'm just... collateral. Maybe this isn't about me at all."

Domingo watched her with unreadable calm. "Denial is a path many walk, Sia Mason. But the world rarely cares for what we want. It only listens to what we are."

She said nothing, retreating inward, her thoughts a churning storm. Grief for Mia. Guilt. Fear. A thread of something deeper, shame, perhaps, that she hadn't wanted this path, that she wasn't ready.

Domingo let the silence stretch, respectful.

When he spoke again, it was quieter. "There are practical matters to address. Ella must be healed. She cannot protect you until she recovers fully. Tobias and Eric must be made aware of what they're guarding, and what dangers follow you now."

He leaned forward slightly. "Dobahold is no longer safe for you. The breach has been opened, and shadows crawl closer with each passing day. I had hoped this sanctuary would hold, but it was never meant to be a prison for destiny."

Sia looked up slowly.

"You will go to a place called Ebenezer's Stead," Domingo said. "It is an outpost far to the north, buried in cold stone and older magic. Few know of it. Fewer still would dare approach it."

Tobias nodded faintly. "I know the place."

"Good," Domingo replied. "You'll take her there. Stay hidden. Give her time to think, to grow stronger. The world won't stop, but at least we can give her the space to catch up."

"And after that?" Sia asked.

Domingo's gaze settled on her again, steady and sharp. "After that, you choose who you become."

CHAPTER 17

Echoes in the Flame

A rebirth out of spiritual adversity causes us to become new creatures.

James E. Faust

THE FIRST THING ELLA noticed was the silence.

Not the sterile quiet of a hospital, or the mechanical hum of machines, but something older, deeper. The air was still and warm, scented faintly with ashwood and lavender. She lay on a thick bedroll layered with furs and handwoven quilts, the kind made with care by hands that remembered every stitch.

Her body ached, sharp and deep, but it was a duller throb than she expected. When she blinked her eyes open, the stone ceiling above her was carved with spiral glyphs, glowing faintly. Someone had tended to her.

"About time," a voice said from nearby, feminine, dry, and laced with just a hint of sarcasm. "Thought you were going to keep hogging the drama. If you're worried about going crazy again, we extracted the shadow curse you were under and we've warded you from it happening again. Try not to cuddle Hellhounds in the future."

Ella turned her head with effort and blinked again. A young woman lounged in a high-backed chair beside the cot, legs crossed over the armrest. Her black jeans were torn, boots scuffed, and a tattered band tee clung to her under a dark jacket layered in chains and charms. Her hair was jet black with a vivid red streak curling near her face, and her violet eyes practically glowed in the dim light.

"Who..." Ella croaked.

"Becca," the woman said. "One of the locals. Dragon, in case you were wondering."

Ella's brows furrowed faintly. "You don't look like a dragon."

Becca grinned. "Thanks. Most of us don't, until we want to. You looked like hell, by the way. Lucky for you, I'm nicer than I dress."

She leaned forward and pulled a small silver knife from her belt. Without fanfare, she pricked her thumb and let a single drop of crimson fall onto a folded cloth.

"What, "

"Shh. Draconic blood is potent. Yours is stubborn. This'll speed things along."

Becca pressed the cloth to Ella's side, just above a slowly healing wound that pulsed faintly with old pain. As the blood touched her skin, Ella gasped.

A warmth bloomed inside her, hotter than fire, but cleaner, like golden light poured into her veins. Her wounds didn't just close, they sealed, knitted from the inside out by invisible threads of power. The ache in her muscles vanished, and her breath came easier.

She stared up at Becca in wide-eyed shock. "How...?"

"You've got dragon in you too," Becca said, casually wiping her thumb on her jeans. "From your mom's side. Thought you might. The way your body responded to the blood? Textbook."

Ella sat up slowly, the stiffness all but gone. "She never told me."

"Lot of moms don't," Becca said with a shrug. "Sometimes they're scared of what it means. Sometimes they just want you to live a life that's your own. But power doesn't really care what you know. It wakes up when it wants to."

Ella looked down at her hands, flexing them, feeling the subtle hum of something new there, something waiting.

"What happens now?" she asked.

Becca tilted her head, her red-streaked hair catching the light like fire in shadow. "Now? You decide what to do with it."

Ella swung her legs off the cot slowly, bracing herself as her bare feet touched the cool stone floor. Her limbs felt unfamiliar, stronger, lighter, as if some hidden weight had been lifted. She crossed the room toward an old brass-framed mirror leaned against one of the stone walls.

Her breath caught.

Among the waves of golden hair that framed her face, a vivid streak of sapphire blue now ran from root to tip on one side. It shimmered faintly, like it didn't quite belong to the same spectrum as the rest of the world.

Becca grinned from behind her. "Yeah. That happens sometimes. Side effect. Blood does weird things when it's waking up old bloodlines."

Ella touched the blue strand gently, her reflection blinking back with something like awe.

The door creaked open.

"Hey," came a familiar voice, soft, but laced with concern. Marcus stepped into the chamber, hands shoved in his pockets. "I heard you were awake. Thought I'd check in before Domingo's horde scooped me up with the others."

Ella turned toward him, trying to mask her surprise at how good it was to see him. "Domingo's meeting with the others?"

He nodded. "Yep. Sia, Tobias, Eric... They're all up there. Council showed up not long ago. Looks like they're hashing out next steps. You got out of it on account of being mostly dead."

Ella smirked faintly. "Lucky me."

Eric's voice drifted in from the hallway behind Marcus. "Becca, mind cleaning up in here? These two are going to need the room again tonight, and it looks like a wyvern exploded."

Becca rolled her eyes. "Fine, fine. I'll scrub the stone with my bare hands and polish the glyphs with dragon spit, shall I?"

Eric leaned into the doorway, smirking. "This is why I don't bring Becca anywhere nice."

Becca shot him a look over her shoulder. "You'd be lost without me, cousin."

Ella blinked. "You're related?"

"Unfortunately," they said at the same time.

Eric chuckled. "Yeah. Our mothers are sisters. She got the fire, I got the charm."

Becca snorted. "He got kicked by a horse as a child and never quite recovered. But he's not totally useless."

"Love the enthusiasm," Eric called back. "Come on, Ella. You're overdue for some food that doesn't come through a straw."

Marcus stepped aside and Ella followed Eric out, her bare feet finding balance on the cool stone floor. The hallways were alive now with murmurs and movement. She stayed close, trailing behind as they made their way through the tunnels of Dobahold.

Soon they stepped into a wide, vaulted space that opened into what looked like a mess hall, though that term hardly did it justice. A cafeteria carved from ancient stone stretched before them, its high ceilings webbed with glowing crystal veins. Long wooden tables filled the center, and the scent of grilled meat, fresh bread, and something floral but spicy wafted through the air.

Dragons in human form clustered near the hearths, laughing and passing steaming bowls. Elves with ivy-wrapped braids leaned close in quiet conversation. A pair of fey creatures shimmered like mirages near the far wall, nibbling petals off a shared plate of glowing fruit. And near the serving line, a stocky dwarf in a thick apron barked cheerfully at the cook behind the counter.

Ella slowed, taking it all in.

Eric bumped her shoulder gently. "You'll get used to it."

Marcus gave them a brief smile. "I'll go grab us something. You look like a burger girl, Ella."

Ella gave a tired nod. "I'd eat anything right now."

With a two-fingered salute, Marcus disappeared into the line.

Eric led her to a quieter corner of the hall where a stone bench met a low wooden table, and the ambient hum of conversation muffled around them. He sat across from her, leaning forward, elbows on his knees.

"So," he said with a crooked smile, "want the cliff notes version of what you missed upstairs?"

Ella raised an eyebrow. "Does it involve Sia finding out she's secretly royalty or something?"

"Close," Eric said. "Turns out she's the twin half of a magical prophecy, Gomath, the creepy shadow-mage we've all been having nightmares about, didn't kill Mia like we thought. He took her. Body, soul, probably wardrobe. Plans to do the same to Sia if we're not careful."

Ella went still, eyes narrowing. "She's alive?"

Eric nodded. "Yeah. Sort of. Domingo said she's been corrupted, but not lost. And Sia... well, she kind of had a meltdown. Can't blame her."

Ella exhaled slowly. "No. I can't either."

Eric's smirk faded to something more sincere. "She's strong, though. Like you."

Ella met his eyes then, catching a flicker of warmth beneath his casual facade.

He hesitated a second too long before adding, "I mean, you both scare the crap out of me sometimes, but like, in a good way."

She smiled, just a little.

He looked down at the table, drumming his fingers. "Just... glad you're okay, El. I mean it."

A beat passed between them, warm and oddly peaceful. The clamor of the mess hall receded into background noise, the clang of plates, bursts of laughter, the low thrum of distant conversation. It felt almost normal. Almost safe.

Ella rested her arms on the table, watching Eric closely. "You know, for a class clown, you're not so bad at the serious stuff."

He grinned. "I've got layers. Like an onion. Or a spell circle. Complex and prone to explosions."

"More like an overripe peach," she muttered.

He laughed, and the sound felt good in her chest. She hadn't realized how much she'd missed that kind of easy comfort.

Marcus returned with a tray stacked with burgers, fries, and bottles of sparkling water, sliding it onto the table like a waiter in a nicer world.

"One extra crispy and one still mooing, just in case," he said.

Ella gave him a grateful smile. "You're a lifesaver."

They dug in without ceremony, the three of them eating together beneath the soft glow of crystal-lit arches. The world outside could wait a little longer.

Whatever came next, they'd face it on full stomachs and, for the first time in days, with something like hope.

CHAPTER 18

Straight Through the Mirror

"I think we dream so we don't have to be apart for so long. If we're in each other's dreams, we can be together all the time."

A.A. Milne

SIA FOUND HERSELF STANDING in front of four full sized dragons. Right out of the ancient fairy tales, they were massive, perhaps 30 feet tall, looking up in the massive dark cavern under the town. Each one looked down at her with a head the size of her entire body. Their large rounded eyes glowed in the dark, deep and reptilian in their massive faces. They were scaled, large lizard like creatures with powerful front claws, large folded weblike wings and sharp looking horns curling back from their temples. They one thing that differentiated from all of the classic imagery she had seen in the past was their eyes. The glow was almost phosphorescent, a low shining blue light that seemed to come from within. She had trouble moving, the beings were simply that awestriking. After what felt like a lifetime of hyperventilating and attempting not to wet herself, Eric gently shook her by the shoulders.

"As I was saying... Elders, this is the girl. The daughter of Blessed Peter and Singer Maria. She's what's been giving us so much trouble with the demons of late."

The titles of her parents and her situation caused enough distraction for her to momentarily forget she was surrounded by gigantic beings. She carefully reminded herself that Eric was one of these monsters. Even if his form was much smaller than what he had informed her were the eldest of the dragons in the Hold. Sia took another breath, to her relief, one of them began to assume human form. The effect was not terrible, the dragon's form became a hollowed image, like a hologram, then an outline of light before it shrank into a form less than 6 feet in height. The man was thin, though not overtly tall like Sia's father. He smiled, with long black hair that was slicked back and tied into a tail. His handsome face carried a reassuring smile, the dark olive of his skin and his dark eyes reminded her of the black scaled dragon he had been moments before.

He approached the two and held out his hand to Sia. She nervously took it and was surprised when he kneeled and kissed the back of her hand like a smooth gentleman. He spoke in a thick, Arabic accent, but his English was quite good. "Ms. Mason, I am Lord Domingo, one of the four current Elders of Dobahold. We are pleased to meet you."

Sia found herself blushing at his attentions, until one of the other dragons made a quaking, rumbling noise. To her humor Sia realized the dragon was making a coughing noise to get Domingo's attention. The man straightened and smiled. "Excuse me, you look so much like Maria I was distracted." He let himself chuckle, and Eric made a face that almost made Sia break out giggling. Domingo bowed his head. "We understand you are the Prophet and while you dwell in Apple Grove you are under our protection. We will guard you from those that wish to turn your role into something terrible."

"Sir... Mister Domingo, what could possibly be more terrible than the end of the world?" Sia asked, her voice hopeless, she was starting to lose herself in the knowledge that her parents had imparted to her already.

"Simple, Miss Mason... the thing more terrible than the end of the world could simply be how it ends. An end is not always final; ends can make way toward new beginnings." He smiled warmly at her, and his words brought her some comfort. "Remember, just because the world ends does not mean it cannot be rebuilt. Heaven and Hell believe the world will end in one of two ways. Your role is to decide that. We'll keep you safe in hopes that Heaven wins the day."

Sia stood there for a moment, trying to digest his words. The gravity of his statement hung heavy in the air, but there was something soothing about the way he spoke, like the calm before a storm, a steady hand in a world that was anything but stable.

After spending some time with the elders, and namely the ever-interested Lord Domingo, it was Marcus who finally took to showing Sia around. She couldn't help but feel like an object passed from hand to hand, though Marcus' gaze, soft and caring, made it easier to bear. The warmth in his eyes offered a semblance of normalcy, something she hadn't felt in a long while. She tried to push away the unease that gnawed at her, but it lingered like the taste of ash on her tongue.

The passage they walked through seemed to stretch on forever, its walls adorned with intricate carvings of beasts she didn't recognize, ancient, strange, and utterly alien. Sia couldn't help but wonder how long this hidden world had existed beneath the town, waiting for someone like her to stumble upon it. The dim glow of LED flashlights bounced off the stone walls as Marcus led her deeper into the labyrinthine tunnels, the shadows shifting and moving like living things.

Her eyes scanned the unfamiliar surroundings, cracked stone floors, twisted roots of massive trees that seemed to grow through the walls, and the faint, almost imperceptible hum of something far below. She felt the weight of history in the air, the sense that everything around her had been here long before she ever set foot in it. But Marcus didn't seem fazed by it at all. He walked ahead, speaking casually about the various tunnels and the town above, like this was all part of his everyday routine.

Sia let out a long breath. For the first time in a while, she felt like a human again. There was something reassuring about the mundane act of walking down a hallway, something that grounded her in a reality that wasn't so strange or foreign. But even in the company of Marcus, there was a part of her that couldn't quite shake the feeling that she was far from normal now. Half her town were ancient mythological beasts, the rest were hidden in plain sight. And she... she was the key to whatever was coming.

She glanced over at Marcus, watching as the faint glow from his phone illuminated his face, casting a soft light over his features. For a moment, she wondered what his life had been like before this. Had he always known? Or had he only recently discovered the world that was unfolding around her?

His voice interrupted her thoughts. "It's a lot to take in, isn't it?" he said, glancing back with a slight smile. "But you'll get used to it. I promise."

Sia nodded, though her stomach still churned. The weight of his words lingered, the sense that her life would never be the same again. Everything she thought she knew was slowly unraveling, and the fear of what that might mean for her future pressed down on her chest.

The further they walked, the more she realized that this place, this hidden world beneath her feet, wasn't just a refuge for creatures of myth. It was a battleground, a war zone where the lines between good and evil were constantly shifting, where one wrong move could tip the balance in favor of the wrong side. She was part of that war now, whether she liked it or not.

"Don't worry," Marcus said, his voice warm as always. "It's strange at first, but it's not all bad. There's beauty here, too. You just have to look for it."

She nodded again, though her heart wasn't fully in it. She wasn't sure if she could find beauty in the midst of this strange, new world. But one thing was clear, this was just the beginning.

"What I've got to show you I think you're going to like. You're the daughter of a Blessed and a Singer, so that means you've got mage blood either way. From what I've seen, you have the powers of a Seer... fitting for a Prophet, but you might have even more." He smiled in the dark at her, she could see it in the outline of his cheeks. She looked over him, heard the care in his voice. She didn't have the heart to tell him she didn't crush on him the same way he was crushing on her. Instead she decided to ask questions.

"That's twice someone's called my mother a Singer. She never even recites a limerick, so what does that even mean?" She sighed, getting to know all these new terms was giving her a headache, it was a lot for a girl to absorb in a day.

"A Singer is a special mage who can enchant with their voice. They don't actually have to sing, but I bet if your mother sang we'd all be helpless but to stop and listen till she was done. She encourages you to play music, doesn't she?" He asked curiously, knowing full well she practiced the violin heavily. She nodded, and he tilted his head. "She may have been training you to see if you have her talent then. Singers are naturally good at weaving sound... in other words, playing music."

She considered that, her mother has always been the primary reason she played the violin. She had started long ago; Mia had taken to the guitar instead. Sia walked in silence for some time before asking her next question.

"So what's a Blessed? I've heard some of the people down here calling you that too, not just Dad." She said with a curious drip to her voice. She looked over Marcus who responded with a shy grin.

"Well it's a far more common Mage. Blessed are imbued with the power to control elements with their will. You've seen me control the fires at the winery and fling earth about. We can't create elements out of thin air, but we can use anything at hand. There's varying degrees of strength. I'm very good with Earth Magic and Fire Magic, as you saw. There's also Air, Water and Spirit magic, anything else you see is just a combination of those five elements." He explained, showing her by holding out his hand as they passed a torch and plucking some of the flame off of it and into his hand, it floated there like a glowing ball of ember, inches over his skin without burning it.

Sia watched this in fascination, reaching out gently to see if she could feel the heat of the flame. The flames seemed to bend away from her, the heat never touching her. Marcus raised an eyebrow for a moment before his face settled and he made the flame shrink down to a tiny little flicker, then it extinguished. They stood there for a moment before Marcus spoke up again. "Blessed are said to be given their gifts by one of three forces, those of Heaven, those of Hell, or the Between. I'm a Between gifted."

"I get what Heaven and Hell are, but what do you mean by Between?" Sia asked, her face drawing into another severe, sceptical look. "Are you trying to tell me you're Neutrally aligned or something?"

This caused Marcus to let out a chuckle. "No Sia, this isn't Dungeons and Dragons, have you ever heard of Purgatory?" He asked, and to this, Sia merely nodded, allowing him to continue. "Well you see, it's not actually some waiting area for people to go to Heaven or Hell when they die. It's sort of a realm for beings that aren't a part of the war between the top or bottom. We're just the myths that got lost in between or whose gods have long become obsolete. Well... some of those gods are still around, they just have no part in the struggle you and I got swept into."

"I see..." Sia said, considering all she learned. "So a Singer uses sound to cast spells and enchantments, a Blessed uses the elements around them, so..." She came to the question she felt so self-conscious about. "What's a Seer?"

Marcus took a moment to think of a proper explanation before answering. "The name is old, Seers are sometimes called Diviners or Soothsayers. Their talent is reading fortunes, telling the future, and seeing into events from another perspective. Everyone knows you always seem to skip out of trouble right before it happens. Heck, I noticed you bringing an umbrella to school the other day when no one would have guessed it was going to storm. These are signs. You can tell the future to some extent." His steps slowed a moment as he considered something. "You also told us about your dreams. I think that's part of your power too. Did your dreams ever warn you anything was going to happen? Show you a future event before it occurred?"

Sia slowed somewhat and considered his words, biting her lower lip, because his question left her little room to lie. She had had warnings, signs, things dreams shouldn't do. "Well... I had a dream about Tobias holding a sword, I thought it meant he was going to kill me but it turned out it was a vision of him saving my life. Also... I dreamt about Johnson's car accident before it happened... I thought it was a nightmare so I..." Her voice choked up a little, the guilt had been wracking her for some time now. Only just now she could identify it.

He stopped walking and turned to her, grabbing her and pulling her into a warm, comforting hug. She felt herself go slack, tension leaving her body as she leaned her weight into him. It was another moment of weakness for her, but she had trouble pretending that the hug wasn't helping immensely. Eventually they parted and Sia ran a hand through her messy hair. The girl turned away a little. "A-Anyway... let's keep going."

Marcus merely continued forward, "Now... I don't have any other Seers for you to meet, you're kind of on your own there. But I've read that they can explore people's dreams, even their own and divine all sorts of things within them. Seers are sometimes also specifically called The Dreamers in lore." He said, speaking a bit faster as they approached a doorway, and the end to their privacy. He paused and looked at her, opening the door and showing her that it opened in the back alley of a small shopping center in the middle of town.

She stepped out into the open air, finding it hard to believe she had somehow gotten into town by walking through darkness under the ground, where she'd always imagined there was a sewer. She couldn't have been more wrong for so long in her life, it was unnerving to her.

"That being said..." He warned. "Until we can get you help, you shouldn't try to go into dreams on your own, it could be very dangerous with what you've told me." He led her down the street towards the public library. He led her up the steps to a side door she had always thought was an abandoned entrance to the small library. He knocked in a sequence and the door swung open. Motioning his arms in a flourish, he smiled at her. "Ladies first, welcome to the Cabal."

The Cabal, as Marcus put it, seemed little more than a secretive collection of librarians and book enthusiasts. In a large chamber, which Sia had always thought to be a closed off historical section of the library, tables had been set up and the walls lined with old leather-bound books. People milled about, some reading, some talking, and some doing things that up until now Sia Mason had thought impossible. That is, until she had seen a man wield holy light through a sword and Marcus call up fire from his hands. One girl her own apparent age sat at a table, turning a notebook into a papercraft bird, the curiosity being that she was apparently doing so with her mind.

Marcus led her through to a larger central table where sat five older looking people, two of middling age, one elderly, and two more who seemed to be in their mid-twenties. They seemed deep in a discussion, but at the approach of Marcus they ended their conversation abruptly. It was clear that it was a business not meant for the ears of someone so young and not in their circle. As they approached, Sia's focus became the woman in the center, as something about the elderly lady called to her. The kindly looking old woman had a bun of silver on the top of her head and her two dark eyes seemed to drink in Sia's being, analysing her. There was something about the way she examined Sia that made her feel as though she was being x-rayed. At last, she spoke, "Blessed Marcus, it seems you have brought to us an oddity. Who is this young woman?"

Sia felt her cheeks go crimson at the question but Marcus was ever affable in his response. "Singer Arianna, and the rest of the Council. I present to you Sia Mason, daughter of a Blessed and a Singer. She is a Seer, at least, that is what the Elders at Dobahold seem to believe." He bowed to them and stood aside as though presenting her in a show. Sia tried not to panic as all five sets of eyes levelled on her.

It was the other elderly one, a man with a thinning profile and equally thinning hair on his head who spoke. A slight twinkle in his gray eyes seemed to shine as his deep, rich voice sounded out. "So this is the girl the Dragons have had their eyes on. They have named her Seer have they?"

It was Sia who spoke, though she wasn't sure where the words had come from. "Yes, Singer Rick. That's what everyone keeps telling me."

Her words were met with an utter and complete silence for a few moments. It was in that silence that Sia realized that no one had told her the man's name or his title among mages. She had simply known it and without much effort, had impressed all of them in the idea that she was what they kept telling her she was, someone who could see the future, walk in dreams, and know what she shouldn't possibly know. It took Rick, as that was his name, some time to recover from that. "We have never actually met a Seer before, it has been some time since one even walked the earth, child. Nevertheless, you seem to be the genuine article. But I wonder, why did you bring her here, Marcus."

This time it was Marcus who looked abashed for a moment before he spoke up, "You see, Council, it's just that since no one has seen a seer in human memory, I figured you might at least be able to help her learn the basics of touching and seeing magic. If she's a Seer, she should possess the same base talents all Magi have in common. It'll be important that she learns, so Domingo tells me, if the Dragons have any hope of teaching her what they know of Seers."

The council looked to one another, then nodded their agreement. It was thus that Sia Mason began a new form of training with a secret council of mages in the small town she had once thought of as boring and nothing special at all.

CHAPTER 19

Between Stars and Shadows

You can have peace. Or you can have freedom. Don't ever count on having both at once.

Robert A. Heinlein

SIA'S BODY ACHED. IT was the deep, lingering kind of pain that clung to you long after the battle ended, muscles strained from unnatural movement, bones bruised from too many falls, and the ever-present sting of magical exhaustion that made her head feel like it was suspended in a storm cloud. Her breathing came slow and steady, but the weariness still pressed on her chest, as though the weight of the world was trying to push her down into the stone floor.

Ella lay next to her, propped up on an elbow, eyes fixed on the swirling depths of the underground cavern they'd found themselves in. Despite the heavy silence, the air in Dobahold had a strange comfort to it. The distant hum of ancient magic, the faint warmth that seemed to emanate from the stone walls, the echo of footsteps in forgotten passages, everything felt like it was holding its breath, waiting for the next step.

Ella, ever watchful, had barely moved since they'd settled into the cavern. Her presence was a quiet constant, a steady reassurance in the chaos that had come to define Sia's life. The light from the glowing cracks in the walls cast soft shadows, highlighting Ella's sharp features, her calm demeanor unshaken by the weight of the world around them.

Sia shifted, her eyes drawn to Ella's silhouette. "Are you ever afraid?"

Ella's gaze didn't leave the shadows in front of them, but there was a slight tilt to her head, a brief acknowledgment that she was listening. "Of course. But fear is something you carry with you, not something you let carry you."

Sia let the silence stretch between them. She'd spent so many years terrified, of her own magic, of the world outside, of the overwhelming responsibility now pressing down on her. But with Ella here, it felt... bearable. A little less like she was standing alone on the edge of everything.

"I don't know what to do next." Sia's voice was small, the weight of her words settling like a stone in her gut. "I'm supposed to save everyone, but I barely understand what's happening. I'm just... I'm just trying to keep my head above water."

Ella's hand moved then, slow and deliberate, until it rested on Sia's shoulder, a gesture so simple, but it grounded her in a way that words could not. "You're not alone. Not in this, not in anything."

Sia turned slightly toward her, eyes locking with Ella's for a brief moment. Despite the darkness of their situation, there was a light in Ella's gaze, a quiet hope that Sia clung to. It was the same kind of hope that had been there the first day they met, a spark in the dark that had always drawn Sia in. Ella, in her way, was the sister she never had. Not by blood, but by choice, by bond, by the way Ella had always been there when Sia needed her most. It was the quiet certainty that Ella would always stand by her, no matter how dire things became.

Ella was the kind of person who made silence feel like comfort, and in her presence, the world could feel just a little less heavy.

"I never really thought about having someone like this in my life," Sia murmured, her voice muffled slightly. "Someone who... sees me. Who stays."

Ella's grip tightened slightly. "We all need someone like that. Even the strongest."

Sia closed her eyes for a moment, letting the stillness of their surroundings sink in. The echoes of the underground tunnels, the soft flicker of the distant lights that lined the stone walls, they all blurred together, creating a safe little bubble where, for just a moment, nothing could touch them. The world outside seemed so distant now, its harshness muted by the walls of Dobahold.

But even in the company of Ella, there was a part of her that couldn't quite shake the feeling that she was far from normal now. Half her town were ancient mythological beasts, the rest were hidden in plain sight. And she... she was the key to whatever was coming.

Her thoughts lingered on Mia, the sister she'd once shared everything with. Mia was lost, pulled into a world she wasn't meant to belong to, and Sia couldn't help but feel the weight of that loss every single day.

"Ella," Sia began quietly, her voice breaking the quiet, "I don't know how to save Mia. I keep thinking I'm doing everything wrong... that maybe I can't fix it."

Ella's hand moved gently across Sia's hair, her fingers threading through it in a calming gesture. "Sia... none of this is easy. And you can't do it all at once. Mia's... not gone. She's just... lost right now. You're not alone in this. I'll help you get her back."

Sia nodded against Ella's shoulder, grateful for the unwavering certainty in her words. It was hard to keep believing that Mia could still be saved, but Ella's voice, steady and calm, held a quiet strength that made Sia want to believe, if only for a moment.

"Sometimes I feel like I've lost myself," Sia confessed, barely above a whisper. "Like I'm just... chasing after a version of Mia I can never reach. She's out there somewhere, but I can't even find her. And the longer I go without her, the more I forget what she's really like."

Ella's arm tightened around her, pulling her in just a little closer. "You don't have to chase her. She's still there, inside. You just have to remind her of who she is. The rest... will follow."

Sia let out a long breath, her chest rising and falling slowly. She didn't know how much longer she could keep this fight going, but she couldn't give up. Not when Ella was here. Not when Mia's face still burned in her mind, a memory that refused to fade.

They sat there for a long time, wrapped in the quiet understanding that only the two of them could share. Sia found herself drifting between thoughts of the past and the present, of the world they were fighting against, and of the family she had almost lost.

Ella was right. They needed each other. It wasn't just about saving Mia; it was about saving each other. Together, they were more than the weight of their fears. They were a force, a bond that nothing, no magic, no demon, no curse, could break.

Sia looked up at Ella, feeling something stir inside her, a warmth, a spark that made her feel a little less lost. "Thank you," she said softly, her voice full of gratitude. "For being here."

Ella smiled, the same quiet, comforting smile that had been a constant presence in Sia's life. "Always. I'll be with you every step of the way."

Sia closed her eyes again, resting against Ella's shoulder, letting the weight of everything else fade for just a moment. She had a long way to go, but with Ella beside her, maybe the journey wouldn't feel quite so impossible.

Sia lay still for a moment longer, her body still sore but comforted by the warmth of Ella's presence beside her. Her thoughts drifted between fragments of the day's events and the faint echoes of things she couldn't quite place. The stillness in the air around her, the rhythmic hum of magic beneath the stone, the quiet murmurs of life that didn't belong to her world, all of it blurred into a soft backdrop as her mind began to slip, like the last remnants of a fading dream.

Then, without warning, the air around her shifted.

The temperature dropped, and the cavern grew darker. The walls, which had once seemed comforting, now felt distant, as though they were pulling away from her. The ground beneath her shifted, too, and Sia's eyes fluttered open just in time to see the stone beneath her dissolve into swirling mist.

Her breath caught in her throat. The room was gone.

Instead, she found herself standing on the edge of a cliff, the ground beneath her feet soft as sand. The world around her was impossibly vast, a horizon that stretched far beyond the limits of her mind. The sky was a deep shade of purple, swirling with fractals of blue and gold, like the end of the world and the beginning of something new. The stars pulsed in time with her heartbeat, and the air was thick with the hum of energy, like the very atmosphere was alive, breathing in tandem with her.

Her hands instinctively reached out, feeling the cool breeze that tugged at her clothes, but it wasn't like any wind she had ever known. It was cold, like it carried the weight of forgotten things. Her fingers brushed against something that felt like glass, smooth and clear, yet unbreakable.

Sia stepped forward, her foot sinking into the ground as though it were soft clay. The earth beneath her rippled, like a reflection on water, and she stumbled slightly, disoriented.

The world around her shimmered, flickering like a broken film reel. The sky split open in strange, geometric patterns, revealing glimpses of something, some thing, just beyond the fabric of reality itself. She reached out instinctively, but the world pulled away, receding into shadows that slithered like smoke.

A figure emerged from the void.

At first, it was little more than a shadow, a silhouette, its shape undulating as though made of liquid. The air around it hummed, the fabric of space distorting as it moved closer. As it drew near, the figure solidified into something more, its features, blurry at first, began to sharpen into a face that was almost familiar. A face that should be familiar.

Sia's heart skipped. She could see the outline of a woman's face, pale, with long dark hair cascading like water, glowing eyes that shone like stars, and a cruel smile that chilled her to the core.

"Mia?" Sia whispered, her voice barely more than a breath.

The figure tilted its head, and Sia could feel the cold presence of the dream-world pressing in on her, the edges of her vision blurring. She couldn't look away. The face before her was unmistakable, but there was something wrong, something off.

The smile faded, replaced by an expression Sia couldn't quite place. It wasn't her sister anymore. Not really. It was Mia, but twisted, deformed by something else. The eyes that once held warmth now held only coldness and an impossible depth.

The figure spoke, but the words didn't sound like they belonged to her. They were clipped, cold.

"You're searching for something, aren't you?" the figure asked, its voice echoing unnaturally. It was a voice Sia recognized, but it had changed, grown distant, like it was filtered through a thousand layers of glass.

Sia took a step back, her breath quickening. "Mia? Where are you? What happened to you?"

The figure's gaze narrowed, and the shadows around her flickered, as if responding to her words.

"You will never find me, sister. Not like this." The voice echoed again, and with it, the surroundings shifted, warping into shapes that didn't belong, the ground beneath Sia's feet trembling like the earth was made of glass, cracking and splintering. The stars above flickered, like dying embers.

Sia reached out, desperate to touch her sister, to pull her back from whatever darkness had claimed her. But the air around her crackled, and her hand passed through the figure, as though it wasn't there at all.

The figure stepped back, melting into the shadows as it faded into the blackness.

"You cannot save me. Not yet."

And with that, the world around Sia twisted and shifted again, the dream pulling her deeper into its uncharted depths.

CHAPTER 20

Shadows Beneath the Veil

Nothing shall part us in our love till Death at his
appointed hour removed us from the light of day.
Apollonius of Rhodes

THE AIR WAS THICK with a heavy, almost liquid stillness. The
horizon stretched beyond Sia's vision, endlessly yawning into the
void. Each step she took felt heavier than the last, as though the
world itself was resisting her movement, pulling her back into its
strange embrace. The ground beneath her had softened into an
eerie texture that felt more like water than earth, slick and shifting
with every footfall. It was as if she was standing on the edge of
something, something vast, too large to comprehend, and yet too
intimate to ignore.

Sia stumbled, the ground beneath her quaking, sending ripples
through the fabric of the world around her. The once-stable cliff-
side had begun to crumble, and as the earth fractured, pieces of
it fell away into the abyss, vanishing into nothing. Panic gripped
her chest. She stepped back, but there was nowhere to go, no firm
foundation to stand on, no way to escape the growing sense of
vertigo that clawed at her mind.

Before she could steady herself, a pulse of energy shot through the
air, reverberating through the ground beneath her. It was so powerful
that it knocked her off balance, sending her stumbling. She caught
herself against the air, reaching out for something solid. But there was

nothing but the hum of energy vibrating the very fabric of the world, a hum that she could feel in the marrow of her bones.

She was no longer alone.

A shadow appeared in the distance, its form shifting like liquid smoke, bending the air around it as it approached. It moved effortlessly, like a phantom drifting on a forgotten breeze. Sia's heart raced, her breath shallow as the figure loomed closer. It was tall, the shape flickering like a flame, impossible to fully grasp, yet undeniably present. She felt its presence as if it were an extension of the dream itself, an ancient force that hovered at the edge of her understanding.

When it spoke, its voice was a low murmur, vibrating through the air like a distant echo of something long lost.

"You've come far."

Sia flinched, her mind struggling to process the words. She opened her mouth to speak, but her voice felt swallowed by the oppressive silence. Instead, she simply nodded, unsure of how to respond, but desperate for answers.

The figure stepped forward, its outline flickering in and out of focus like a mirage, and as it did, the world around Sia began to shift once more. The earth beneath her feet seemed to dissolve into wisps of smoke, and the sky above folded in on itself, warping like a piece of parchment scorched at the edges. The stars above twisted into impossible shapes, converging into patterns that made her head ache just to look at them.

It was as though the very laws of reality were unraveling before her eyes.

The figure's voice broke through the chaos, calm and unwavering. "This place is not what it seems. It exists between worlds, between the known and the unknown, the conscious and the unconscious. Here, you are both nothing and everything." His voice was deep, resonating with a faint echo that made the air vibrate around them. A strange, almost unnatural calm radiated from him, and Sia could feel the weight of his presence press in on her like a thousand unseen hands.

Sia's pulse quickened. The weight of the figure's words settled in her mind, sinking deep into her consciousness. This place, this shifting, unsteady realm, was something more than a dream. It was an in-between, a space where the rules of time and space no longer applied, where everything was in flux. It was a threshold, a strange, nebulous place between the worlds she knew and the one she was beginning to understand. And it felt like she was standing on the edge of something vast, too large for her to comprehend.

She opened her mouth to speak again, but the figure continued, its form growing more defined as it approached. Now she could make out its features, no longer a flickering silhouette, but a face, strangely human, yet impossibly alien at the same time. The eyes were pools of darkness, and its mouth curved into a smile that seemed to know too much.

"You are searching for something, aren't you?" The figure's voice rang through her, its tone smooth, like honey. "You are standing at the edge of something vast, but you already knew that, didn't you? That's why you've come."

Sia's eyes narrowed as she instinctively took a step back. "Yeah, right. I've definitely got some deep existential reason for being stuck in this dream. And that's why I came, sure," she muttered under her breath, trying to deflect the mounting unease with a little sarcasm.

The figure leaned in closer, his presence overwhelming her senses, making her feel small and insignificant in this dream realm. She felt the pressure of his gaze like a weight on her chest, but there was something comforting about it, too, something familiar, though she couldn't place it. There was a warmth to his cold, calculated words. It reminded her of something protective, something almost fatherly.

"You've crossed a threshold, Sia Mason. A threshold that leads to more than you understand. To be here is to make a choice. And that choice will define everything that comes next." His words were wrapped in an odd sense of reassurance, as though he were guiding her rather than threatening her.

Sia let out a shaky breath. "You really have a knack for talking in riddles, don't you?"

The figure's smile didn't waver, though there was a flicker of something like warmth in his eyes now, a slight softening of his otherwise cold demeanor. "I speak in truths. You'll understand soon enough."

Sia frowned, her discomfort growing with each word. But there was something in his voice, a hint of something deeper, that made her pause. He wasn't like the distant, ominous force she expected, there was a fatherly quality to his presence, like someone trying to guide her with gentle patience. "Great. The mysterious 'truths' that no one ever explains. I'm sure that'll help."

Sia's eyes narrowed as the weight of the dream continued pressing down on her. "So, what's your name, then? Or should I just keep calling you 'vague, mysterious being'?"

The figure's lips curled upward in a knowing smile, one that was both unsettling and reassuring at the same time. "Thanatos," he said, his voice carrying an air of finality that made Sia's skin crawl. "But you may call me Than, if you so choose."

Sia blinked, her surprise melting into a smirk. "Wait, what? Thanatos? Is that supposed to be impressive? I get it, you're all-powerful and ancient. But Than?" She shook her head, feeling a flicker of amusement in spite of herself. "Well, Than, I don't know how you've survived this long with a name like that. I mean, really, Thanatos? Not exactly a dinner party name, is it?"

Than's smile remained unwavering, but this time, Sia caught the glimmer of something different in his gaze, approval, perhaps? It was hard to read, but it was there. His presence was still immense, but for some reason, she wasn't as afraid of him as she thought she'd be.

"Very well," he said with a slight bow of his head, the slightest hint of affection in his tone. "Than it is. Now, you must understand that what lies ahead will not be simple. What you face... is not just about saving your sister. It is about understanding what lies at the heart of your power and how it will shape everything that comes next."

Sia felt her heart rate increase again, the weight of his words pressing down on her once more, but now, it felt different, more like a challenge than a threat. His tone wasn't just cold and distant anymore. There was something protective in it, as though he was trying to prepare her for what was coming, even if it wasn't easy to understand.

Sia stood still, the surreal world around her pressing in like a thick fog. The ground beneath her still shifted, rippling like the surface of a lake disturbed by an unseen force. Each step she took seemed to sink deeper into the dreamscape, the horizon around her bending in impossible angles. There was no true sense of direction here, just the feeling of floating, of being both a part of the dream and apart from it, as though she existed between worlds.

Than stood beside her, his presence a steady anchor in the chaos. Despite the overwhelming strangeness of the world around them, his calm, unwavering demeanor remained the same, grounding her when everything else seemed to slip away.

"You've been chosen for a reason, Sia," Than's voice rang through the stillness, his tone soft but powerful. "You walk the line between worlds, between life and death, light and dark, the known and the unknown. The power that courses through you is not your own, but a part of something far greater than you understand."

Sia turned to face him, her brow furrowed in confusion. She still didn't fully grasp what was happening, let alone the implications of the words he spoke. "So, what? I'm some kind of... divine tool? Some chosen one who's supposed to fix everything?" Her voice was tinged with frustration, her patience beginning to thin as the weight of her responsibility settled in.

Than gave a slow, almost imperceptible nod. "In a way, yes. You are the vessel for something far older and more powerful than you could imagine. Your magic is but a reflection of that power. But it is your choices, your will, that will decide how it is used."

Sia's heart raced at the gravity of his words. "And what happens if I make the wrong choice? If I don't have what it takes?" Her voice shook slightly despite her attempt at composure.

Than's eyes softened, the deep darkness within them momentarily flickering with something more gentle, more understanding. "You are not alone, Sia. You will never be. But the path you walk is yours alone to choose."

The wind shifted, stirring the strange mist around them, and Sia's gaze lifted to the sky. The stars were fading, their light dimming to a soft glow. The fabric of reality around her shimmered, bending and warping, the edges of the world beginning to unravel as though it were something not quite real. She stepped forward instinctively, drawn to the shifting, pulsing light at the center of it all.

"What is that?" Sia asked, her voice a mixture of awe and trepidation.

Than's gaze followed hers, and a flicker of something ancient passed over his face. "That, Sia Mason, is the heart of the void, the very source of your power. The gateway between realms. What lies within it is beyond understanding, beyond comprehension. But you will need to face it. You will need to understand it before you can truly unlock what you're capable of."

Sia hesitated, a wave of uncertainty washing over her. "What if I can't do it?" she whispered, her words barely audible.

Than's voice was steady, unwavering. "You can do it. But you must trust yourself, and you must trust the bond we share. That is what will guide you, no matter what comes."

Sia looked up at him, her eyes searching his face for any sign of doubt, any hint that what he said might be more than just empty encouragement. But all she found was unwavering certainty. The bond between them, though divine and mysterious, was as real as the earth beneath her feet, and in that moment, it gave her the strength to take the next step.

As she moved toward the pulsing light at the heart of the void, the world around her shifted again. The edges of reality blurred, and the air seemed to crackle with energy. The path was uncertain, and yet, it felt like the only choice she had. The power inside her began to stir, waking from its slumber, pushing at the edges of her consciousness. Her body ached, as though it were being pulled apart and remade in the same breath.

And then, it began.

The voices.

At first, they were soft whispers, barely audible, like faint echoes carried on the wind. They spoke in languages she didn't recognize, their words rolling over each other like the sound of a distant crowd, a cacophony of thought from realms beyond her comprehension. The languages felt ancient, primal, some she instinctively understood, others she couldn't place, but all of them felt wrong, as though they were things that shouldn't exist in this world.

But there was one voice, growing louder, sharper, cutting through the others. It was deep, vibrating in her chest, and as it spoke, the air around her seemed to tremble. The words were not in any language she had ever heard, yet she could feel the power in them, like a distant thunderclap.

"You are the key. You are the one who will open the door. Choose... choose... choose."

The voice rang out, louder now, its power pressing down on her chest. It felt as though it were speaking directly into her soul, its presence dark, ancient, and utterly alien. The words repeated over and over, filling her mind with a sense of dread that settled in her bones.

Sia faltered for a moment, feeling her heart race in her chest as the voice grew louder still, demanding, overwhelming. The world around her seemed to bend, and the pulsing light at the center of the void flickered, as though responding to the energy in the air. She gasped, stepping back, trying to steady herself.

"Choose... choose... choose the way forward. Or lose yourself to what lies beyond."

A chill ran down her spine as the voice grew even louder, deafening now, its power shaking her to the core. But through the fog of overwhelming sound, a part of her resisted, a flicker of clarity breaking through.

"What do you want from me?" she cried out, the words escaping her lips before she could think.

The voice paused, and for a moment, there was silence. It hung in the air like a storm cloud, heavy and oppressive. Then, in the quiet, the voice spoke again, its tone softer now, but no less ominous.

"I am the beginning. I am the end. I am the one who shapes all things. You will be the catalyst, Sia Mason. Your choices will awaken what sleeps. And when it does, you will be the one who stands at the center of it all."

A shiver ran down her spine as she felt the weight of the words settle on her, the echoes of the voice pulsing through her body. The light before her grew brighter, but the sense of dread that had begun to claw at her mind remained.

And then, everything stopped.

She was no longer standing in the strange, shifting world. She was back in the cavern, her breathing ragged, her heart pounding in her chest. The void was gone, the light dimmed, and Than stood beside her once more.

He looked at her with a faint smile, but there was something deeper in his eyes, a knowing, a recognition.

"You have crossed the first threshold," he said softly, his voice full of approval. *"And with it, you have unlocked a power that will shape the world. What happens next... is up to you."*

CHAPTER 21

The Light Between Dreams

To enjoy good health, to bring true happiness to one's family, to bring peace to all, one must first discipline and control one's own mind. If a man can control his mind he can find the way to Enlightenment, and all wisdom and virtue will naturally come to him.

Buddha

SIA STOOD STILL, THE surreal world around her pressing in like a thick fog. The ground beneath her still shifted, rippling like the surface of a lake disturbed by an unseen force. Each step she took seemed to sink deeper into the dreamscape, the horizon around her bending in impossible angles. There was no true sense of direction here, just the feeling of floating, of being both a part of the dream and apart from it, as though she existed between worlds.

Than stood beside her, his presence a steady anchor in the chaos. Despite the overwhelming strangeness of the world around them, his calm, unwavering demeanor remained the same, grounding her when everything else seemed to slip away.

"You've been chosen for a reason, Sia," Than's voice rang through the stillness, his tone soft but powerful. "You walk the line between worlds, between life and death, light and dark, the known and the unknown. The power that courses through you is not your own, but a part of something far greater than you understand."

Sia turned to face him, her brow furrowed in confusion. She still didn't fully grasp what was happening, let alone the implications of the words he spoke. "So, what? I'm some kind of... divine tool? Some chosen one who's supposed to fix everything?" Her voice was tinged with frustration, her patience beginning to thin as the weight of her responsibility settled in.

Than gave a slow, almost imperceptible nod. "In a way, yes. You are the vessel for something far older and more powerful than you could imagine. Your magic is but a reflection of that power. But it is your choices, your will, that will decide how it is used."

Sia's heart raced at the gravity of his words. "And what happens if I make the wrong choice? If I don't have what it takes?" Her voice shook slightly despite her attempt at composure.

Than's eyes softened, the deep darkness within them momentarily flickering with something more gentle, more understanding. "You are not alone, Sia. You will never be. But the path you walk is yours alone to choose."

The wind shifted, stirring the strange mist around them, and Sia's gaze lifted to the sky. The stars were fading, their light dimming to a soft glow. The fabric of reality around her shimmered, bending and warping, the edges of the world beginning to unravel as though it were something not quite real. She stepped forward instinctively, drawn to the shifting, pulsing light at the center of it all.

"What is that?" Sia asked, her voice a mixture of awe and trepidation.

Than's gaze followed hers, and a flicker of something ancient passed over his face. "That, Sia Mason, is the heart of the void, the very source of your power. The gateway between realms. What lies within it is beyond understanding, beyond comprehension. But you will need to face it. You will need to understand it before you can truly unlock what you're capable of."

Sia hesitated, a wave of uncertainty washing over her. "What if I can't do it?" she whispered, her words barely audible.

Than's voice was steady, unwavering. "You can do it. But you must trust yourself, and you must trust the bond we share. That is what will guide you, no matter what comes."

Sia looked up at him, her eyes searching his face for any sign of doubt, any hint that what he said might be more than just empty encouragement. But all she found was unwavering certainty. The bond between them, though divine and mysterious, was something real. She could feel it, pulsing beneath her skin, as though it were a part of her very soul.

With a deep breath, Sia stepped forward, her resolve slowly hardening. "Alright. I'll do it. I'll face whatever's coming. But I don't know how to stop it, Than. How do I stop a force that's been waiting for eons?"

Than's gaze softened as he placed a hand on her shoulder, a protective gesture that filled her with warmth. "You will stop it, Sia. Not through strength alone, but through your understanding. Through your choices. And in that, you will not walk alone."

The air around them began to hum, the world seeming to respond to her words, to the decision she had made. Than's presence grew stronger, and for a brief moment, the world seemed to hold its breath.

Than's voice, usually calm and controlled, softened further. "There is more to you, Sia, than you understand. It is time you learn what lies within. I will share with you a fragment of my memories, a gift to guide you."

Sia's breath caught, and she turned to look at him, confusion and curiosity mixing. "Your memories?"

"Yes," Than said. "I am of the Dream Realm, and I hold knowledge of the ancient forces. I will pass a small piece of that knowledge to you, so that you may understand your power and how it connects to the realms you now walk between. This gift will help you in the trials ahead, for they are coming."

Sia nodded, uncertain, but she knew she had no other choice. She closed her eyes, and almost immediately, she felt a strange pull, an unseen tether between her and Than. A sharp sensation, like a jolt of electricity, ran through her body as his memories flooded into her mind. Visions of ancient battles, forgotten spells, and divine rituals swirled before her eyes. The power of the Dream Realm, of gods and immortals, of magic beyond her understanding, rushed through her, imbuing her with a sense of ancient knowledge.

Her body trembled as the power coursed through her, but Than was there, steadying her with his presence, guiding her through the storm of knowledge that flooded her mind. She saw glimpses of herself, of her own magic, woven into the tapestry of the realms, part of something far grander than she had ever imagined.

The visions stopped as abruptly as they had started, leaving Sia breathless, disoriented. Her hands shook as she steadied herself, the weight of the knowledge sinking in. She opened her eyes to find Than watching her closely, his expression unreadable, yet full of understanding.

"You now carry a fragment of my power, Sia," he said softly. "You are ready, but the path ahead will not be easy. What you've learned will guide you, but you must choose when and how to wield it."

Sia swallowed, her mind still reeling from the experience. "I don't feel ready for all of this."

Than's gaze softened with a flicker of affection. "You are more ready than you think. You've always had the strength within you. Now you simply know how to use it."

Sia closed her eyes, focusing on the energy within her, she could feel it now, the magic she had always struggled to understand. It was different now, more fluid, more attuned to the vast powers of the realms she was tied to. And with it, a deeper sense of responsibility settled in her heart.

She nodded, a new resolve solidifying within her. "Alright. I'll face what's coming. But I'll need your help. Always."

Than placed a hand on her shoulder once more, his touch warm and comforting. "You will have it. And together, we will see this through."

With that, the weight of the unseen lifted slightly. Sia felt something within her change, like the first light breaking through the fog. She was ready, or at least, ready enough to face what lay ahead. And she wasn't alone.

The dream faded like smoke through her fingers.

Sia opened her eyes slowly, breath catching in her throat. The stone ceiling of the borrowed chamber in Dobahold greeted her, its arching construction clearly chiseled by practiced hands, symmetrical, purposeful. The room was lit by a single hanging lantern that swayed faintly from its iron chain, casting soft golden circles on the smooth, flagstone floor. The quiet creak of the chain echoed in the stillness, a reminder that even underground, the world moved. The air held the scent of carved stone and warmed metal, touched by the faint tang of old spellwork, like something ancient had breathed once and never quite left. Her body felt weightless, yet heavy at once, as though part of her still lingered in the dream-realm. Her heart pounded with the echo of what she had seen, what she had felt.

She tried to move, but something warm and soft pressed against her side.

Ella.

The other girl had curled up against her during the night, one arm draped protectively over Sia's waist. Though she was awake, Ella's eyes remained half-closed, her breathing steady and calm. She wasn't asleep, Sia could tell, but she wasn't entirely present either, watching over her with the kind of peace Sia rarely saw from her.

"Hey," Sia whispered, voice dry.

Ella smiled faintly without opening her eyes. "Welcome back."

Sia blinked. "You... stayed?"

"I figured if something tried to steal you through a dream, I'd punch it in the face."

Sia chuckled softly, then winced. Her body still ached, even if the pain felt distant.

"You okay?" Ella asked.

Sia nodded slowly. "Yeah. I... I saw him again. Than."

Ella blinked. "Than? Is that the same one from your dreams?"

Sia nodded again. "Yeah. He's the one I always see there. Thanatos, he told me his full name this time. But I call him Than. It feels more... manageable."

Ella looked at her now, more alert. "Did he help?"

"Yes," Sia said. "And he gave me something. Knowledge. Like a... map made of memories. I don't understand it all yet, but it's there."

To demonstrate, she held out her hand and let her fingers spread slightly. A soft, silvery glow gathered in her palm, flickering like moonlight on water. The magic danced gently along her skin, effortless, calm.

Ella's eyes widened. "That... that didn't used to come so easy."

Sia nodded, a small, confident smile curling on her lips. "I know." But even as she said it, a flicker of doubt crossed her eyes. The magic felt different now, stronger, deeper, but also heavier. Older. She wasn't sure where it ended and she began. The thought unsettled her, just enough to dim her smile.

Ella brushed Sia's hair back gently, revealing her forehead. "Then we'll figure it out together."

After resting a little longer in silence, the two girls found fresh clothing laid out for them, brought quietly while Sia slept. A small gesture of hospitality, folded neatly on a nearby bench. Sia's was simple, practical: a soft charcoal sweater, a plain tunic, and fitted trousers with reinforced seams, just like the kind she preferred to wear back home. Ella's was far more stylish, flared dark jeans tucked into calf-high boots, and a fitted jacket over a layered tunic dyed in elegant jewel tones that shimmered faintly under the lantern light.

They washed quickly, brushing away the last remnants of dream-stiff limbs and the grime of their earlier trials, and dressed in quiet companionship. There was comfort in the normalcy of it, hands running through tangled hair, boots pulled on with practiced ease.

Only once they were ready did they step from their chamber and into the heart of Dobahold. Their boots clicked softly against the well-polished stone walkways, the sounds of their steps swallowed by the vaulted corridors. The deeper they walked, the more obvious it became, this place had not been carved by monsters, but built with care and precision. Wooden beams lined with metal bands supported doorways, glowing crystal sconces illuminated intersections with a steady warmth, and stone murals along the walls depicted tales of dragons and magic in clean, deliberate detail. They found Marcus and Tobias waiting in the cavernous main hall. The space buzzed faintly with activity, distant voices murmuring in low tones, the ring of metal on metal from a forge hidden beyond a nearby archway, and the steady hum of enchantments etched into the hall's foundations. The golden glow from overhead lanterns gave the chamber a gentle warmth, casting long shadows across the banners that hung between carved columns bearing the old runes of dragonkind. Tobias leaned against a crate, checking his gear, while Marcus chatted with one of the elder wardens.

Lord Domingo approached as they neared.

"You've rested?" he asked, his voice gentler than usual.

Sia nodded. "As much as I could."

Domingo's gaze shifted to Ella. "Then it is time."

He drew from his side a sheathed weapon wrapped in deep crimson cloth. With reverence, he offered it to Ella.

"This blade was forged in the heart of Dobahold, cooled in dragonfire and blessed by our wardens. It has never been drawn. You will know when to unsheathe it. Do not do so until then."

Ella accepted it with both hands, her face solemn. "Thank you."

Tobias approached next, one of the younger dragons handing him a crate.

"Restock," the youth said. "All the blessed blades you lost. Glyph rounds too. We even fixed your old throwing knife with the cracked handle."

Tobias grunted approval, already checking the edges. "About time someone showed some respect for good tools."

Finally, Sia turned, and found her pack and umbrella resting neatly beside Marcus's boots.

"I thought I lost these," she murmured.

"You did," Marcus said with a smile. "But Dobahold is good at finding what's still needed."

Sia picked up the pack and slung it over her shoulder. Her fingers curled around the umbrella's worn handle, runes faintly gleaming where her palm touched them. It felt... heavier. More real. Like it remembered everything she had just seen.

As the others finished checking gear and preparing to leave, Sia stood quietly, her eyes drawn to the echo of the dream still ringing in the back of her mind.

A storm was coming; but now, she carried a spark to meet it.

As they made ready to depart, Marcus remained by the edge of the chamber, his arms crossed, his expression thoughtful. Sia looked over to him, a flicker of expectation in her chest.

"You're not coming with us?" she asked.

Marcus shook his head slowly. "Not yet. Eric needs me here. The mages who helped start your training, some of them are... uneasy. They sense the shift in power. In you. In Dobahold. There's tension brewing under the surface, and Eric's been doing his best to keep it calm, but he can't handle it alone."

Sia tilted her head. "They're afraid of me?"

"They don't understand you," Marcus said. "And people fear what they don't understand. But give them time. Once you've shown them who you really are, they'll see."

There was a softness in his voice, one that lingered just long enough to leave an ache in her chest. She gave a reluctant nod.

"Then I guess we'll see each other after," she said quietly.

"You'd better," Marcus said with a faint grin. "Don't let anyone steal your umbrella again."

Sia hesitated for a moment, then stepped closer, eyes locking with his. "Thanks for finding it."

Marcus opened his mouth to reply, but before he could, Sia leaned up and pressed a swift, warm kiss to his lips. It wasn't long, just enough to say what words couldn't. Her hand lingered on his arm a moment longer before she stepped back, cheeks flushed but eyes steady.

Marcus blinked, surprised, then offered a crooked, stunned grin. "You, uh... really like that umbrella."

Sia laughed softly, already turning to join Ella and Tobias. "Shut up, Marcus."

CHAPTER 22

Night Bleeds After Us

And can you offer me proof of your existence? How can you, when neither modern science nor philosophy can explain what life is?

Masamune Shirow

THE ENTRANCE TO DOBAHOLD, hidden behind the wooded hills on the outskirts of Apple Grove, vanished from view as they drove away. The heavy stone doors had sealed silently behind them, cutting off the path to the underground sanctuary, the last refuge of dragons, guardians of ancient power locked in a secret war with demons and darker things. Above ground, the quaint town of Apple Grove looked quiet, peaceful. But beneath its sleepy surface, Dobahold had armed them, warned them.

Now they were alone in the open world again, and the evening haze thickened like a veil behind them. The air beyond its protective walls felt raw, like something waiting had been let in.

Tobias drove, hands steady on the wheel, eyes flicking between the road and the mirrors. The muscle in his jaw worked in a slow rhythm. He hadn't said much since they crossed the outer wards. Sia sat in the passenger seat, arms crossed over her stomach, staring out the window as if trying to catch the last glimpse of safety.

Sia hadn't spoken much since Dobahold, not after the last meeting with the wardens, not after the unsettling way Tobias had ordered her into the car with a tone that invited no argument. The passenger seat felt too empty beside her. She kept glancing into the mirror, unsure of what to look for. All there was for her at the moment in the world anymore was herself, Ella and Tobias.

Sia pressed her palm against her chest, trying to calm the rapid beat beneath her ribs.

"Everything's fine, right?" Sia asked finally, trying to sound casual. "No one's following us?"

Tobias didn't answer right away.

"We should've gone west," Ella muttered from the back seat. Her voice was tight, focused. She'd been watching the road just as sharply as Tobias, though with less certainty in what she was looking for.. "You know they'll expect us to head toward the Rift. Everyone does."

"We're not everyone," Tobias said flatly. "And they're already following us."

Sia blinked. "Wait, what?"

"I saw the tail three intersections ago. Black sedan, mirror tint. Never passed us, never turned off."

Ella leaned forward, tension creeping into her voice. Her fingers curled around the door handle as she glanced back through the window. . "Do you think they're Church?"

"No," Tobias said. "Too smooth. Too calm. They're not watching us. They're herding us."

Sia swallowed. "Demons?"

"Worse," he muttered. "Demons that think like people."

In the rearview mirror, the black sedan was still there. Headlights low, calm, steady. Too steady.

Then a second car appeared, this one gray, unremarkable, slipping in behind the first like a shark's fin beneath dark water.

Tobias's knuckles whitened on the wheel. "Buckle up."

"What are you, " Sia began.

The accelerator hit the floor.

The pickup truck roared to life, tires screaming against the cracked asphalt. The rear bed rattled under the sudden torque, sending Ella scrambling to climb out the back window and into the truck bed. Sia joined her a second later, bracing herself with one hand on the roll bar, the other already beginning to draw a glyph in the air.

They had seconds.

From the alley shadows, something moved, too fast, too silent. A shape peeled from the wall, human-shaped but elongated, smeared like it had been painted in shadow and set loose. It bounded toward the truck, its feet not touching the pavement.

"On your left!" Ella shouted.

Sia turned, flicked a lighter and blasted it with a jet of concentrated flame. The creature shrieked as it dissolved mid-air, leaving a smear of oily smoke.

Then came more, three, five, eight of them, racing along the walls, leaping across rooftops, some scrambling on all fours like starving things.

Tobias swerved to throw one off, his knuckles white on the wheel. "Hold on!" he barked.

Ella crouched as the truck jolted, slashing out with her dagger as one shadowy figure landed on the tailgate. Her blade met its chest, and the thing split open into strands of black mist.

Sia spun around, casting wide arcs of lightning that danced like silver whips. Two of the creatures were flung off the truck, their forms collapsing mid-leap.

The pickup's speed wasn't saving them, it was drawing more in.

More shapes dropped from the overpasses, hunched things with suits that melted into the night. One landed on the hood with a thud, clawed hands punching toward the windshield.

Tobias ducked and swerved the csar clipping into a cement column. The impact knocked the creature off, but also shattered part of the front bumper.

"We are not going to make it if we stay on the road!" Sia called.

"I know!" Tobias shouted, spinning the wheel.

He veered down an access ramp toward the industrial district. Around them, shadows pursued like a plague, leaping onto fences, sprinting across parked cars, howling with inhuman glee.

Ella's dagger flashed again. Sia threw a barrier behind them, catching a pursuing group mid-charge, the spell exploded into a concussive wave that sent bodies flying.

The mall loomed ahead, its half-collapsed sign flickering like a dying star: Hollow Echo.

"We make our stand there!" Tobias yelled.

And then they were swallowed by the dark.

Sia twisted to look out the back window. One of the "drivers", a tall figure in a too-tight black suit, blinked out of existence for a half second, only to reappear closer. Its eyes glowed faintly red through the windshield.

"They're not even trying to be subtle anymore!" she shouted.

"Then neither will I," Tobias snapped.

He took a hard right, barreling into a half-flooded alley. The car bounced, scraping its undercarriage. Sparks lit the air. Ahead, a barricade loomed. He didn't slow down.

"Sia, shield us!"

She flung up her hands and cast raw magic in a wide cone. The barricade exploded outward in a burst of kinetic force, splinters and rust flying. They burst through the smoke and landed hard onto a descending service ramp.

The black sedan clipped the edge of the barrier and spun, but the gray car followed perfectly, too perfectly, gliding through the chaos like it wasn't touching the ground.

Ella reached down, drawing a short silver dagger from her boot. Strapped along her other thigh, barely visible beneath her coat, was one of Tobias's spare short swords, compact, matte-bladed, etched with faint warding runes. She hadn't asked to carry it. Tobias had given it to her wordlessly before they left Dobahold. She'd worn it since, feeling the weight of his trust every step of the way. Her eyes burned with quiet resolve.. "We're not going to outrun them forever."

"We're not," Tobias said grimly. "We're heading somewhere we can make a stand."

Sia looked at him sharply. "Where?"

"The Mall," he said. "The Hollow Echo."

Sia's heart sank. She remembered the stories. Hollow Echo Mall had been shut down during the last global pandemic, left abandoned when the town never fully recovered. Locals claimed strange things still moved inside after dark, and rumors of hauntings had given it a second life as a place to avoid. No one went there willingly. Certainly not at night.

Nobody walked out of the Hollow Echo Mall after nightfall.

Not unless they were dragged.

CHAPTER 23

Hollow Echoes Beneath the Skylight

To live is to suffer, to survive is to find some meaning in the suffering.

Nietzsche

THE HOLLOW ECHO MALL had once been a monument to consumerism, glass atriums, indoor fountains, a vaulted skylight that opened above the central plaza like an artificial cathedral. Waterless fountains stood cracked and bone-dry, their ornate basins filled with dirt and wind-blown leaves. Fake plastic trees, faded and dust-caked, curled around planters like frozen sentinels from a long-lost artificial forest. Statues of shopping families with wide smiles and permanent welcomes lined the halls like the ghosts of capitalism.

Some of the shops remained half-lit or open just a crack, never fully closed, only abandoned mid-collapse. Faded signs promised last-minute sales, mannequins stood naked or askew behind smeared glass, and old pop music warbled from broken ceiling speakers like the last breath of a dying world.

Storefronts gaped like open mouths. The light filtering through the cracked skylight above painted everything in a haze of gray and decay.

The trio moved cautiously through the lower concourse, heading toward the main atrium. Sia's spell lit the space in flickers, while Ella covered their rear with dagger in hand. Tobias led, eyes narrowed, moving with practiced caution.

"They stopped following," Ella whispered.

"No," Tobias said. "They're waiting."

A sound answered him, low and slow, like bone dragged across tile.

Sia shivered. "They're already inside."

They reached the central court, a vast open space beneath the broken skylight. Overgrown plants curled through shattered benches. A ruined escalator jutted like a ribcage from the floor, its metal teeth twisted and rusting. Glass elevators loomed like skeletal towers, their tracks stained with grime, some cracked open where demons had already begun to climb through. The second-floor walkway encircled the court, lined with busted railing and gaps where the floor had collapsed inward. Fake trees cast twisted shadows as old music hummed and warbled, echoing from broken speakers in surreal mockery of normalcy.

Suddenly, motion above, shadowy figures crawling upside-down across the walkways, dropping with animal grace to the floor below. From every hall, every ruined stair, they poured in, Men in Black Suits, faces waxen and too-perfect, eyes glowing faintly red. With them came things that had never been human, shadows walking in broken geometry, claws scratching along the walls, scaling support columns and leaping from balconies like insects in coordinated swarm. Tobias shouted, blades drawn, as the first wave charged.

They fought.

Sia's magic danced through the air, fire and lightning splitting the dark. She hurled a blazing arc into a pack crawling down the escalator rails, sending the whole contraption shuddering and catching fire. When a shadow leapt from the second-floor railing, she diverted it midair with a gust of concussive wind, smashing it through the glass of an old perfume shop.

Tobias vaulted onto the central kiosk, using the height to sweep his blades across two oncoming figures. He kicked over a mannequin to trip a crawling shadow, then dropped and finished it with a precise stab through the neck. He moved like he knew every inch of the terrain, leaping from a fallen fountain basin to a toppled bench, keeping their flanks clear.

Ella had climbed halfway up the cracked elevator track. With Tobias's sword in hand, she used the steel frame for leverage, swinging down like an executioner on a shadow beast scaling the wall beneath her. When she landed, she slammed the blade into the tile, sending a small holy shockwave rippling outward. Around the girl luminous armor had suddenly formed and there was a golden light to her eyes that had not been their prior. Tobias regarded this even as he sidestepped a demon's claws to slice it's arm off at the shoulder. He had seen this only once before, a Templar had been chosen as a vessel. All he could do now was hoped the angelic force that had suddenly joined with her would protect his sister.

They used everything, the planters, the fountains, the shattered upper railings, to funnel, divide, and trap their enemies. The mall was no longer just a place. It was a weapon in their hands.

Sia pivoted to defend Tobias's flank, casting a spiraling shield of light that cracked under the impact of three diving shadows. One got through. Claws like obsidian raked across her side, tearing into fabric and flesh. She screamed, the force of it sending her crashing into a cracked display window. Glass rained around her, slicing skin, catching in her hair. Her coat was in tatters now, her blouse soaked in blood from a wound that pulsed with searing heat.

She forced herself up, one hand glowing with healing light, the other still clutching her focus. Her magic stitched the flesh just enough to keep her standing, but her limbs trembled, blood trickling down her arm. Her fingers curled tighter around the thing she used to channel her power, not a wand, nor a staff, but a familiar, battered black umbrella. The fabric had long since burned away, leaving only the polished handle and slender iron ribs, runes scrawled haphazardly along its length in multiple languages. A ridiculous thing, once chosen for convenience. Now it was bound to her will by repetition and ritual, a conduit shaped not by tradition, but by sheer defiance at having nothing else to work with and the quickened ingenuity to use what she had at hand.

Ella saw the hit and lunged forward, driving her blade through the creature's back with a shout. She didn't say a word to Sia, but the look in her eyes said everything, Get up. We need you.

Sia staggered back into formation, breathing hard, her magic sparking wild in the air around her.

As Sia staggered back into formation, breathing hard, a new sound resonated through the shattered halls of Hollow Echo Mall, a rhythmic chant, deep and resonant, echoing like the tolling of ancient bells.

"In nomine lucis!"

A burst of radiant white light exploded from one of the side corridors. Through the blinding glow stepped a squadron of Templar warriors, armored in battered steel and flowing white tabards marked with crimson crosses and embroidered holy runes. More practical kevlar and tactical coats draped over the reliquary gear reminded all that they had not suddenly gone back in time. The guns at their hips an slung along their backs helped with this as well. Their leader, Garran, a towering figure with silver-streaked hair and piercing blue eyes, raised his blade high. Divine fire wreathed the sword's edge as he roared a command, his voice booming over the chaos.

"For the Light!"

The Templars surged forward, their blades and spell-guns blazing. Glyphs carved into their armor shimmered brilliantly, deflecting claws and dark energy as they plunged into the horde. Garran moved at their head, wielding his relic blade with calculated fury. Every stroke cleaved through shadowy forms, leaving trails of holy fire in its wake.

"Late as usual!" Tobias shouted, slicing through another demon as Garran's squad approached.

Garran laughed sharply, parrying a clawed strike and cleaving the attacker in two. "Saving your hide again, Tobias? Feels like old times."

"Couldn't let you get bored in retirement," Tobias shot back, spinning gracefully to decapitate a shadowy figure lunging from above.

Garran glanced toward Ella, eyes widening slightly at the shimmering holy aura and ethereal wings glowing behind her as she struck down another demon.

"By the Saints, Tobias, does your sister have an Archangel whispering in her ear?" Garran called out, voice tinged with genuine awe.

Tobias smirked despite the chaos. "I can only hope it's something like that! Just try to keep up, old man!"

Two Templar women flanked Garran, each a seamless blend of grace and lethal precision. One spun fluidly, chanting ancient prayers, her blades releasing luminous glyphs that exploded on contact, scattering demons in burning fragments. The other knelt briefly, steadying her rune-carved spell-gun and firing bolts of silvery light, each shot a precise invocation that punched through demonic armor, igniting foes from within.

The Templars moved as one, disciplined and fearless, carving a path of salvation through darkness. Their arrival turned the battle, briefly stemming the tide and giving Sia, Ella, and Tobias a critical reprieve.

One of the Templars, a man in a soot-smeared tabard, face half-hidden behind a rune-inscribed scarf, paused just long enough to place a hand on Sia's head. A soft glow passed from his palm into her, warm and weightless like sunlight on water. Holy magic surged through her wounds, knitting flesh, erasing pain. The blood vanished. The searing edge of her injuries dulled to a memory.

Her clothing, however, remained in tatters. Smoke-stained fabric clung to her in ribbons, the remnants of her coat hanging limp, the hem of her blouse scorched and shredded. Yet she stood straighter now, steady, renewed. And the umbrella in her grip gleamed faintly, as if it, too, had been reminded of its purpose.

Ella stood at the center of it all, holding the line with grit and prayer, her angelic wings blazing defiantly.

But then the air trembled.

From the far corridor came a new presence.

Sia turned.

And froze.

She stepped out of the smoke and ruin as if the mall had opened itself to her. Long black coat, heels striking the tile like hammers, wings flared behind her. Horns curled from her brow, and her crimson eyes gleamed like twin coals.

Mia.

Sia couldn't move. Couldn't breathe.

Her sister was alive.

And terrifying.

Mia raised a single hand. The demons halted mid-charge. Then they bowed.

Sia's voice broke on her lips. "Mia...?"

Mia smiled. Cold. Regal. And utterly not herself. She pointed through the ruined glass atrium above.

"You want answers?" she purred. "You want me?" Her voice turned sharp, sing-song. "Then follow me, sister."

Sia looked up, and saw it. Through the broken skylight, just beyond the crumbling edge of the parking lot, a fracture in the sky shimmered like oil on water. A gate. Open. Breathing. The real sanctum was not inside. It was waiting just outside the mall.

Sia ran.

Ella and Tobias followed as the shadows gave chase.

The Templars regrouped, holding the corridor.

"Go!" Garran roared. "We'll hold them here!"

The women with him nodded once, moving in unison to cover the retreat. Their spell-guns lit the mall in flashes of blue fire and scripture.

Tobias met Garran's eyes one last time.

"Don't die on me."

"Not planning to," Garran grunted, raising his blade with grim determination. "You still owe me a drink after this."

Then came the roar of the enemy.

The shadows surged again, thicker this time, snarling as they poured in from shattered display windows and buckled escalators. The floor groaned beneath their weight. Spell-guns cracked in divine rhythm, hurling streaks of silver and flame into the tide, but still the tide rose.

A massive figure barreled through the fog, a horned brute with armor made of bone and shadow. Garran met it head-on, his relic blade slamming into the creature's gut in a blaze of righteous fire. The two women Templars fell into motion beside him, one chanting mid-spin as glowing glyphs burst from her blades, the other laying down cover fire with her spell-gun, every round a miniature invocation that seared sigils into flesh.

"Go!" Garran bellowed again over the chaos, voice raw.

Sia didn't look back. She couldn't.

The trio tore down the corridor, boots hammering cracked tile slick with ichor. Smoke and red light painted the walls around them in flickering streaks, and the mall screamed, a cacophony of inhuman howls, shattering glass, and burning scripture.

They burst through the shattered doors into the night air, lungs heaving, heat at their backs.

The gate pulsed ahead of them, suspended above the parking lot like a great wound in the sky. It shimmered, breathed, called.

Sia felt it tug at her very bones.

Behind them, the mall belched fire and fury, the Templars still fighting, still holding.

And so the trio ran, into the dark, into the threshold.

Toward fate.

CHAPTER 24

Where the World Unravels

Life can only be understood backwards; but it must be lived forwards.

Soren Kierkegaard

THEY BURST FROM THE mall's shattered front into a landscape twisted by something deeper than magic, something mythic. What had once been a cracked parking lot was now a yawning dreamscape, half-remembered from nightmares. The earth sloped in unnatural curves. Pavement curled like parchment exposed to flame. Cars floated in the air, suspended mid-twist as if frozen mid-explosion.

Above it all, the sky churned, not with clouds, but layers of color and static, like a corrupted aurora. Lightning forked sideways. The stars blinked in and out, each in their own rhythm. A broken moon hovered low and close, casting fractured silver light like shattered glass.

And in the center stood the gate.

It rose like a jagged monolith, an open wound in reality. Its frame was composed of twisted metal and bone, stitched with strands of golden thread that pulsed like veins. Stairs spiraled upward into it, steps made of stone, smoke, and memory. With every rise, the stairway shimmered like heat on summer asphalt, vanishing and reforming depending on how one looked at it.

Sia stepped forward slowly, the tug in her chest now a roar. "It's not just a portal. It's a passage into a place between what is and what was meant to be."

Ella followed close behind, armor catching the unnatural light. "This... feels like walking into someone's dream."

Tobias scanned the landscape, knives drawn. "No," he said. "Worse. We're walking into a god's unfinished thought."

Behind them, the ground shuddered.

The mall, still whole and crumbling, vomited flame and shadow. The sound of battle had changed, replaced by the shriek of unstable geometry. Demons poured from the front, howling. Shadows streamed in from beyond the treeline, circling, converging. The entire world groaned as if in rejection of the gate's presence.

Sia turned, panicked. "They're coming."

Ella's eyes narrowed. "Then we hold here."

Tobias grabbed Sia's shoulder. "You go. We'll hold the line."

"No," Sia said. "Not without you."

"You said it yourself," he growled. "The sanctum is beyond. You're the only one who can get through."

Ella lifted her blade. "You save your sister. We'll buy your time."

The first wave hit, shadow-creatures streaking across the distorted earth like cracks in glass. But Tobias and Ella didn't flinch.

Tobias surged forward, blades glinting in the stuttering dreamlight. His cloak, black, heavy, edged in deep red, fluttered behind him, bearing the unmistakable cross and twin keys of the Templar order. The hood was pulled low over his brow, but not enough to hide the wear and blood caked into his jawline. Old wounds reopened beneath torn armor, a thin red trail sliding down his left side. But he still moved with coiled strength, sharp and relentless.

As he ducked beneath a slashing claw, he took a mental inventory: four throwing knives left, one blessed dagger, two charges in the last holy glyph crystal on his belt. No time to reload, no time to hesitate. He kicked off a crumbling bit of curb, flipping mid-air to drive both daggers into the shoulders of a horned monstrosity. It collapsed beneath him, and he rolled free before the next could pounce.

"Still got a few rounds left in me," he growled, parrying another beast's claws with a clang that echoed like a bell warped in water.

Ella was radiant beside him, a holy fury anchored in calm resolve. Unlike Tobias, she seemed untouched by fatigue. The divine magic that flowed through her lit her from within. Translucent golden armor shimmered over her body, an ethereal second skin woven of light and will. Her face was serene, composed, yet her eyes burned with righteous clarity. Where Tobias fought like a shadowed blade, she was the flare of dawn.

Her wings unfurled to their full span, casting divine light across the nightmarish terrain. She pivoted low, sweeping a shadow's legs from beneath it, then brought Tobias's sword down in a clean arc that sent shockwaves through the ground. Her long coat still trailed from beneath the armor, torn from the earlier fight but untouched by blood, as though the sanctity within repelled the world's decay.

They fought like they were buying seconds with blood, and they were. But those seconds mattered.

Behind them, Sia paused at the threshold, looking back one last time.

"You don't have to do this," she called.

Tobias didn't stop moving. "We already did."

Ella turned, eyes fierce beneath her halo. "Go. This is our stand."

And so Sia turned away, the sounds of war growing distant with every step up the spiral. But Tobias and Ella remained, two figures of fire and steel holding the line at the edge of a world that had already started to fall.

Sia turned away as the noise swallowed her name. Her clothing hung in shreds, charred at the edges from the spells she had loosed in the mall, stained by dust, ichor, and smoke. Torn sleeves revealed the healing scars of earlier wounds, closed by magic but not erased. Her boots were nearly ruined, one heel broken. Her arms trembled as she reached for the stair, yet her gaze never wavered. She looked like someone dragged through fire, yet still walking. Still burning.

The stairs shimmered under her feet, each one humming with power. She stepped forward, and nearly stumbled. Her legs shook beneath her, muscles still raw from battle. The first stair rose higher than expected, and when she stepped again, the space beneath her foot warped, stretching the distance until her limbs burned with the strain.

Around her, the world buckled. Geometry dissolved into curves and contradictions. Time pulsed. On one stair, she saw the reflection of herself as a child, playing in the orchard. On the next, her worst fear, Mia, dead, eyes glassy and cold. She flinched and almost fell, catching herself on a rail that hadn't been there a moment before.

Sounds twisted into music and static, laughter one moment, whispers the next. A phantom breeze tugged at her ruined clothes, carrying the smell of fire and flowers, of old parchment and forgotten rain.

She climbed, breath ragged, her body aching with every step. The weight of magic clung to her like chains and wings at once. She had to fight for each rise, not against a foe, but against the unreality that tried to convince her she had never been climbing at all.

One stair crumbled beneath her foot and rebuilt itself backward. Another pulsed with heat like a heartbeat. There was no rhythm. No mercy.

But she kept going.

Because at the top, beyond this spiral, beyond this madness, was Mia.

And Sia would break the world open again to reach her.

She climbed.

The dream grew darker.

And the world unraveled behind her.

And the world became silence.

CHAPTER 25

The Last Bond

The only way to make sense out of change is to plunge
into it, move with it, and join the dance.

Alan Watts

THE SANCTUM'S DOORS HISSED open with a breath like dying gods.

Sia stepped inside, alone.

The chamber was vast, domed, blackened by smoke, the walls
etched with pulsing red veins of hellstone. Runes slithered across every
surface, never staying still. Overhead, a fractured sun hung in the air,
casting shifting shadows across the floor like searching hands.

At the center stood Gomath, or rather, what he had once chosen to
wear. As she approached, his flesh split open like rotted bark peeling
from a tree, and something far worse stepped free.

He rose from his mortal shell like a god of nightmares. Towering, obsidian-skinned, molten-veined, his every movement cracked the
floor. Horns spiraled from his skull like jagged black lightning, and
behind his burning eyes swam too many faces, all screaming, none his
own. His mouth split open in a grin too wide for anatomy, and when
he laughed, the echoes came from the walls, the floor, the air itself.

"You expected robes and riddles," he said, his voice like tectonic
plates grinding together. "You thought this would be clever. But I am
not a game. I am not a man. I am the knife that cuts Heaven's throat."

Sia froze. Magic trembled at her fingertips, unruly and uncertain.
Her heart raced, the magnitude of him anchoring her in place. He
wasn't just a monster, he was inevitable.

And then her eyes found Mia.

Bound in coils of shadow-forged chain, her twin knelt like a conquered queen at Gomath's feet. She looked almost like Sia, nearly identical in face and frame, but the resemblance was framed by something far darker. Mia's skin was a dusky, charcoal hue, marked with faint veins of glowing red. Two curling horns swept back from her brow, polished and ridged like obsidian. Her eyes, once ocean-blue like Sia's, now glowed an eerie, unholy crimson.

Wings of leathery black stretched behind her, torn but still vast and powerful, and a sinuous tail coiled against the floor like a waiting serpent. Despite the chains and her kneeling posture, there was a feral elegance to her, something predatory and tragic all at once.

She was Sia's reflection warped through flame and shadow. A mirror image rewritten in the language of hell.

Her crimson eyes didn't even blink. Her wings, torn but terrible, flexed like living blades.

"She won't hear you," Gomath purred, each syllable dragging power. "She's perfect now. Fearless. Loyal. Yours no longer."

Sia's voice caught in her throat. "She's still my sister."

"Then let's find out," he murmured, and the chains snapped.

Mia moved like lightning, a blur of flame and shadow. One moment she was kneeling. The next, she was on Sia.

They struck the ground with a thunderous crash that shook loose the loose stones and dust around them. Mia's claws came down like curved daggers, glinting with demonic fire. Her teeth bared in a snarl not quite her own, too wide and too cold. Sia twisted just in time, the razored strike missing her by inches as it carved a gash into the stone where her heart had been a second before. She scrawled a warding glyph mid-air, the lines burning with hastily summoned light, but Mia's talon sliced through it with a guttural roar, shattering the spell as if it were paper. The energy burst apart in a crackle of sparks that stung Sia's cheek, leaving the scent of scorched ozone in its wake. Sparks and blood danced in the air.

Sia didn't raise her hand to strike. Every part of her screamed to defend herself, to retaliate, but she held fast to restraint like a lifeline, refusing to hurt the sister she had only just found again.

She dodged, deflected, cried out, but she wouldn't harm her.

"You remember me," she gasped between blows. "You have to, Mia, please!"

But Mia was silent. Her face unreadable, her movements mechanical. Like something remote was piloting her body while the real Mia watched from behind glass.

Sia was slowing. A claw nicked her cheek. Another tore through her coat and the skin beneath, shallow but stinging. Mia straddled her now, pinning her to the floor. Her eyes glowed a deep, soulless crimson.

"You never really knew her," Gomath called from above. "She always hated being weaker. She envied you. She came to me gladly."

"Liar," Sia hissed, even as Mia's hand curled around her throat. "She loved me. We, "

"She was always meant to rise without you. And now, she will finish what I began."

Mia's hand tightened.

Sia fumbled with one hand in her pocket. Found the old charm bracelet, bent, burned, but still whole. She raised it between them.

"You gave this to me... when we were seven," she choked out. "Said we'd always match. Even when we fought. Even when we were scared."

Mia paused.

A tremor in her grip. Her claws shook.

And somewhere else entirely, inside, something shifted.

The air rippled, the sanctum's stone briefly flickering away to reveal a different place. A vast corridor of silver glass and drifting fog, where the ceiling arched like the sky yet bore no stars. The ground felt both solid and weightless, like walking on memory. There were no walls, only endless reflections, mirrors that showed Mia's face in countless variations, each twisted by regret or rage or loneliness.

The real battle wasn't in the sanctum now. It was here, in this place behind her eyes, where Gomath's whispers echoed louder than screams.

Mia stood in a place of mirrors and smoke, chained in a hall of twisted memories. She saw herself through Gomath's eyes: monstrous, triumphant, cruel.

But then, she heard Sia's voice.

Not a scream.

A memory.

We always match.

The chains cracked, first a spark, then a shuddering rattle that echoed like a funeral bell. The mirrors shivered as if struck by wind in a place where no air moved. One shattered. Then another. With each memory reclaimed, the fog receded, and the reflection staring back at Mia became more her own.

Her reflection changed.

In the sanctum, Mia blinked. Her claws withdrew. She stared at Sia, not as prey, but as a sister.

"I remember..." she whispered.

Gomath bellowed. "NO!"

Sia reached up, touched her sister's cheek. "Come back to me."

The spell-forged chains on Mia shattered like glass.

And the bond between them flared into light, bright, soul-deep, undeniable.

Together, they turned toward Gomath, who had begun to swell in size and wrath. His body twisted, doubling, tripling in size, clawed limbs sprouting like branches from a burning tree. His molten veins burned brighter as his skeletal wings unfurled and scraped the chamber walls. With every breath, the air grew hotter, thinner, like it was rejecting the presence of life.

The ground split beneath their feet as Gomath howled, the sound splitting the air with enough force to rupture stone. Reality bent at his presence, walls bled shadow, light inverted, and the runes in the sanctum thrashed as if trying to flee from their master.

But the sisters did not flinch.

Sia raised her hand first, the gesture fluid, precise, and full of purpose. Golden fire spiraled around her arm, curling like a dragon waking from slumber. Across from her, Mia mirrored the motion, her infernal magic wild and crackling, red lightning skipping across her skin like a living thing.

Their spells were not incantations but declarations. Their bond had become the incantation.

As one, they drew sigils into the air, light and shadow intertwining, not opposing, but completing.

Sia's voice rang out, firm and clear. "You took her from me."

Mia's followed, sharp and unflinching. "You tried to unmake us both."

Then, together: "We remember who we are."

Their magic collided into Gomath's center, a storm of divine brilliance and abyssal fire. The chamber erupted in light that roared like oceans and screamed like wind through dead leaves. The force was not a beam or a blast, it was a rewriting. A refusal.

Gomath shrieked as his form unraveled, limbs disintegrating mid-motion, wings torn from his back by invisible hands. The darkness within him writhed, desperate to find purchase, but there was nowhere left to run. The bond had found him wanting.

And Hell remembered what it was to burn.

CHAPTER 26
The Gate That Would Not Fall

Mankind is poised midway between the gods and the beasts.

Plotinus

THE SANCTUM'S GATE PULSED behind them, a jagged wound of dreamlight and ruin. Sia had vanished within, and the silence that followed was deceptive, because the battle outside had only begun.

Tobias stood at the edge of the cracked stone walkway, blades drawn, boots braced in the dust of the collapsing mall. His breath came steady, trained, but something twisted under his ribs as he stared into the charging horde. Sia was in that gate, somewhere beyond what he could understand, and for all his years of training, the things she faced now made his weapons feel like sticks.

Still, he fought.

Grudgingly, he admitted to himself that she had surpassed him. Not in technique. In force. In truth. He had been shaped to kill monsters in shadows. But Sia? Sia had stepped into the light of something divine, and Tobias was both proud and afraid of her.

Demons poured from the structure behind him, some crawling, others flying, all hungry. They came in waves: howling, skittering, slavering beasts twisted from flesh and memory, shaped by the same nightmare realm Gomath had opened.

Beside him, Ella glowed with holy light. Her armor shimmered like glass bathed in sunrise, her wings arcing wide in radiant arcs of energy.

Her sword hummed with restrained divinity, as though it, too, could feel the gravity of what was happening beyond the threshold.

"We can't let them reach the gate," Tobias growled, parrying a clawed strike and driving a blessed dagger through the throat of a leaping creature.

Ella nodded, spinning her blade in a high arc that burned through three beasts in a single swing. "We hold. As long as it takes."

The horde surged. Fire fell from above. Shadow-bound hounds and skeletal horned warriors emerged from the wreckage like smoke given form. Tobias moved like a wraith through them, each motion economic, exacting, deadly. His cloak billowed around him, the cross of the Church a red stain on black.

Ella stood firm, the light around her flaring with each invocation she chanted. Despite the blood streaking her armor and the burns rising along her arms, she felt no panic. The power within her guided her hands, filling her lungs with breath, even when her muscles screamed. Her sword felt like an extension of that light, not forged but called. She moved not just with training, but with trust. Her wounds stung, but did not slow her. It was as if the divine magic flowing through her smoothed over the edges of pain, made serenity possible even on a battlefield of ash.

She did not yield.

And when Tobias fell back beside her, she pivoted into him without needing to look, their movements so practiced, so natural, it felt choreographed by instinct. A massive demon, its mouth a vertical maw splitting its chest, surged toward them with three smaller shadow creatures flanking it. Tobias ducked beneath a snapping jaw, sliding low as Ella vaulted over him, bringing her sword down with a cry that cracked the air.

The blade hit true, severing one of the demon's arms, ichor spraying across the scorched stone. Tobias sprang up behind her and slammed a blessed dagger into the creature's spine. It shrieked, staggering, but didn't fall. The shadow monsters lunged, claws scraping over Ella's armor. She twisted, shielding Tobias with one wing as he spun and drove his second dagger into the nearest wraith's eye.

"I had that one," she muttered through gritted teeth.

"You're welcome," he shot back, barely dodging another strike.

They moved as one, light and shadow in perfect harmony, not needing to speak. As the demon reared back for one final charge, Ella raised her sword overhead, her voice becoming a song of judgment. Tobias stepped in front of her, both arms crossed with daggers raised, eyes burning with purpose.

Together, they struck. Her blade came down like a sunbeam turned blade, his daggers piercing deep. The demon convulsed, and burst into light and smoke.

But more were coming.

And still the demons came.

The next wave hit like a thunderclap. A dozen snarling beasts, all scale and sinew, charged through the smoke with eyes like molten coals and maws too wide for their skulls. Behind them slithered tendrils of animated shadow, creeping, clinging, whispering obscenities in tongues older than language.

Tobias and Ella stood in the center of it all, back to back, breath heaving.

It felt endless. Not in duration, but in weight.

Every second dragged like minutes. Every heartbeat became a drumbeat echoing across a killing field. Blades struck flesh, and flesh struck back. Ella's sword met bone with a crunch that sent vibrations up her arm. Tobias parried with a grunt, slamming his elbow into a beast's snarling jaw before finishing it with a twist of his dagger.

Their muscles burned. Blood slicked their hands and boots. The air reeked of sulfur and scorched ichor, and the noise, gods, the noise, was deafening. Screeches, howls, divine incantations, the crash of bodies and steel and claws.

Ella's light dimmed with every blow, but she pressed on, breath rasping like wind through shattered glass. The fire in her veins carried her, no longer as strength but as necessity. Tobias moved with the grace of the dying, precise, efficient, because there was no room for anything else.

He saw a shadow-beast leap for Ella and hurled a dagger with all the force of his fear. It struck true. She didn't look back, but he heard her whisper, "Thanks."

He didn't answer. He was too busy saving her again, and again, and again.

It was a storm of blades and light and death.

And still, it wasn't enough.

From the ruptured sky overhead, a monstrous silhouette descended, a creature of bone and molten iron, stitched together from the remnants of fallen archons. It landed with a quake, its roar sending cracks through the ground.

Ella faltered.

Tobias stepped in front of her, weapons crossed. "We can't stop that."

"Then we delay it," she replied, teeth gritted.

The creature lunged.

And then, The world shattered.

A wave of silver-blue force erupted from the east. Demons were thrown like leaves in a gale, scorched to cinders mid-air. Tobias was knocked to one knee, his breath ripped from his lungs. Ella fell back, shielding her eyes.

When the dust cleared, someone stood at the edge of the battlefield.

A cloaked figure.

Tall. Still. Hood drawn low.

Behind them, other shapes emerged, blades glowing, spells charging, strangers whose faces were hidden by glamour and shadow. Their silhouettes moved with the grace of old warriors, and their armor gleamed with subtle hints of scale motifs and dragonbone inlay. One wore a sigil shaped like a twisting horned serpent, barely visible beneath their cloak. Another whispered in a tongue that made the shadows recoil. Though Tobias did not know them, something in his blood stirred, an instinctive recognition, ancient and buried deep. The figure raised a staff, and the entire battlefield trembled.

Then, just briefly, the wind shifted the cloak.

Tobias saw a glint of hair, red as blood and flame.

His breath caught.

But before he could speak, the light flared again, And the gate swallowed everything.

CHAPTER 27

The Catalyst

The supreme paradox of all thought is the attempt
to discover something that thought cannot think.
Soren Kierkegaard

SILENCE LINGERED AFTER GOMATH'S final scream, not peaceful
but thick and hollow, as though the world itself was struggling
to remember how to breathe. The stillness carried weight, like
the moment after a symphony's final note has rung out, too full,
too sharp, too alive to be empty. In the distance, the faint echo
of chimes lingered, though no wind stirred them. Somewhere
beyond the broken walls, a low, harmonic hum resonated like
the pluck of a string from a forgotten god's harp, soft, endless,
and just slightly off, as if reality itself was holding its breath. The
sanctum was no longer a structure, it was ruin. The floor was
fractured glass and melted stone, the walls torn open to a sky that
had forgotten its color. A slow wind stirred dust and ash in aimless
circles.

Sia swayed where she stood, her knees trembling as the gold-
en fire around her sputtered. Beside her, Mia clutched her arm,
breath ragged, her other hand still glowing with embers of infernal
magic. They had done it. They had destroyed Gomath.

But something remained.

At the center of the scorched chamber, a ring of runes still pulsed,
low, red, and hungry. Gomath's spell, unanchored from his will but
not undone. It had grown unstable, its foundation cracked but not
collapsed. The glyphs pulsed in sequence, drawing not from a vessel

now, but from the raw, open leyline Gomath had torn through Sia's presence.

"It's not over," Sia whispered.

Mia looked up. "What do you mean?"

"The spell is still active. It's feeding on what's left of the rift. And if it doesn't close soon..." She didn't finish.

Beyond the gate, the void yawned wider, shapes twisting inside, echoes of what lay beyond the threshold of life and death. The space between. The Realm of Forgotten Gods.

Sia turned to Mia, eyes glistening. "It needs a sacrifice. A soul that matches the original signature. It's still trying to use me."

Mia's breath caught. "No. No, you're not, "

"I have to finish it. Not with rage. Not with hate. With choice."

Mia dropped to her knees, grasping Sia's coat like it might anchor her to the world. "I just got you back. You don't get to leave me again."

Sia bent down, resting her forehead to Mia's. "You were strong enough to come back. Let me be strong enough to stop this."

And then she stepped into the spell.

The glyphs surged upward, wrapping around her like a cocoon, but they did not devour, only held. Bound. Judged. The sound of them was like a choir submerged underwater, notes stretched and reverberating with unnatural grace. Her heartbeat slowed in her chest, each thump joined by the solemn toll of bells that no longer existed, yet she could hear them, one by one, counting down the end of something and the beginning of something else.

Light spilled out, and with it, Sia's awareness unraveled and expanded.

She stood in a place where time had not been born. Where language was feeling and thought was law. The mirrors of Mia's dream-space paled compared to this, an endless gallery of starlight and concepts, where every truth was both hidden and revealed.

And something... noticed her.

It did not have a name, but the world had called it many: The Source. The Flame. **Yaldabaoth.**

It drifted closer, not a creature, but an idea made flesh. Serpentine wings unfolded from a spiral of symbols, crowned with eyes that blinked in patterns rather than rhythm. Its voice was a vibration through her bones.

You are not one of mine, it said. But you are of what was before.

Sia floated in the center of it all, pulsing with power and pain. "Why me?"

Because you are the wound and the salve. The question and the refusal. You were never meant to be bound by their law.

The universe bent inward. Possibilities collided.

And from her mouth came a word she had not learned, but had always known.

"Verum."

Truth.

The spell did not consume her.

It completed her.

Light tore through the sanctum like an orchestra erupting in crescendo. It sang through the space, a chorus of soundless voices and harmonic bursts that defied understanding. The corruption howled as it was swept away, the rift sealed with a final chord that reverberated through the marrow of stone and soul. It wasn't just a purge, it was a requiem.

And when the dust fell, Sia hovered at the center, radiant, unfamiliar.

Her hair floated around her like a halo. Her skin shimmered with celestial markings. Her eyes were no longer blue, but white-ringed, like eclipses.

She touched down, light still coursing over her skin in fine threads.

And for the first time since entering the sanctum, she smiled.

Ashes and Embers

EPILOGUE

Everyone who observes himself doubting observes a truth, and about that which he observes he is certain; therefore he is certain about a truth. Everyone therefore who doubts whether truth exists has in himself a truth on which not to doubt.... Hence one who can doubt at all ought not to doubt the existence of truth.

St. Augustine

MIA BLINKED AGAINST THE wind as the final light faded. The sanctum lay in ruins, cleansed, silent, and utterly alien. It no longer felt like a battlefield or even a place. It felt like a memory held too long, brittle around the edges.

And at its center stood her sister.

Gone were the scorched leathers and battle-scarred fabric she'd worn during the fight, garments torn by claw and spellfire. Now, Sia was adorned in a gown of flowing silk, pure white and impossibly clean, as though it had never touched the world. The fabric shimmered faintly with ethereal threads, trailing behind her like the wake of a falling star. It was not stitched or bound, it became, wrapped in seamless perfection around her form, a symbol of rebirth and transcendence.

Sia was... changed. Not just alive. Not just victorious.

Transcendent.

The glow around her wasn't the crackling chaos of a spell or the unstable heat of magic. It was something quieter, more terrible. The kind of stillness found in sacred things too old for worship. Her eyes, those beautiful, blue eyes, were now white-ringed and radiant, pupils like eclipses, full of understanding no mortal should bear.

Her skin shimmered like moonlight seen through rain, runes shifting beneath the surface like they were remembering something from a previous life. Her hair lifted gently in a wind Mia couldn't feel.

Mia's throat tightened. Her knees nearly gave out.

Sia turned slowly to face her. The smile was there, gentle, familiar. But Mia felt the distance. A quiet separation between human and divine.

"You came back to me," Mia whispered, unsure if her voice could even reach.

"I never left," Sia replied, and for a moment, she sounded like the sister Mia had grown up with. But behind her voice echoed a second tone, like a chord sung beneath the melody, a resonance that did not belong to this world.

Mia stepped forward, her tail brushing ash, her wings dragging. She reached out, hand trembling.

Sia took it.

Warm.

Grounded.

Still her.

But Mia couldn't shake the feeling that she was holding the edge of something vast.

Above them, the wind howled. Not just wind, voices. Whispers tangled in the air like silk threads being pulled taut. Mia turned her head, eyes narrowing.

She wasn't alone in hearing them.

A chill danced across her spine as she realized what they were saying:

> *She is unbound.*
> *She carries the flame.*
> *She will awaken what sleeps.*

The prophecy came unbidden, slipping into Mia's mind like a memory she'd never lived:

> *The false gods will tremble.*
> *Hell will rise.*
> *And they will come not to kill her, but to claim her.*

Before she learns to wield what was hidden.
Before she becomes what cannot be controlled.

Mia looked back at her sister, standing radiant in the ruins, and a single truth burned brighter than all the others:

This was not the end.

It was only the invitation.